THE NEW NATURALS

ALSO BY GABRIEL BUMP

Everywhere You Don't Belong

THE
NEW NATURALS

a novel

GABRIEL BUMP

ALGONQUIN BOOKS OF CHAPEL HILL 2023

Published by
Algonquin Books of Chapel Hill
Post Office Box 2225
Chapel Hill, North Carolina 27515-2225

an imprint of Workman Publishing
a division of Hachette Book Group, Inc.
1290 Avenue of the Americas,
New York, NY 10104

Printed in the United States of America.
Design by Steve Godwin.

The publisher is not responsible for websites (or their content) that are
not owned by the publisher.

This is a work of fiction. While, as in all fiction, the literary perceptions and insights
are based on experience, all names, characters, places, and incidents either are products
of the author's imagination or are used ficticiously.

Library of Congress Cataloging-in-Publication Data

Names: Bump, Gabriel, author.
Title: The new naturals / Gabriel Bump.
Description: First edition. | Chapel Hill, North Carolina : Algonquin Books of
Chapel Hill, 2023. | Summary: "After losing her child and seeing the world
as an increasingly dangerous place, a young Black woman from Boston decides to
construct a separate society at an abandoned restaurant in Western Massachusetts.
She locates a benefactor and soon it all begins to take shape, but it doesn't take
long for problems to develop"— Provided by publisher.
Identifiers: LCCN 2023025843 | ISBN 9781616208806 (hardcover) |
ISBN 9781643755342 (ebook)
Subjects: LCGFT: Novels.
Classification: LCC PS3602.U474 N49 2023 | DDC 813/.6—dc23/eng/20230608
LC record available at https://lccn.loc.gov/2023025843

10 9 8 7 6 5 4 3 2 1
First Edition

For Lauren and Simone, my mountains.

PART ONE

Naturals

THE NEW NATURALS were formed in a basement, under flickering light and frayed nerves. In those nascent days, Gibraltar and Rio worried about their unborn daughter. The world was imploding in certain places, exploding in others, melting, sliding, boiling. Gibraltar and Rio were academics living in Boston, at a liberal arts college with a progressive mission. They taught Black people to white children. They had met in graduate school in North Carolina, fell in love with each other's research, discovered each other's bodies during a Christmas karaoke party, in a one-person bathroom.

Rio was the brilliant one, the beautiful mind. She studied slave revolts, was descended from a post-Emancipation Black executive from an all-Black town. She could trace herself to a lush grove in Florida.

Gibraltar studied modern athletics and its connections to slavery. He wanted to write a bestselling book and get paid lump sums to comment on race for media conglomerates. Gibraltar was born to hustlers in Little Rock, Arkansas, an untraceable lineage, a web of false identities convoluted in the Jazz Age. There was a distant uncle, a war hero, sent to die in Europe, exploded.

After graduation, followed by a luxurious fellowship in the Berkshires, Rio took the job in Boston; Gibraltar rode her star; Rio took six different pregnancy tests; Rio found an OB, scheduled an appointment; they waited weeks; Gibraltar paced around the house; Gibraltar paced in the hallway; Rio sat up on the hospital bed, looked at pictures of her womb; Gibraltar stood in the hospital room, cried at the black-and-white images of his baby, no bigger than a bean.

Gibraltar admired his wife's growing stomach, cared for her aching joints, cried when they found out the sex, a baby girl. Gibraltar rubbed healing butters on Rio's stretching body, kissed her collarbone when they maneuvered through sex, twisting, gentle, prioritizing comfort.

Rio looked around and hated what her new perspective revealed. When she first moved to Boston, she'd admired her colleagues, lifelong New Englanders, who drank wine and whiskey by the bottle, toughed through blizzards, lamented what they saw as our cultural mettle softening. These were people descended from Pre-America, colonizers, in the literal sense. Immigrants, too, escaping famine, war, divorces, abuse. A calculus professor, from Neapolitan parents, had put his arms around Rio and Gibraltar after orientation, when they were milling about, minding their business. The calculus professor sandwiched his face between their faces and said he understood, you know, what it was like—didn't they know Neapolitans were the Blacks of Europe? Sure, whatever, it was charming, a misguided attempt at comradery.

She walked around Boston's twisting and impractical streets, imagined her daughter popped out her belly, walking at her side, holding her hand, growing a foot a minute until she was taller than Rio, taller than a bus, taller than the new multipurpose luxury structure in her neighborhood. She'd look up at her giant daughter, see her giggling when a cloud tickled her nose.

Her giant daughter squatted behind Rio during a committee meeting, her giant head a floor above, listening in on a two-hundred-level debate about Jonathan Franzen. This was a new committee, one created for Inclusion, Diversity, and Representation. Rio, the only Black person in the room, held her notebook over her face. The calculus professor said something about affirmative action, a dismissive statement, or Rio guessed it was dismissive because a sociology professor threw a glass of orange juice at the calculus professor's face. Rio wasn't listening. Rio was worried about her giant daughter, who was twisting with boredom, just like Rio.

There was a neighborhood meeting in a church basement, to discuss a new pizza place, which promised to serve organic toppings and local beer. Rio stood close to a rear wall, leaned against her daughter's ankle. When her daughter's gigantic muscles twitched, Rio felt the aftershocks, felt her own body convulse. A white woman, new to the neighborhood, a minor executive with a minor-executive husband, with a new glass house built where an old wood house once stood, rose from her foldout chair and gave a speech about settling this neighborhood as a new world without violence, drugs, poverty, vandalism, and petulance; it's about safety, a world for our children, who here feels safe?, raise your hand if you feel safe, when you're walking down the street at night and some junkie is sitting at the bus stop, how can you feel safe, with that stuff around?; and your homes, your investments, imagine your home doubling in value, tripling in value, how is that going to happen with junkies at the corner store, standing around, laughing, smoking cigarettes, howling?; and that stabbing, disgusting, the looming threat of violence, the lowest human urges, how is that going to improve our investments?; imagine, Clean Boston, imagine, a utopia, imagine. Rio's daughter stomped, twice, jerked Rio alive. The white woman was receiving applause from the other attendees, all white and minor rich in warm coats from London and Paris and Turkey. Rio stood where she stood, hands twitching against her hips, realized, here too, she was the only Black person in the room, removed from the applause, removed from the new world, under construction, all around her. She clutched her daughter's big toe when the white woman stopped her speech, removed her white fur cap, took a deep bow. Rio left, found the sidewalk illuminated by her daughter's towering glow, found for-lease and for-sale signs where she didn't before, found a small ramen place crowded with white people in suits listening to hip-hop, found her apartment building, a white man walking through the front door, looking over his shoulder, seeing Rio coming, shutting the door as Rio waved for him to wait. She rode the elevator in silence with the man and her giant daughter, who filled the entire elevator shaft.

She found Gibraltar on the couch, grading papers, watching the Celtics, eating gourmet popcorn from a new gourmet popcorn store around the block, turning his head when she entered, asking how it went, turning his head back around when she didn't respond and went into the bathroom, understanding it was a long day with classes and meetings and tensions he didn't understand. He turned his head, again, and tried to catch a glimpse of her closing the bathroom door. That was a moment they had learned to love, that brief second where one was shutting away and smiling at the other, knowing they'd see each other again soon. Gibraltar didn't catch her this time. Small defeat paused him, head twisted like it was, trying to catch quick love before she disappeared.

He heard the sink start up, water creaking up the pipes, rumbling the walls. He remembered again to call the landlord about the pipes, how the creaking and banging, whenever a neighbor took a piss in the night, jolted them awake at night, how his wife was pregnant and needed her sleep. Rio had told

Gibraltar to make her the excuse, always, if he wasn't getting anywhere.

One afternoon, a few weeks ago, he was watching European soccer while Rio was at work, enjoying the lazy solitude that had mostly vanished from his life. He was transported back to a couch he'd shared with three others, in college, in a house off campus, a neighborhood blended with families and young idiots. From that couch, he could turn left and see the street; right, there was the backyard; straight ahead, above and beyond the screen, the neighbor's kitchen. That afternoon—high a little, a little hungover, typical—Gibraltar heard a ruckus. He shook himself out of the stupor, saw glasses breaking in that kitchen. Woman yelling at man. Man yelling back. Objects flying from an unclear hand—who did it?

Woman out the front door, on the sidewalk, standing there, getting her breath. Her belly bigger than it was a month ago. Her hand on her lower back. Gibraltar felt the pain: in her body, swelling on her face.

Man out the back door, in the backyard, bent over, crying into his knees. Standing, now, breathing, deep, deep. A scream loud enough for Gibraltar to feel. Like a low-flying plane, close enough to the highway, for a moment, it felt like a historic catastrophe, a forever horror.

Gibraltar had turned the volume up, cheered for the Spanish team, made several vows to himself: to never live with a girlfriend, to never bend a knee in the beautiful wheat field, to never negotiate with caterers, to never, ever, purchase an ice sculpture, to never kiss the bride, dance with his mother to

Elton John, to never buy a house in a college town, blow up in the kitchen, storm out.

Now, whenever he had an afternoon off, whenever European soccer came on, Gibraltar remembered how that college afternoon ended. Right before the final whistle, he saw them again, man and woman, in the kitchen. He watched them hold each other, exchange tears, yell apologies. Then later, right before graduation, weeks from move-out day, Gibraltar, from the couch, a little high, hungover a little, saw them come up the sidewalk with a stroller. He saw them in the kitchen, man holding baby, dancing swaying; woman taking pictures. In the backyard, he saw them, aflame with joy, rolling in the grass. Joy he felt, hot, searing love and joy. There was time and love collapsed on each other. Future, past, and present on a couch, a little high, a little hungover.

Now, looking at his wife and unborn daughter through the closed bathroom door, he felt seared with love. He could see them through the flimsy wood. He could see them when they were miles away, walking home, walking to class, riding the T, taking a break on a bench. He felt ridiculous and corny. A cornball. He understood his luck, the rarity. Rio didn't happen to most people. Waking up next to Rio, watching Rio read, grade papers. He was a simp. He was pathetic in his love.

Now, Gibraltar stood at the bathroom door, his forehead knocking, soft.

"Hello?" Gibraltar asked.

"I need a minute," Rio said.

"Can I come in?" Gibraltar asked.

"A minute," Rio said.

Rio heard another soft knock. His forehead. It annoyed her, a bit, when he acted like this: a big baby, whining. He needed to toughen up if they were going to keep going, make it through. She couldn't scream in overwhelmed moments like this because when she screamed, Gibraltar would hold her and whisper something boring and comforting, which wasn't comforting, just flat and flimsy, not true. Something like "tomorrow is a new day," or, worse, "I will carry you across the river, I will bury you in the sand," or, the worst, "We will float on our power." Something about water in his mind, it poked all these horrible and romantic neurons. She liked him better on the couch, staring at the screen, lost in action, a European soccer match during the weekday, for example, or, like now, the Celtics, the Grizzlies, the Bulls. She loved his ability to detach, ignore the world. They were leveled through Rio's intensity, her ability to see and feel each particle in the universe, throughout history, galactic dust drifting across blank space before the big bang. Leveled by Gibraltar's inability to hear a train coming, a bus coming, a jogger coming up from behind, asking him to move left.

They were unleveled when Gibraltar got like this, head against doors, whispering, asking to feel the universe with Rio, to hold her and whisper assurance and protection. When they felt too much, the floors went slant, jars fell off the spice cabinet. She wanted him to go back to the couch, sit and wait for her to appear, to let her walk over to him, put her feet in his lap, ask him to rub.

Another knock. "Rio," Gibraltar said.

"Gibraltar," Rio said, grabbing the sink.

"I'm coming in," Gibraltar said.

"Don't," Rio said. "Please don't."

Gibraltar twisted the knob.

Rio stomped her foot.

Gibraltar stopped twisting his wrist. Instead, his ankles twisted and moved him back to the couch, papers, basketball, and worry.

Rio released the sink, sat on the toilet, head on her daughter's ankle. An urge for flight, which she fought, pushed down on her throat. All of it. She wanted to leave it all, all of it, every meeting, each paper, each class, each forced exchange with a colleague, a student, a stranger on the sidewalk forcing her aside, sorry, excuse me, fuck you. This world. She fought several urges at once. She sunk deeper into her giant daughter. Urges, like a horde, running up her nose, right into her brain, that impulse part, the delicate one. Violent urges. Less violent urges. Taking a sledgehammer and smashing a skull; taking two muffins and paying for one. The urge to march right down to city hall and demand more money for teachers, less money for cops. The urge to commandeer a stealth bomber and free the Uyghurs, free the homeless. These jumbled, nonsensical urges transformed from hordes into colorful ribbons pouring out her eyes and ears. Something was wrong. What the hell is happening to me? Not Boston. Not Gibraltar. Not the baby. Of course, not the baby. Not you, Rio thought and sunk deeper into her giant daughter, the unborn monstrosity engulfing her, the vision, the hallucination. I'm busted, Rio thought. Downright losing it, Rio thought. Deep breaths. One, two, slow down, one, two, too fast. She was gone. She was down the slope, flying down. Dizzy. She was one long rainbow streamer floating around the small bathroom, these creaking pipes, fix these damn pipes, fix the damn world. How can you explain a sensation, a spiral, like this? How can you explain a baby, five stories tall, unborn, giggling? She had to stand up. Stand up, Rio thought, you must. Rio, you must. Stand up. Rio looked up, saw her daughter looking down. No ceiling above, no upstairs neighbors, no rooftop social area with a grill and uncomfortable lounge chairs. Just a big smiling face looking down, smiling back. Stand up.

Rio stood up.

Rio went down.

Gibraltar watched Rio twist in the hospital bed, tangle up some tubes, wake a bit, moan, free herself from a nightmare. He knew what came next. He scooted his chair closer to the bed.

Rio jolted.

"Gibraltar!" Rio yelled.

Gibraltar grabbed her hand.

"Here," Gibraltar said. "Here. Here."

A nurse, a doctor; an onlooker hooked up to an IV on a rolling pole type deal taking a walk. They all stepped into the doorway, asked if everything was okay.

"She's awake," Gibraltar said, without turning around, trying to lock into Rio's drifting gaze.

"Everything alright?" the doctor asked.

"I don't know," Gibraltar said.

"I'll get someone," the nurse said.

"You are someone," Gibraltar said.

The nurse and doctor weren't Rio's nurse and doctor. They kept walking. Gibraltar wanted to follow them, get some help, she was awake. Rio squeezed his hand.

The onlooker stayed watching.

"What happened?" Gibraltar asked Rio.

"I was flying," Rio said.

"Oh," Gibraltar said.

Rio closed her eyes, went somewhere else. Gibraltar felt a deep and frightening urge to explode with fear and sadness.

"I'll yell for someone," the onlooker said, then yelled.

A nurse appeared, told the onlooker to keep it quiet, there are sick people here. The onlooker pointed to Rio and Gibraltar. The nurse walked in, looked at charts, touched the machines and tubes.

"She's awake?" the nurse asked.

"Yes," Gibraltar said. "I don't know what's going on."

"Her eyes are closed," the nurse said.

"She's awake." Gibraltar shook Rio's hand.

Rio kept her eyes closed.

"I'll get someone," the nurse said.

"You are someone," Gibraltar said.

The nurse left; the onlooker stayed.

"I'll keep you company," the onlooker said. "You look troubled."

"Please," Gibraltar said to Rio, to the onlooker. "Please. Make sense."

A doctor nudged the onlooker aside, knocked on the door. A nurse followed.

"Mr. Hurston," the doctor said.

"I'm Mr. Donohue," Gibraltar said. "She's Ms. Hurston."

"She's your wife," the doctor said.

Gibraltar held up Rio's hand, kissed it, not knowing why, at the moment, he felt the desire.

"Seems like you got it handled," the onlooker said.

The onlooker kept walking, pulled his IV along, shouted thanks for the miracle, shouted thanks for protecting our mothers and our babies, shouted, pleaded for a miracle of their own, a miracle to suck the poison from their blood. If there were any miracles left, by chance, after today was done. Imagine that, the onlooker shouted, waking up to a miracle.

And the onlooker was gone.

"Rio," the nurse said, holding her bicep. "How are you feeling?"

"You had a scare," the doctor said. "You're in a hospital."

"Are you feeling okay?" the nurse asked.

"Is she okay?" Gibraltar asked. "Please tell me she's okay."

The doctor turned to Gibraltar, serious, dour.

"We don't know," the doctor said. "There's no way to know."

"I'm fucking fine," Rio said. "How's my baby?"

"Rio," the doctor said. "You had a fall, a spell."

"I guessed," Rio said.

"Do you need water?" Gibraltar asked.

"I had some water and drank it," Rio said.

"Your husband was very worried," the nurse said.

"My baby?" Rio asked, rubbed her stomach. Still there. The size.

"The baby is fine," the doctor said.

"Your baby is fine," the nurse said.

Rio sunk in relief, found Gibraltar, noticed, finally, his hand squeezing hers, noticed his worry. That overbearing worry. Annoying now as always. Embarrassing, now, with the small crowd.

"Can I have a second?" Rio said.

"Of course," the nurse said.

"We need to talk," the doctor said to Rio, stern. "There are things to discuss."

"I want my husband," Rio said. "My family. Please."

The nurse pulled the doctor out.

In the hallway, the nurse slapped the doctor's gut. Between them, standing in the hallway, all the things left unsaid, things said late at night in the cafeteria, in the parking garage, on the phone driving home, in their separate driveways, their separate families waiting inside, the children, the children, mistakes spoken, mistakes in action, all of it between them, that couple in that room, that baby—don't you want that too? Of course I do. We can't. Not here.

Alone, Rio squeezed Gibraltar back. Crying, he rubbed her stomach, felt for life.

"I'm fine," Rio said. "Please stop."

"I heard a crash," Gibraltar said. "I saw you there, on your face."

Gibraltar couldn't describe further. How can you put that fear into words? Your world on the bathroom floor, on their face, breathing, a little, not responding to your shouts.

"I'm okay," Rio said.

Gibraltar nodded, put his face away.

"She's okay," Rio said.

Gibraltar twisted his body away, contorted in the chair, sobbed and shook. What do you say about that? The dreadful possibility?

"Listen," Rio said. "Look."

Gibraltar turned back, looked.

"I saw something," Rio said. "In my head."

"A dream," Gibraltar said.

"I know about dreams," Rio said. "This wasn't a dream."

"You knocked your head," Gibraltar said.

"I saw colors," Rio said. "Twisting thin fabric. Transporting me."

"Okay," Gibraltar said, pulled away.

"I was caught in an updraft," Rio said. "Lifted by rainbow streams."

"It's okay," Gibraltar said.

"Then I landed," Rio said. "Careful. I was placed on grass. Green sturdy grass."

Gibraltar tried to touch her forehead. Rio grabbed his wrist.

"Stop that," Rio said.

Worry came back to Gibraltar. Strong worry and fear.

"A hill," Rio said. "An overlook. A river. A bridge, a bridge named after royalty, a royal bridge. French something.

German. One of those. Hawks soaring, in the updraft, diving down, swooping low, circles and circles."

Gibraltar backed up.

"Don't do that," Rio said. "Don't look scared."

Gibraltar recognized her eyes, hyperalive, looking into the future, clear. He wouldn't call them visions. She hated that word, felt it too dark-velvet room and incense and beaded strings instead of doors. She hated dreams, too. That was just noise in your head. A dream, Gibraltar thought. Maybe it was a dream.

"A dream," Gibraltar said.

Rio rolled onto her side, showed Gibraltar her back, her gown opened, her ass.

"It wasn't a dream," Rio said. Outside her window, the harbor, streets that didn't make sense, narrow cobblestoned messes, the T, the crowded platform, remembering the years they spent, her and Gibraltar, in the Berkshires, driving to Alewife, parking, running late, catching the train to the Common, holding hands, Rio's head on his shoulder, switch, Gibraltar's head on her head, rocking, visiting friends at Emerson, coming back home at a reasonable hour, back to Alewife, taking Route 2 all the way back, in the dark, in the happy dark, in the tipsy, dangerous dark, not sure what was a mountain and what was a valley.

Rio rolled back over, showed her ass to the city.

"It wasn't a dream," Rio said.

"Tell me what you need," Gibraltar asked.

"Get me the fuck out of Boston," Rio said.

So, they moved to Western Massachusetts.

They rented a small house in a small hill town. They were filled with wild energy, moving fast. Racing against Drop's arrival. They found small jobs at a small private college, teaching small classes for small money. Rio had saved. There was money inherited from an aunt in San Diego, a businesswoman without kids, dead now going on five years.

Gibraltar finished a long-dormant book proposal, sent it around, waited to hear back, figured his idea was genius. It was a book without a title. It was an idea. Something about largesse in professional athletics demonstrating a clear sign of America's collapse; these grown men playing games and getting paid more than bankers; hundreds of millions; billion-dollar athletes with wineries and production studios and real estate empires; what are we doing here, where is all this money going?; the athletes aren't to blame, of course, the athletes are playing a game, the athletes are artists; what does it say about our society, that these beautiful artists aren't satisfied with art, these beautiful artists want to live like hedge fund managers—what does that say about us? Nothing good. Something was coming, Gibraltar warned, we should be prepared.

Gibraltar started a Twitter account, retweeted videos of mudslides in Appalachia, explainers on elitist money laundering, threads and articles that illuminated urban housing crises. Once, he retweeted a video from a fringe conspiracy theorist, someone who thought public schools were turning children into frog people. Gibraltar didn't agree with everything the man had to say. Still, he'd made good points on urban food deserts. Friends, reading the desperate tenor of these social media posts, called them, concerned about their mental states. Gibraltar felt surveilled.

"Let's go dark," Gibraltar said to Rio.

Rio and Gibraltar deleted their accounts, smashed their phones on rocks near the creek, started using a landline.

They waited for their daughter; they ignored invitations to dinner and drinks; they skipped faculty meetings; they enjoyed their new quiet universe. They hired Jamaican apple pickers to build a tall fence around their yard.

Out here, their baby wasn't a giant. She was safe in Rio. She was calm, small, growing like normal, partying when caffeinated, doing cartwheels at odd moments.

Rio, glowing anew, talked more about destiny and purpose. Gibraltar nodded, rubbed her stomach, massaged her back and feet, moisturized her sides.

Somewhere in New York City, a young Black woman was abducted by police officers and sold into sex slavery. Somewhere in Atlanta, a young Black man was mistaken for a thief and shot by a grocery store owner. Down in Memphis, schools closed and children sat on slanted stoops all day, stared into their potholed street, saw time pass like violent rapids. Out in Chicago, a closed school turned into a microbrewery with farm-to-table appetizers.

The president changed. The nationalistic weirdos, for a moment, took over the Capitol, lit the steps on fire.

Gibraltar and Rio talked about the American Experiment

in their windowless basement, how it had failed, how the ship was sinking.

Rio hung a ten-foot world map on the south wall, drilled it in place, marked red Xs on unsafe places. She attacked the map with her red marker when a police officer killed a civilian, when a protest against the status quo turned violent, when a law was forced into legislation through gerrymandered evil majorities, when an innocuous spark churned into a crawling wildfire, when a ship filled with immigrants capsized in beautiful water, when a virus sprouted and tore apart economies and hospitals.

Gibraltar sat at a foldout table and watched her pregnant body work. Sometimes, he told her to slow down, watch her step, careful on that stool. She'd tell him to keep reading the news, shut up, worry about himself, what's happening in Argentina, sorry, sorry. Then she'd climb off the stool, walk over, kiss Gibraltar's head, let him rub their unborn daughter, feel her kick. Then he'd tell her about Chinese aggressions toward India's sovereignty. She'd run back to the map, slash Xs along the Sino-Indian border. They shared an office on campus that was always locked and hollow. They went to doctor appointments, the grocery store, the hardware store, a nice bakery a few towns over.

Except for those occasional trips, they stayed home and fortified. Rio ordered security cameras online, Gibraltar hid them in bushes and trees, nailed them above doors and windows. Rio could monitor their surroundings on her phone. On slow news days, they left the basement. They would sit in the living room and read history to their daughter, safe in the womb. They told her about Brazilian quilombos, the Great Dismal Swamp, Sojourner Truth, Frederick Douglass, Marcus Garvey. They told her about the Back-to-Africa movement, how it failed, why it failed, why it was a joke. They told their daughter about a new idea.

Rio wanted to try again, complete what her forbearers started. Gibraltar and Rio talked about a new utopia. They cooked modest vegetable dishes; they broiled white fish; they composted; they discovered wild strawberries in their backyard.

Violence erupted in France, migrants attacked in Italy, militants sprang up in Cameroon, ice shelves tore apart in the Arctic, wind currents intensified in the Caribbean.

Rio attacked her map.

In Southern California, a forest fire ate through a suburb. In Idaho, moose populations grew erratic and aggressive.

In Boston, sea levels crept above levees.

In their bed, Rio and Gibraltar held each other at night and Rio dictated her thoughts to Gibraltar. She'd talk about a perfect world until her powerful voice turned into a mumble, until she stopped altogether and snored just before sunrise. Then, Gibraltar would kiss his wife's forehead and stroke her hair until falling asleep, arm draped across her stomach.

Then, Rio was due.

Gibraltar had the route memorized. He anticipated turns while telling Rio to breathe, hang on, we're almost there. He stood in the delivery room, doctored-up in scrubs. He listened to Rio scream, cheered her on, let her hand crush his hand, let her eyes rip through his chest. He heard the baby scream.

He felt love and joy, in a powerful concentration, take over his blood and wreck his mind.

He saw his small daughter curled against his wife's chest, both of them covered in sweat and slime. He saw his younger selves lined against the wall, all those fools chasing insignificant dreams. All those lesser aspirations he desired all his life. This was it. This is how he would die: serving these beautiful women.

Gibraltar and Rio declined to eat the placenta. They rested. No one came to visit because there was no one else. This was everything and everyone. The hospital kicked them out. Gibraltar took the turns home with slow care, held up traffic, let motorcycles pass, checked his rearview for daughter and wife bundled in the backseat, blew a kiss to Rio, who didn't see, who was looking at their daughter, who couldn't look away, who promised their daughter safety, I'll never let you go, I promise.

"We're here," Gibraltar said after parking.

Rio didn't move.

"Rio," Gibraltar said. "We're here. Come on."

"I promise you," Rio said to their tiny baby. "I promise you everything."

Gently, softly, Gibraltar helped mother and daughter out the backseat, through the front door.

They didn't sleep for days and weeks. They sorted through names on the living room sofa.

Drop.

They liked the hard sound, the power.

They stopped reading the news. They didn't talk about the world as unsafe. They didn't speak about anything beyond their house.

Drop, with her wonder, her blooming joy. With her father's face, with her mother's grip. Drop and her tiny fingers, not letting go. Drop, asleep, smiling, hopeful. Drop, swaddled, her hugging parents looking down.

Drop, perfect, Drop.

Then, one cold day with a bright sun, Drop coughed.

They took Drop to the doctor. The doctor said she was fine. Young parents worry.

The next day, Drop coughed and coughed.

Again, the doctor turned them away, wouldn't run the tests Rio wanted.

The next day, Drop stopped coughing.

Drop stopped breathing.

Then, the sun went away, the cold intensified, and Gibraltar hit his turns to the hospital with reckless speed. He skidded into the parking lot, left his keys in the ignition, took his daughter, left Rio crying in the front seat.

Please, please, please, he said to the emergency room attendant. My daughter, he said.

She's purple, he said.

He handed his daughter to a male nurse with a ponytail.

He collapsed in the lobby.

Rio didn't leave the front seat. She cried with her door open, ambulances with roaring sirens honking for her to move, she can't park there, this is an emergency lane only.

How does a couple survive such a loss? Celestial beauty is gifted to you in this brilliant small package, with eyes like mother and cheeks like father. You see the universe in a swaddled mess of tears and shit and piss. Then—how do you prepare for the doctor to pull you aside and explain how vulnerable your daughter was to air and sickness? How does wife tell husband that she wants to die, too? How does husband tell wife that life is still meaningful? Gibraltar asked the doctor, "What the fuck? What now? Why didn't you listen to us? What the fuck?"

Gibraltar asked to say goodbye. Rio held him up. There was Drop, little Drop, pale and frozen on a small table.

They sat in the waiting room, while they waited for their daughter's ashes. They couldn't say anything. They hid in their respective minds. They took a vacuum-sealed box from a sad male nurse with bangs and forearm tattoos. Gibraltar, careless with his turns, almost hit a ditch. Rio rubbed his shoulder while looking out her window.

They took their vacuum-sealed box to the basement. They sat at their foldout table, on opposite sides. They turned on the flickering light. Gibraltar noticed his wife's beauty, her strength shown in a hard scowl. He saw shadows on her face and knew this wasn't the end. Rio leaned back in her chair.

"I know," Rio said.

"You know what?" Gibraltar asked.

"We had the wrong idea," Rio said.

"What idea?" Gibraltar asked.

"Underground," Rio said.

"I don't understand," Gibraltar said.

"We're too focused with the surface," Rio said.

She stood and walked to her world map, wiped dust from South America, spiderwebs off Siberia. She studied the map. Gibraltar studied her back, the muscles tensing and shifting under her loose shirt.

"I don't understand," Gibraltar said.

"The surface doesn't matter," Rio said.

"I think we need sleep," Gibraltar said. "Some rest."

"We need to go underground," Rio said.

"We're in a basement," Gibraltar said.

"We need to go deeper," Rio said. "There's nothing up here for us."

Rio studied the map, ran her fingers over the topography. She looked at their location, marked with a blue heart. She rubbed the old mountains and small hills.

"Tomorrow," Gibraltar said. "Can we talk about this in the morning? After breakfast?"

"I can't sleep," Rio said.

"Me neither," Gibraltar said.

"We need pamphlets," Rio said. "We need people."

"For what?" Gibraltar said. "What people?"

"We need blueprints," Rio said. "We'll need engineers, workers, and chefs."

PART TWO

Sojourner

IN FOXTONHOLLOW, MASSACHUSETTS, months ago, Parks &
Recreation had been forced to test for lead levels in the public
water. Forty-five minutes away, another small town in Central
Massachusetts had been dealing with a health crisis—sick
children, birth defects, warped brains, brown liquid squirting
from faucets. The victims were Black, Hispanic, Sri Lankan,
Cambodian; refugees and immigrants, poor Americans, people unable to relocate, unable to pick up and find clean water
elsewhere.

The city council considered threats to health and safety in
other small towns' emergencies. If it could happen there, they
figured, why wouldn't it happen here?

Sojourner's beat was local government. She was assigned the story. She attended the meetings. She read the reports. She grew attached to the story, as she often did.

The Department of Environmental Protection had tested the water, claimed that they'd found acceptable lead levels. Still, the city council drafted and sent a letter to the governor demanding new water infrastructure and regular testing for lead. The letter claimed clean drinking water was a right of all citizens. The governor sent a letter back. She respected the city council's concern for future generations. She hoped more communities would take action, write letters, post videos online, protest. She finished with a few sentences about self-determination and American grit. Sojourner wrote a final story on the matter: our water is safe; their water is not safe; no one is going to do anything about it; some people deserve safe drinking water, other people do not. Sojourner had gotten used to not mattering. She wanted her work to help change the world. She, too, wrote a letter to the governor, included her stories about lead poisoning, pleaded with the governor to consider signing the bill into law. The governor wrote back, thanked Sojourner for her concern and her journalistic service, called her an inspiration to young people, said she was going to a summit, in Aspen, with other governors and she would bring up the issue alongside other pressing issues, such as economic development in historically underserved areas and clean energy farms.

Yesterday, months later, in her office, Sojourner had seen a headline about another small town, another crisis, more lead, more deformities, more calls for action, more brown water.

Is that what set her off? The continuing crisis. The worsening. Or, was it the growing apathy from the newsroom, the editors, her sources, the public? The declining readership. The moving on. Was it knowing she was the only one still fighting? That cold feeling.

Sojourner wasn't sure. When she left the office that day, she didn't feel changed in an irreversible way. She was upset, sure. She was often upset. She often hated her job and drove home upset. Was there something special about yesterday? In the morning, she didn't know. There, in bed, on her day off, Sojourner replayed the previous workday. Her drive to the office. Her walk into the building. Her body in her chair at her desk, sipping her coffee, still not waking up, still half-asleep, two blinks, sitting on the toilet, closing her eyes, leaning against the stall, praying no one found her, three blinks, back in the car, back in her bed, a blur, a pressure in her stomach, a desire to run and keep running.

There, beside her, sleeping and drooling, Rascal kicked in his sleep, punched at the air, moaned the way he always moaned: scared and empty. Sojourner shook him awake. He drooled during his night terrors and, somehow, it made them harder to bear. Everything wet and dramatic.

"Me," Sojourner said into Rascal's nightmares. "Me. Me. Me."

"CHAPPAQUIDDICK!" Rascal yelled into the darkness, eyes closed.

Sojourner played her fingers against his chest.

"Me," Sojourner said again. "Me and you. Me and you."

Rascal punched past Sojourner's face, kneed her thighs.

Sojourner pulled at his hair, stuck a finger in his ear.

"MARY JO!" Rascal yelled through his teeth.

Sojourner dodged another punch, went to the bathroom, slapped her face, pulled her eyes open, put her face inches from the smudged mirror, studied the red lines vibrating from her irises. She slapped her face again, felt her way to the kitchen. She slept in socks. She slipped on the kitchen tiles. Sometimes, with a good running start, she could glide from the oven to the living room couch.

She pulled a beer from the fridge, considered the hummus gaining crust on the top shelf, considered the salami curling up next to the browned kale.

She took her beer, took her socked feet off the porch. She went into the field out back, sat in the dawn's young light, listened to birds wake, the cooing doves, catbirds and their meowing, the hammering woodpeckers, a brilliant and obnoxious blue jay. She scanned for bears.

Okay, Sojourner thought.

"Okay," Sojourner said.

She often spent mornings like this. She often felt her screws loosen, felt like a made-up version of herself.

She chugged her beer, tapped the empty bottle against her thin knees, counted different birdsongs, scanned again for bears, saw a deer staring back at her, just a small thing out in the clearing.

She tipped her beer back again, forgot it was empty. Sometimes, she had embarrassing impulses. Now, for example,

she wanted to throw her empty beer at that stupid small thing
out in the clearing. She wanted to know if she was strong
enough to make direct contact, send the small thing running back home, back into those stupid and beautiful woods.
She didn't want to harm anything; she wanted to know her
strength; she hated it here, there.

She walked down the porch, toward the deer, long damp
grass tickled her ankles—she hated tickling. She thought about
ticks. She scanned for bears. The deer remained. Too stupid,
Sojourner thought. She squeezed her empty beer, adjusted
her grip. Thirty feet, Sojourner thought. Twenty-nine, twen-
ty-eight, twenty-seven.

"Run," Sojourner said to the deer.

Twenty-five, twenty-four, twenty-three, twenty-three.

"Run," Sojourner said, standing still.

Again, she tried to chug the beer. Again, she held the bottle
at her side, squeezed the glass. Twenty-two, twenty-one. Was
that a hawk circling up there, over there, above the tree line,
swooping down? Sojourner noticed a black spot on the baby
deer's stupid snout, a big black spot. She wondered, standing in
the damp expanse, if stupid baby deer had birthmarks, if each
one was unique in their babyness and stupidness. Like her,
were they worried someone would laugh at their birthmark?
Sojourner's was a blotch—faded at the edges, swirled in the
middle—on her upper back, large and jagged, running from
her upper vertebrae, between her shoulders, to her middle ribs.
Did stupid baby deer feel like her, empty, stuck, a void in their
guts like her, a hollow rock like her? Did stupid baby deer walk

down to the river, tongue at the water, feel watched, hunted, hated; did they hate themselves, like her?

Sojourner sat in the grass, extended her arms.

"Come here," Sojourner said to the deer.

The deer twitched, remained standing, blinked, snorted, wiggled its stupid little tail.

Sojourner fell back in the grass, sat up on her elbows, kept her eyes on the deer, scanned the horizon again. That, at the tree line? That shadow.

Sojourner looked at the deer; the deer looked at Sojourner; Sojourner looked at the tree line; the deer looked at Sojourner; Sojourner looked at the deer; the deer looked at the tree line. That shadow moved.

"Nope," Sojourner said.

Sojourner sprang up, walked backward to the porch, faced the rising sun, now brilliant and full above the tree line. This deer, Sojourner thought. The deer remained still, kept eyes on Sojourner. This deer isn't right, Sojourner thought. The head, tilted at an unnatural angle; the knees buckled too far. Not a normal deer. Someone help this deer, Sojourner thought. Sojourner looked back for the shadow, didn't see it.

"Nope," Sojourner said.

In bored moments, Sojourner wondered how this place would kill her. First, she thought she would kill herself. A tick could do it. Just one tick, left to suck and get fat with blood. One tick tucked under her armpit, in a place she never checked—that could do it. Rabid foxes, a foaming pack, could take her down no problem, in a second. A bear, yes, of course.

Once, months ago, a man saw a baby moose on a dirt road somewhere close. That baby moose trampled that man and crushed his insides. Sojourner wrote an article about the funeral. She focused on the widow, stoic in a red pantsuit, in the front pew, expressionless. The widow knew, Sojourner thought then in the chapel, looking down from the balcony. She'd seen this coming, Sojourner thought. Poor woman, Sojourner thought, forced to live in a place like this.

The New Naturals

THE MOUNTAIN CAME to Rio on a walk through the woods. She had told Gibraltar not to worry. She was coming back. Settle down: it's just a stroll.

Gibraltar had hovered in doorways as Rio called real estate offices and architects. He'd tried to talk her down. Then he'd shut his mouth. He'd go to the kitchen and eat oranges in silence, leave her in the basement with her maps. He hoped it would pass, this urge to save the world, this savior complex.

He remembered their younger selves on a trip to Miami, in a bar with a courtyard and tropical trees providing shade, during a school break, dissertations driving them insane. A

third pitcher of sangria. Those fried plantains eaten without forks, just greased fingers, giggling, dropping pieces. In
a different bar, this one without a roof, Rio danced by herself while Gibraltar waited for their tequilas. He could see her
hair, head, neck, shoulders, moving in a fluid chaos, each part,
it seemed, pulling in a different direction, different currents
pushed by the moon. He didn't remember getting those tequilas, spilling them on his way back to Rio. He didn't remember drinking them. The night went black except for Rio. Her
warmth against his body. His sweat and her sweat. There she
was in the blackness with radiating waves. She guided him.
He followed, hands on her ribs. He would follow her everywhere, wherever she led. Just like he'd followed her to Miami.
Just for the hell of it. Last-minute tickets, no swimsuits,
no sandals.

In the morning, there she was: standing in the hotel bathroom, drinking water from the tap, rubbing her forehead,
promising to never drink again, asking if he was a saint, if
he'd go and get six bagels with butter and bacon. Gibraltar
met her in the bathroom, puked in the toilet. There she was
behind him, above him, rubbing his back, grossed out and loving. They ate their bagels in bed, watched the sun move along
outside their window. "I love you," he said. "I love you," she
said. "I love you forever," he said. "I love you forever," she said.

Now, peeling an orange in the kitchen, this is how Gibraltar
pictured his wife: in the elevator, packed bags at her feet, sunglasses sliding down her nose, sweating, sick, smiling at him,
putting her hand into his hand, leaning in to say "I love you"

again, for the hundredth time, to say "I hate Miami, I hate tequila, I love you."

Now, unpeeling in the kitchen, Rio blurred across the hall.

Gibraltar met her at the front door. Coat over her robe, she was putting on her boots.

"Settle down," Rio said. "It's just a stroll."

Gibraltar watched her from the doorway, saw her disappear without looking back.

Rio followed a half-trail, reached up her hand and slapped droplets from leaves. In the wild, she thought of her great-grandmother, all her kin, hiking from Georgia to Florida with post-Emancipation worry and glee. She tried to imagine freedom that strong, how it must have shook their bodies. She looked across a field, opened up in her path. She thought of her grandfather, as a child, running away from home, playing a game, wanting everyone to find him, finding himself in a swamp, climbing a mangrove, dangling his feet above the water. Rio's grandfather told her about that swamp. He told her about Florida. He found it hard to describe. He would put Rio on his lap, go silent. A place like that, he would say, doesn't exist in real life. Their town was a dream. Except it wasn't a dream. It was a place removed. The outside world, past the swamp and orange groves, was violent, upside down. They lived in peace, they never had to leave. There were schools, gardens, streams for fishing, trails that led from the streams to the schoolrooms, covered trails with smaller trails spreading to hangouts and quiet places. Everyone had their own space. If you felt in love, you could take your girlfriend to the river and kiss in the water. If you felt overwhelmed, you could disappear into the woods, take your time, and come back before dinner, and no one would worry because everyone was safe and no one, besides them, knew where they were. They understood the key to safety and happiness wasn't blending into society, making yourself part of the whole, but making your own community with your loved ones, caring for each other. What else did you need?

Her grandfather would go silent again. He would ask Rio to imagine it: all those Black people living in peace for the first time in their lives. Then he would take Rio off his lap and tell her to go play. And Rio would run into the backyard, thinking about peace and freedom. Then Rio's mother would yell about bedtime from the window, brushing her teeth, changing into pajamas, kissing her grandfather goodbye. Years later, Rio's mother would take Rio to the nursing home, when her grandfather couldn't remember any of their names. Then Rio's mother would take Rio to visit his grave every August to sing "Happy Birthday" and lay down flowers. Then Rio's mother would take Rio to visit Florida. Her grandfather's town was now a strip mall. The swamp was now a golf course. The orange groves were now a private prison, the biggest employer for miles. Rio's mother would tell Rio about the world's trajectory, how it was spiraling downward to a calamitous end. Standing in that strip mall, Rio had felt history balled up over her head. She felt the world about to drop.

Now, looking across the open field, standing on the edge, Rio started to run.

She ran to the other side, tripped on a log, got up, kept going.

She ran through more woods and got scratched up.

She ran onto Route 2, ran on the edge of traffic. She felt a truck carry a wind gust against her back, carry her forward.

She reached French King Bridge out of breath.

And the Mountain came to her. There, on the other side, poking up, looming down. There was an abandoned restaurant on its peak, looking like it might break off and slide into the road.

Rio couldn't catch her breath. She could see it all.

Her ancestors crossing the Florida–Georgia line, carrying their bags across foreign terrain, swatting away mosquitoes.

Her grandfather, as a child, living in a dream. Her grandfather, as a man, unable to speak, looking into the sky, smiling. All those Black people living in peace for the first time in their lives.

Her mother cursing the world.

Rio could see it all in the Mountain.

She and Gibraltar would bring them here. They would burrow inside, create a dream, let them in, anybody, everybody— they would make a place for everyone.

This was the one. This was it.

She gaped upward and understood freedom. And it shook her. She felt freedom vibrate her shins. Hot freedom in her sweat.

She would do it.

Gibraltar was in the front yard, on his back, pressing his palms into the grass, when Rio appeared above his face.

"I found it," Rio panted.

Rio pulled Gibraltar up, pulled him into the house, pulled him into the basement, pulled him to a map.

"Rio," Gibraltar said. "What happened?"

"Aren't you listening?" Rio said. "Here."

She pointed to the French King Bridge, dragged her finger to the Mountain. Gibraltar turned away.

"I'm going upstairs," Gibraltar said. "I'm getting you some water."

"I don't need water," Rio said. "I found it. It's right there."

"I need some water," Gibraltar said. "I need to lay down."

"It's here," Rio said. "I'm telling you. It's right here."

"I can't do this," Gibraltar said. "We can't do this."

"Where do you think you're going?" Rio asked.

She followed him halfway up the stairs, grabbed his wrist.

The power in her grip put Gibraltar down. He sat down on the bottom step and looked up at his wife.

"Don't you understand?" Gibraltar asked. "This is impossible."

"It's always impossible," Rio said. "We're going to build something impossible."

"How?" Gibraltar asked.

Rio told him how. She laid bare the contacts, phone calls, donations, construction. She said how they would make a place for everyone. She told Gibraltar about Florida and swamps, peace between the groves, crossing into a new world that could last forever, freezing time, escaping into infinite love.

"Can't you picture it?" Rio asked, bent over her husband, panting still.

"No," Gibraltar said. "I need some water."

He walked up the stairs and closed the basement door behind him. He wondered, halfway to the sink, if slamming the door would have made his point clearer. He wanted it to stop.

He took his water to the window and looked out at their yard. The quiet was eroding his senses. He missed cities, how their noise kept him alert. He missed walking up the street and grabbing a beer by himself, catching a game, a few quarters, a few innings, walking back home, kissing Rio on the couch before going to bed, hearing the cars before sleep. There were only birds up here. Birds and coyotes. He'd forget about the coyotes until it was three in the morning and they came into the yard like frat boys, whooping. He thought of Rio in Miami. He thought of Rio in Boston. He thought of Rio on a trip to Chicago, to see family, for a funeral; how Rio made them drive past Fred Hampton's house, drive down Emmett Till Road, stop at that mosque on Stony Island, near the expressway; how Rio had held his hand on Lake Michigan, looked back at the city and asked if they could move to Chicago. How long until the Mountain was like Chicago: a nice passing idea, a moment?

Rio heard Gibraltar upstairs, pacing across the floorboards, sending the creaks onto her head. What wasn't he seeing? How could he not feel the world on fire? Just yesterday, the aggressions in Kashmir. Didn't he understand? It was all coming to an end.

They needed the Mountain.

Rio sat at the table, pushed the maps aside.

She listened to her husband, above her head, stop, then move again, stop.

Sojourner

RASCAL MET HER in the kitchen, yawning.

"Couldn't sleep?" Rascal asked, rubbed his short beard.

"You need a doctor," Sojourner said, moved past him, opened the fridge, pulled a bottle, inspected the kale.

"You need to stop that," Rascal said, pointed to Sojourner's face.

"My day off," Sojourner said, looked for the opener.

"Mine too," Rascal said.

"None of your business," Sojourner said.

"What should we do?" Rascal said.

"Get a magnetic one," Sojourner said. "For the fridge."

"What?" Rascal said.

"You need to work on your organization," Sojourner said.

Sojourner slammed a drawer too hard, startled herself. She put the beer bottle down—again, too hard—faced Rascal, leaned against the sink. Rascal's face was worried. What is his problem? Sojourner thought. That stupid face. What was she doing here, with him, with her life, with all this stupid, with him always on the couch, reading his books about nothing, writing his papers about nothing, keeping her up with his stupid dreams—what was his problem?

"What is your problem?" Sojourner asked.

Rascal turned away from Sojourner. He stared at a bare wall, water-damaged up where it met the ceiling. Sojourner watched his back spasm up near his shoulders. He said something Sojourner couldn't hear. She asked him to say it again.

"Not today," Rascal said. "I'm not fighting."

He wanted to sit around with Sojourner and do nothing. And feel nothing. She couldn't do it anymore.

"What did you say?" Sojourner asked.

Rascal went into the bedroom and closed the door, coward. Sojourner picked up her bottle, opened the cap on the counter. She tried to down the whole thing in one continuous pour. She couldn't. Choking, she coughed into the sink. She couldn't breathe. She spat and coughed until liquid left her body and air rushed in. She felt emotionless tears slide down her nose.

From within the bedroom, behind the still-closed door, Rascal called out, asked if everything was okay out there.

"Fuck off," Sojourner said, quiet, into the sink. She turned the water on, put her mouth on the faucet. She tasted metal.

She imagined tiny lead particles cutting into her cheeks, getting into her blood, messing up her brain. She felt connected to the other poisoned families. Their shared rage was a red, glowing ball behind her closed eyes. Pure rage. And nothing to do about it.

Rascal called out again, muffled, frightened.

"I'm fine!" Sojourner yelled back, not wanting to see him again.

Sojourner took her bottle off the counter, pulled another from the fridge, opened the new bottle on the counter with a slam, a flex.

"It's in the drawer!" Rascal yelled out.

"I'm going for a walk!" Sojourner said.

"I love you!" Rascal yelled out.

"I love you too!" Sojourner yelled from the open screen door.

If something was going to kill her, rip her apart out in the field, past the tree line—she hoped to find it. Maybe she could kill it first.

Outside, again. Nothing visible in the field. Just thin fog hovering like a poison gas cloud. She knew there were crickets and ants and ticks and spiders in the dewed grass, hopping, crawling, slipping. Still, she couldn't see them. She started walking, sliding her socked feet across the grass. The deer was gone. She checked the tree line again. No vague beast, lurking. She headed that way, toward the woods, into the fog, double-fisting her beer, warmth spreading through her limbs, heart, and head.

Today, Sojourner thought.

"Today," Sojourner said.

Today, today she would find a way to escape. No, she thought, escape is too strong a word. Leave, she thought. Leave was right. I'm not trapped, she thought.

"I'm not trapped," Sojourner said.

All she had to do was look Rascal in his stupid face, framed with that stupid hair, and tell him to fuck off. Then, while Rascal cried, she would pack a small bag, call a cab, head to the airport, fly back to Chicago. She didn't know which cab company to call. She didn't know how she'd pay for the cab and the plane ticket and rent in Chicago and groceries. She didn't know anyone there anymore. Her neighborhood, gentrified; her family, gone. She tripped over a stick and forgot about Chicago. She spilled beer down her leg, just a few drops, nothing dramatic. She regained balance and thought about Rascal. She wondered if he was still hiding in the bedroom, waiting for attention. She wondered if she hated him. No, she thought. Not at all, she thought.

"No," Sojourner said. "No, no, no."

When she thought of life without Rascal, she didn't imagine herself with someone else. She didn't picture a taller and tanner person cooking multicourse lunches, making love to her in exciting and exhausting ways, paying their taxes on time, taking their dogs on long walks. She didn't picture anyone in her life without Rascal. Instead, she imagined herself in a small room by herself. In this small room, opened windows and urban noises poured over her, kept her from sleep. She

heard buses in her fantasies, laughter, sirens, people threat-
ening each other, dirt bikes; salsa, rap, rock, and heavy metal
pumping from busted cars' radios. Downstairs, beneath her
small room, she heard a couple screaming, throwing pans,
breaking glass, crying and crying. She heard the couple forgive, moan, climax together, laugh. She heard a newborn
bawl. She heard all the fights and cheers as that newborn grew.
Outside, when the school bus arrived, she heard the couple
say goodbye. When college came, the couple couldn't believe
it: their child, an Ivy League institution. The couple bragged
about their little lawyer. In her bed, looking out her opened
window, Sojourner glowed with contagious pride. Sojourner
heard that little lawyer cry when his first marriage didn't work.
Sojourner heard the couple spoil their grandchildren, make
them fat and happy with home-cooked meals. She still heard
the couple fight, scream, throw pans, break glass; she still
heard them forgive, moan, climax together, laugh. She heard
a constant and humming love, a love that brushed against her,
made her warm, gave her all the love she thought she needed.
She would remain alone, happy and content, absorbing whatever love the couple spared.

Then, one week, Sojourner didn't hear anything. Then, one
day, Sojourner heard ambulance sirens pull up outside. Then,
one morning, Sojourner heard the little lawyer crying, asking
how he's going to live without them.

Then, days later, Sojourner heard a new couple oohing and
aahing at their new apartment, so much bigger than the last—
all that room for a new life. Warm again.

Now, back here, Sojourner stood at the tree line, cold, love-less, looked into the woods. She tossed one bottle, finished, in a dead-stick pile.

There, up ahead, a twisted and worn trail.

There, two years ago, transported, in her mind, next to her grad school best friend, Robert, a man from Oregon, stuck, like her, in Buffalo for two years; getting the same Masters in Literature; reading the same lumpen proletariat books, Dahlberg, Steinbeck; writing the same response to *Tortilla Flat*; feeling the same way about each other; wanting, stand-ing there, to hold hands, feel platonic, not a shred of romance between them. Just a sweet boy from Oregon. Just a sweet girl from Chicago. Friends. Looking into the quarry and thinking about jumping. Promising to jump if the other jumped.

No romance between them. Not a shred. Just their feet, almost touching, a step away from the depths, say about thirty feet from the depths, the blue that is black now due to the night, the clouded sky without lights, the spring breeze. That sweet man from Oregon willing to jump with her. A year of depths. A year staring down a thesis and contemplating pur-pose, staring at academia, the professors, hollowed out, grants accepted, grants declined, grants offered to competition, com-petition over nothing, deciding between getting a doctorate or adjunct positions at a college two hours away. And what for?

I won't jump, I'm sorry, I have a family dog, back in Oregon, an aunt that sends me gigantic chocolate bunnies for Easter and Christmas. That's okay. That's okay to step back, walk to the car, drive back with the radio low, the windows down, two cigarettes burning in the dark, those thin ones the sweet man from Oregon brought from home, which Sojourner wouldn't smoke on a usual night. This, not a usual night. This, alive again.

Alive, like the Wednesday after college graduation, sitting in the crowded coffee shop, watching the doorway, waiting for her best friend since freshman year, Rosaline from Tampa, waiting for one hour, waiting for two hours, waiting for three hours, until they closed, waiting on the sidewalk, calling them again, never hearing back. Alive, like leaning against the closed coffee shop, waiting to hear back. Alive, like curled up in bed, after they found the body. Alive, like listening to voice-mails from sophomore year, when her friend took an improv class, when Sojourner didn't pick up the phone and her friend left joke messages in bad accents. Alive, like her friend imitating Patrick Stewart. Alive, like her friend imitating Lawrence Olivier. Hello, Sojourner, this is your friend, are you alive?

Sojourner heard her first therapist, saw her, in a dream-like current, sitting across the room, leaned back, gentle, saying: "This family history is significant. This death. And your friend. That is significant."

Family history: the time Sojourner stood in the doorway, when her mother, eyes closed, heard about her baby brother, Sojourner's Uncle Ross. All that sadness, hopelessness, despair, twisted metal, balled up in a ditch, hurtled off the expressway at seventy miles per hour; her mother, eyes closed, curled up on the carpet, howling, unlike anything Sojourner had heard before or since. A tragedy like that, of course that breaks a person. Of course, her mother changed and Sojourner changed and the house changed and the atmosphere dropped in pressure, or was the sadness thick like tar? Of course the house broke and her mother walked around with her eyes closed and knocked into walls and grasped through the darkness at something to hold, anything to hold, to feel steady, to feel grounded.

"Sojourner, how do you feel?" the therapist had said.

She'd felt like running then.

Now, she felt like running. Not away from death. Toward life.

Stand up, Sojourner.

The New Naturals

-- --

RIO CHECKED OVER her list of potential investors, coconspir-
ators, like-minded folks.

First, she tried Kofi Auburn, a tenured economics professor
from outside Chattanooga, a man with whom she'd shared a
pitcher of margaritas at an academic conference in Columbus,
Ohio. Kofi answered the phone on the first ring.

"Lord," Kofi said. "Rio. Is that you? Are you okay?"

Word had spread through their circle that Rio had suffered
a mental breakdown after her daughter's death. Kofi had heard
they were living in the mountains, hunting for their food, gone
feral. Kofi made Rio repeat herself.

"A what?" Kofi asked. "A society?"

"We can dig into the mountain," Rio said. "We can use bunker technology."

Kofi went silent on his end. He let Rio explain. He reclined in his chair. He remembered his brother, the morning before his suicide, calling over and over, speaking about the doomed world, the unavoidable disasters, speaking too fast to catch it all.

"I'm sorry," Kofi said.

Kofi hung up. He didn't move until his son knocked on the door and asked if they could go to the park, toss the baseball around, get ice cream after, and a hot dog. Kofi hugged his son until the boy had to squirm away.

Rio tried Georgia Hubble, a veteran anarchist from outside San Francisco, a writer of pamphlets and ignored articles for ignored journals. Georgia loved the idea. She cut Rio off. She had some recommendations: What about a militia? What about attack plans? What about sabotage? The best coders in the world, super hackers—what about them? Did Rio know about our election systems, how those computers could crack in minutes? Don't you see how we can bring it all down, watch it burn?

Georgia was still talking when Rio hung up. She called back and Rio didn't answer. She kept calling back and Rio had to block the number, block her e-mails.

She called deans, adjuncts from old money, associate professors, assistant professors, one provost, a chancellor. She ran through people from public and private institutions, nonprofit organizations with radical missions, for-profit universities with online degrees in sports management, lawyers, bankers, real estate developers. They hung up. She hung up. They threatened to call the authorities. They tried to co-opt her mission. All she wanted was peace and quiet. All she wanted was a place for people to live and love and hide. Was that too much? Was that impossible? Yes, they said. What's the point? Where's the income, what are your margins?

Two days passed and Rio hurt all over. Her eyes, legs, chest, arms, and ears. She stood and shook. She howled and collapsed. She heard Gibraltar beat down the stairs. She felt Gibraltar put arms around her body, lift her up.

"What's wrong with them?" Rio asked Gibraltar's chest. "What don't they understand?"

"Sleep," Gibraltar said. "Come to bed."

He helped her up, tucked her in, closed the blinds, closed the door, stood in the hallway, hoped this was the end, hoped they could get back to the world.

Rio didn't leave bed in the morning. Gibraltar brought her orange juice, toast, and bacon on a tray.

Rio didn't leave bed in the afternoon. Gibraltar slid into the covers, asked if she needed anything else.

Rio didn't leave bed at night, the next morning, the next afternoon, the next night, the next morning. Gibraltar didn't leave either.

A week passed. Gibraltar helped Rio roll up the maps, put them in plastic trunks, put them in the garage next to an unused lawn mower, tools they never used, stacks of plastic water bottles.

They sat on the couch, watched action movies, shared bowls of popcorn. They took showers together, soaped up each other's backs, sang oldies in bad harmony.

Gibraltar saw a glow return to Rio's face. If sun came through the window, splashed her cheeks just right—Gibraltar caught her smiling.

They even talked about trips abroad, Spain, Morocco, Macau, getting drunk and spending fistfuls of cash on baccarat, spilling their drinks when they hit it big. They had savings. They could move to Lagos, work at an English-speaking university. They could spend a summer in Tokyo. There were crowded beaches in Australia, zip lines through Costa Rican rainforests. They weren't dead. The world was dying. They had their health. They had their love. They were alive. They cooked dinner together and danced while the lamb roasted.

Rio would make coffee in the morning, feel failure tapping on her head, stand outside, muster strength and accept her smallness. She wasn't a person that could change the world. She'd tried. Most people don't try. She would take a vacation. Mexico City. She would visit museums, hold Gibraltar's hand, point out details in portraits, a curved line, a smooth gradient.

Gibraltar watched his wife sleep in her new hammock, worried she'd tip over in the breeze. He enjoyed this type of worry. He imagined his route to her, if she would fall. He imagined falling in the grass, too. Maybe they'd hold each other. Maybe, someday soon, they'd have another baby.

Gibraltar put his coffee down. One foot was off the ground, moving to the door, when the phone rang.

"Is this Gibraltar?" a woman asked.

"Who's calling?" Gibraltar asked.

"Is this Gibraltar?" the woman asked again. "Is your wife Rio?"

"Who is this?" Gibraltar asked again, froze.

"I know your idea," the woman said.

Gibraltar watched his wife wake up.

Rio saw Gibraltar, in the kitchen, on the phone, looking right at her. Like his eyes were melting. Like his head was turned upside down.

The Benefactor

- -

SHE WAS A voice, an obscene bank account. She got their number from a friend of a friend of a friend. Someone passed along the idea. The Benefactor loved it, had spent nights in Hawaii, looking at the sunset, wondering how the next stage looked. She had a paradise here, on the archipelago. Another paradise in Utah, in the mountains. Paradise in Dubai. Paradise in Argentina, Nigeria, New Zealand, and Kyoto. She could go anywhere and find beauty, find someone to scrub her feet and rub her shoulders. It was a boring comfort. It was glorious boredom without purpose.

THE NEW NATURALS   57

Each time she visited her mother in Durham, her mother didn't recognize her daughter, hair like that, clothes like that, private security, would comment on her eyes and smile. Her mother would pick up a picture from the mantel, hold it up to the Benefactor's face, show her a smiling child on a canoe, on a river, brave and happy and filled with purpose. That's you. Where did you go?

Then her mother had died, two years ago, and that didn't matter anymore; a disconnect from her old self, whatever that meant.

The Benefactor had been a college-aged genius. A visionary. The mind behind Polonaise, high-speed servers capable of handling galaxies full of data. Her servers were small, could fit in a closet. They were powerful, graceful. Polonaise was beloved across borders, both ideological and physical, the Rio Grande, in Juarez and El Paso, for example. Her capitalistic mind was perfect for the moment.

She was a growing conglomerate. A scourge of Congress. An antitrust behemoth.

She grew too big for restraint and kept growing.

Then, on a beach in Hawaii, she felt empty. For the first time, she felt a hole where her soul should be, right between her ribs and gut. She had conquered the moneyed world. She could charge small-minded executives $100,000 for an hour lunch. She would share her worst ideas with them; they would kiss her hand, call her back, and she wouldn't answer.

On the Hawaii beach, in her stolen paradise, she decided to

spend her money on something ridiculous, improbable, fun, maybe world-changing, who knows. She wanted to feel full. She needed something to do. She called her advisor.

Her advisor was on the beach in fifteen minutes, out of breath, still wet from a shower.

"What should I do?" the Benefactor asked.

"You could have children," her advisor said.

"That's not interesting," the Benefactor said.

Her advisor took a step back, grimaced.

"What about sports?" her advisor asked. "You could win a Super Bowl."

"Jerry Jones won a Super Bowl," the Benefactor said. "No thank you."

"I'll figure it out," her advisor said.

Her advisor didn't figure it out.

The Benefactor, in her New Zealand compound, another stolen paradise, received a call from a college friend, who had received a call from a colleague, who had received a call from Rio. The chance to build a better world, to think centuries in the future. In tech they called it longtermism—making investments today that would pay off in a thousand years. Instead of going to space, why not go inward, down?

Sure, the Benefactor figured, staring at a lush valley, an underground society, a blueprint for the future. An attempt at perfection through isolation. She remembered a history class in college. Whole communities of runaway slaves in a swamp straddling Virginia and North Carolina. The Great Dismal. She recalled runaway slave communities in the Amazon.

Quilombos. She could build something like that underground. Not just for slaves. For anyone. For everyone. The Great Dismal and the quilombos would have welcomed everyone, if their intentions had been pure, if they could have joined their missions against oppression and exploitation. She could try to get it right. That has purpose. That will help. Whatever they want.

Sojourner

RASCAL HAD FOUND this trail when they first moved in, when he'd wandered around out here, looked for hidden cameras and wiretaps. He had hustled back, grabbed Sojourner, showed her, asked her if this trail looked like a Police Trail. Sojourner didn't know what a Police Trail looked like. Rascal tried to explain; he often didn't make sense.

That was nine months ago. Sojourner was prepared to leave then. She was prepared to leave Rascal the night she met him.

She'd been new to town. Rascal was sitting in a beer garden, smoking cigarettes with other PhD candidates. His back leaned against an ivy-draped brick wall. Sojourner was there with a colleague, a male sports reporter with thin skin and improper intentions. Rascal had this laugh—an obnoxious boom. Sojourner sipped her beer and looked past the sports reporter whenever a boom careened her way. The sports reporter was talking about sports, or something. Rascal and his friends were talking about Shakespeare and Ibsen and O'Neill and August Wilson, talking loud enough for the whole beer garden to hear their intelligence, their ability to connect dots between works created centuries apart. One grad student called Ibsen "unhinged." Rascal hollered with joy. Someone in the crowd yelled, "'Reason is dead and gone; long live Peer Gynt.'" The sports reporter stopped talking about corner-backs, or whatever. Sojourner excused herself. She sat at the bar inside and watched the sports reporter outside thumbing through his phone, looking for scores, or who cares. She wanted to see how long he would wait for her to return. She watched as Rascal excused himself, headed straight for her.

Now, in the woods, stopped, hunched over, gasping for breath, Sojourner thought about that first moment, when Rascal had walked in and sat next to her, asked if she needed a drink, even though her drink was almost full. That short hair, cropped close, even and tight. He tried to hide his nerves. He couldn't stop his leg from bouncing. He'd take a sip and choke and try to hide his choking. Sojourner wanted to understand him better. He was an adorable curiosity. His face like a teenager's, soft and pimpled.

Her memory was interrupted by a noise. A snap. Sojourner felt her dilated eyes wobble. Her heart pumped extra blood to her organs and limbs. Fuck, Sojourner thought. It's here to kill me.

"Fuck," Sojourner said.

She stood, prepared to sprint and hurtle back to safety. When she tried to move, however, her muscles locked. She froze. At a time like this, with certain danger, unseen, coming for her. She looked down, saw a centipede linger on her ankle. She tried to scream and nothing came out. She tried to run, again, and nothing moved. Except her heart, gone wild. Except her eyes, darting about, wild, too.

She closed her eyes; she didn't want to look death in the mouth. Fuck, Sojourner thought.

"Fuck that," Sojourner said.

She opened her eyes; clenched her teeth; chugged her beer.

"Come on!" she screamed into the morning.

Then she saw it. Standing proud next to a boring tree, right in front of her: the baby deer with a black spot.

"You're fucking kidding me," Sojourner said, laughed.

Her body, drowned in adrenaline, vibrated. She forgot about the centipede until she felt one hundred feet move up her thigh. She screamed again, danced, swatted the insect into a dead log. Still, the baby deer looked at her.

Sojourner settled, sat, caught her breath, grabbed her heart, felt her pulse, didn't keep track of the beats, figured she wasn't dying. It was just her and an unflinching deer out here, with nothing to talk about. They stared at each other as the woods resumed their mundane routine. The deer didn't move when three squirrels cartwheeled down a sapling; Sojourner didn't move while a mosquito sucked on her earlobe.

She wondered if this was meditation. Once, another therapist, a nice white therapist in a dashiki, suggested Sojourner take some quiet time to sit and reflect. Just a few moments, the therapist suggested, to think about yourself, to thank yourself. Thank herself for what? Sojourner left the office and wrote the therapist a bad review online.

Now, she and the deer were stuck in a mental loop, exchanging souls, it felt like. Her and this strange deer. This unnatural deer. Both of them blinked, sure. Still, they were deep into something Sojourner had never felt. A connection. Nonromantic. Sojourner was loose, relaxed. Her body slumped and her jaw unclenched. The deer, she saw, was relaxed, too. She expected the deer to sit down, like her. She thought about all the deer she had seen: shooting across highways, frozen in meadows, high alert, muscles poised to gallop. She thought about the deer sitting down, cool, maybe taking a drink. Sojourner motioned for the deer to sit. Nothing. Okay, Sojourner thought.

"Okay," Sojourner said. "Your choice."

This was meditation. Sojourner knew it. She closed her eyes, didn't mind the bugs swirling along her shin, buzzing in her face. She grinned at her calmness. See, Sojourner thought, I'm meditating. I'm at peace, Sojourner thought—calm. She forgot her beer. Her beer slipped, spilled. She didn't mind. She kept her eyes closed and tried to leave her body. For a moment, she did.

She was floating, looking down on herself and the deer, going higher, knocking into large and slim branches, not feeling a thing except calm.

She was flying above the tree line, circling their house, scanning the meadow. No Rascal. No nothing. She kept going. She sped above the empty dirt road, took it to the highway, rode the highway to town. There, her office: the paper. That small gray building with too few windows. Below her now: Main Street, pizza places, coffee shops, Thai restaurants, Chinese restaurants, Japanese restaurants, organic markets, yoga studio, Pilates studio, spin studio, weight rooms, and an upscale French place, closed for renovations. Now: The College; different architectural eras contained on a sprawling campus, a flagship; new glass buildings next to faded redbricked dorms next to concrete offices with serrated facades—a visual mess. There: Rascal's office, the English department. Fuck this place, Sojourner thought. I can't stay here, she thought. If I stay here, she thought, I'm going to combust. She couldn't look at it anymore. She never wanted to see it again. Dead ends everywhere. Purposeless everywhere. Disgusting.

She wondered if, in her state, she could go anywhere. She thought about Rome and found herself, in an instant, dipping into the Coliseum, raking her fingers in the Tiber.

Sojourner thought about Los Angeles, San Francisco, San Diego, Oakland. She didn't want California. She wanted home.

She thought about Chicago. She found herself on the north coast, with those suburban mansions with private beaches. She thought about her father and his new family, drinking margaritas, feet in the sand, underneath umbrellas. She thought about how people change and how that change can hurt. She flew south, along Lake Shore Drive. She passed downtown, thought about her mother, her new family, their condo, their private schools and tutors. She flew south, hovered over South Shore. She thought about her first life. Mom and dad yelling in the kitchen, yelling in the car, yelling in the front yard, yelling in the bedroom, real yelling, wall-shaking yelling. Sojourner remembered the boys at school asking why her mother was white and her father was Black—where could they meet a white woman? Sojourner remembered the girls pulling at her long brown curls, poking at her freckled nose, poking her sunburns, admiring her light eyes. Sojourner remembered studying herself in the mirror, pulling at her long brown curls, poking, poking, wondering about herself, where she fit in the world. Would she always feel different, outside the conversation, an interloper? She would go to college, meet other girls and boys like her, have circular conversations about race and identity, how identity is more than race, more than long brown curls and light eyes; she would move on from race, stop talking about it, stop engaging, she would graduate to other existentialisms, like her current emptiness, a purer, less-complicated wondering, what is the meaning of life, what is the meaning of anything.

Beneath her: their old house, the stucco painted a different color—red, not blue—the basketball hoop on the garage still crooked, leaning to the left, large and thin spider webs along the backboard. Why did this new family cut down all the trees?

Overcome, Sojourner flew straight up, fast. Wet clouds splashed life back into her face, rinsed her tears.

Now, she busted through the ozone and felt power unlike anything she had imagined before. Now, she busted through space, right through the moon, right toward the sun. She felt wonderful heat toast her heart. She heard voices calling her name. She called back, said "I'm here! I'm here! I'm burning up! I'm here!"

Now, there was a hand on her shoulder, pulling her back, slowing her down, digging fingernails into her shoulder, tearing at her flesh.

Now, she was back in the moon, cometing backward, loud screaming voices pumping through her walls, water rising from her floor, her ceiling lowering onto her terrified face.

"What the fuck!" Sojourner yelled.

She opened her eyes.

She was back on earth, sitting on a stump, in a place she wanted to leave. No deer. A hand on her shoulder.

"WAKE UP!" Rascal yelled.

He stood behind her, hand on her shoulder, fingernails dug into her flesh.

"I heard screaming," Rascal said. "I came running."

Sojourner slapped his hand away, stood, wanted to strangle him, looked for her deer.

"Why'd you do that?" Sojourner asked.

"You were screaming," Rascal said. "I thought a bear got you."

"There was a deer," Sojourner said.

"Did it attack you?" Rascal asked.

"I was meditating," Sojourner said.

Sojourner pushed past Rascal, ran back toward the house, stopped in the meadow, caught her breath, kept running, busted through the front door, locked the door behind her, went into the bedroom, locked the door behind her, went into the bathroom, locked the door behind her, turned the shower on cold, didn't close the curtain. She sat like that—cold water running over her body—until the shaking stopped, however long that took.

Okay. Leave.

Wrapped in a towel, Sojourner zipped her suitcase.

Rascal followed her through the kitchen, onto the porch.

"Please," Rascal said. "What's wrong?"

Bare, Sojourner couldn't speak. She shook her head, closed her eyes. In her darkness, she heard his continued pleading, his asking. She kept shaking her head. She did this whenever she felt like crying and didn't want anyone to see: hid herself, imagined herself invisible. It was just her and darkness and Rascal's voice trailing in hopeless directions and, now, morning sounds beating against their bedroom windows. She found herself in a twisting helix, shooting backward through time. And there was Rascal coming through her old apartment door with coffee, bagels, spreads, kissed, all delivered with a silly voice, a bad imitation of Sean Connery. And there was Rascal fumbling in bed, trying to make her feel good and failing, earnest, heartfelt. Enough, just the thought. And there was morning coming through Sojourner's old apartment window, rubbing against Rascal's face, not waking him, just causing his eyes to twist under their lids, just adding color to his nocturnal tantrums, soft yellows and oranges. Sojourner had begged him to see a specialist, take medications, do research. Back then, over bagels and coffee and spreads and crumbs in Sojourner's old bed, Rascal explained to Sojourner how he couldn't do that kind of research, he was a doctoral student, he studied books, researched connections and themes throughout history, looked for missing links, tried to think thoughts no one had ever thought before. Tried to have an original mind. I know, Sojourner had said. Rascal, back then, chewing on an untoasted onion bagel with strawberry cream cheese, kept talking about his original mind and his night terrors as reflection and proof of his original mind. Sojourner had listened and hated him, chewed on a toasted plain bagel with plain cheese cream, thought, maybe, she just hated everybody and, considering other people, Rascal wasn't so bad—the person she hated least of all. Months later, they'd moved in with each other. Somewhere in between, they fell in love. Or, decided falling in love and moving in together was easier than breaking up. Sojourner wasn't sure, then, when Rascal led her up the meadow, up the porch, into the kitchen, into the bedroom—our place!

And that's how unsure love turned into ambivalence and hatred. They would get into bed, turn away from each other, try to talk, fight, stop talking, go to sleep angry.

One night, they watched *All the President's Men*. Rascal went on a lame rant about self-importance in journalism.

What has changed? Rascal said, Are politics any less corrupt?—imagine how politicians spy on each other now, imagine the tricks, the schemes, the lessons learned from Nixon.

"For example," Rascal said. "Your story. The lead."

Sojourner turned to him.

"Don't look at me like that," Rascal said. "It's not a scan-
dalous story. 'People in small towns getting sick.' You have to
make people care. Do you even care?"

"No," Sojourner said, insincere. "I don't."

"You don't care about anything," Rascal said. "You're the
problem with journalism. You give up too easy."

Sojourner had turned over, faked sleep, was finished with
Rascal. She was finished with the story. All that work. For
what? For Rascal to call her a failure? For nothing to change?

Sojourner had started sleeping on the couch with old television shows playing over and over, shows she would never
watch when lucid, network sitcoms about chaotic families, predictable shows with laugh tracks and reused tropes,
numbskulls and aghast supporting players. She wanted to stop
thinking. In this way, Sojourner had felt her emotions dull.
Her laugh turned hollow. When Rascal mounted her, on rare
and drunk occasions, she kissed him when it finished, didn't
feel a thing, floated into sleep.

Like she was floating, now, standing in front of him.

She opened her eyes.

"Please," Rascal said.

Of course, he was crying. Of course, she was crying.

"I need to get dressed," Sojourner said.

"What am I going to do?" Rascal asked.

"You can do this," Sojourner said.

"No," Rascal said. "I can't. You can't."

Sojourner nudged Rascal out of the way, closed the door. She took work clothes from the closet: professional slacks and a blouse. She pulled elegant underwear from her drawer. She got dressed, cried, listened to Rascal tap his head about the door, tapped her feet to his rhythm. She felt cruel and broken, refreshed. She caught herself in the mirror, flexed, gritted her teeth.

Clothed, she called a cab.

As she walked through that house for the last time, she didn't see Rascal. He was hiding somewhere. She wouldn't see him again.

The New Naturals

RIO AND GIBRALTAR debated, first, if this was a place only for Black people, if the plan, now that the plan could become reality, was an extreme form of resegregation, a return to the peaceful, prosperous isolation of All-Black Towns, Black Wall Streets, and the like; if the plan was resettlement, a modern version of Marcus Garvey's Black Star Line, or Liberia. Would they offer Black Americans a chance to go underground, remove themselves from white society, forge a new world? What about other marginalized folks? Native Americans, Latinx, Uyghurs, Migrant Workers. What about them? Would they have a place? Of course they would. What about a hypothetical young man from Kansas City, white, football star, with a hollowness in his chest, a sleepless sense of not belonging, a young man adrift? What about them? Of course. They were welcome.

They were the New Naturals.

Soon, the Benefactor brought in advisors. She formed a board comprised of former CEOs, heads of states, consultants, Effective Altruism gurus. They would operate with anonymity. They would communicate through secured telephone lines. Never meet in person. Never share personal details. A faceless cabal.

During their first conference call, Rio and Gibraltar declared their project was for anybody who needed them. They would spread the word through existing community outreach programs, shelters, soup kitchens, gyms. They would move through whispers and nudges.

Next, they needed to build.

They called in favors, got zoning officials to look the other way, pay no mind to the dump trucks, the industrial drills. The excavation. The constant noise. They hollowed out the Mountain. They called the Benefactor, asked for more funds, asked for better equipment, revisited the blueprints, debated whether the workout room should go next to the garden room, debated the number of classrooms, the number of libraries, the number of rooms without a purpose, without decoration, rooms for sitting in silence. The debates seemed endless. They kept revisiting Rio's blueprints, found aspects of the design infeasible or underwhelming. Rio wasn't an architect. Rio's original design called for a simple floor plan, two intersecting hallways with rooms built off the hallways. Her plans looked like a boring state-college dormitory. The board wanted avant-garde. They wanted more rooms, more privacy. They wanted curves and flow. They wanted the garden room and the brewery far away from the nursery and the kindergarten. They kept building down, more levels, more space. They added a pool. They added lab space for experiments and research. Maybe, if they attracted the right scientists, in time, the New Naturals could cure cancer or develop a strawberry that lasted forever, without federal agencies looking over their shoulders.

And this restaurant. Why not tear it down and replace it with trees, a monument, something, anything, the board asked? Rio wouldn't budge. She thought the restaurant was a beacon. It had meaning. It was staying. The board asked Rio to explain. The board didn't understand her rambling about the Mountain, the bridge, the chipping white paint, how it pulled you upward, pulled you inside, to rest, to relax, to eat. The board agreed to let the restaurant stay, for now. There were more pressing concerns: how many beds did they have to order?

Anyone could come. Fine. But who would come? How would they fill this place? The board needed answers. The engineers needed specifics.

Rio and Gibraltar called up a former graduate student, Julian from Albuquerque, told him about a secret project, low-cost, good experience. They told him about the Mountain. They asked what he was doing, where was he working, how was he feeling about life, society. He was teaching back home, at a community college, Native American Literature. The state legislature was planning to cut his department and all departments associated with books and reading and understanding history. He delivered groceries at night, to pay rent. He felt like an aimless blob on a whitewater rapidly bouncing, without emotion, toward a sharp rock, the sharpest rock he had ever seen. Sure, Julian from Albuquerque would come.

Rio and Gibraltar called other former students, other friends in shrinking positions.

"Help us build," they said. "Help us try again."

Concrete was poured, holes were drilled, mattresses were ordered, and people came to the Mountain.

After a year, the New Naturals were real.

Sojourner

- -

SHE WALKED INTO the office, head up, suitcase and briefcase in either hand, swinging them in defiance. She sat in her cubicle, laid her head on the keyboard. After a few moments, a voice over her shoulder. Matteo. Half-awake, voice still weak and scratched.

"It's your day off," Matteo said.

Matteo noticed her suitcase, rolled his head around his thick neck, patted his thick stomach, arched his weak back.

Sojourner noticed Matteo notice her suitcase.

They both contemplated the suitcase.

"I'm behind on a story," Sojourner said.

"What are you going to do?" Matteo asked.

"I have family in Chicago," Sojourner said. "I have family in Boston."

"I meant the story," Matteo said.

"Just calling leads," Sojourner said, hid her face.

Matteo patted Sojourner on the shoulder, headed back to his office, stopped, turned around.

"If you're going to leave," Matteo said, "give us a heads-up."

Sojourner looked around, checked to see if other people heard. In the corner, the sports reporters were yelling about Black quarterbacks and white receivers, how the whole culture had turned upside down overnight. The other reporters were shushed, typing, whispering into their phones, texting, tweeting. In a glass room, the columnists took turns raising their hands, writing notes on a long whiteboard.

Sojourner took out her notebook, turned on her computer.

With the lead fiasco behind her, the job had returned to boring, slow. Sometimes, of course, a city council member was caught using taxpayer money for a three-day New Year's Eve bacchanal.

Once, a former school board president fathered biracial children with an El Salvadorian refugee, a teenager with little English and a mature mind, cunning. Her name was Esther. Sojourner interviewed Esther. She had a sixteen-year-old's body and face—arrogant, not confident; insecure. Her mind, however—her mind. She spoke like an oracle, an ancient soothsayer. She understood broken hearts and despair and love's joys better than Sojourner, or anyone Sojourner knew.

She spoke in wonderful parables. She compared love to molten rock, shifting and rocking the earth's crust. She asked Sojourner about her present life, her past life, her future life, her loves. On a walk down a dirt road, during a final interview, she asked if Sojourner was happy, fulfilled. Of course not, Sojourner said.

"Are you even trying?" Esther asked.

"I don't think so," Sojourner said, stopped walking. "I don't know."

"That little bird," Esther said.

A sparrow hopped in their path, pecked at the dirt.

"What is the bird saying?" Esther said. "Listen."

Sojourner listened to the chirps, listened to a gust pass through, a car on a different road, somewhere she couldn't see, driving too fast.

"I can't hear the bird," Sojourner said.

"Try and listen to the bird," Esther said.

Sojourner went home confused, wrote a profile, won awards.

Most days, she sat in twice-a-week city council meetings that were too long and too filled with conceited people complaining about their lawns and college students fucking on their lawns, reciprocating oral sex in their greenhouses, vomiting on their sidewalks, denting their car hoods with their fucking.

This week's meeting promised the same.

St. Patrick's Day and Spring Break were coming in two weeks.

After what had happened last year, Sojourner was assigned to report on the town's preparations for the siege. Off the record, the town's police chief told Sojourner he wanted to coordinate tactical drone strikes on Frat Row, raze the horn-dog bastards. On the record, transcribed in her notebook, the police chief said they would work with student council to ensure peaceful crowd control. Off the record, the police chief couldn't understand it—this wasn't the March on Washington; this was drunk teenagers wandering around like sex-crazed zombies. Didn't these fuckers have homework? Tests? Hobbies? What ever happened to fishing?

Last year, for reasons still unclear, the students had turned into animals. Some people blamed the planetary cycle, Jupiter rising. Some people blamed Republicans, this Repressive Era making young people ache for expression, freedom. Some people blamed cocaine. More than a few blamed rap music and these young rappers acting like fools in public for social media followers: Everyone wanted to get famous doing stupid shit on camera.

Last year, around noon, Friday before Spring Break, a concerned citizen called in about a group of students sitting on a front porch, drinking beer, yelling, playing music too loud. That was the first call, a tame one, one that was handled by one squad car pulling up and telling the kids to take it inside—to quit acting like jackasses. From eyewitness accounts and the official reports, the students went inside, turned their music down, turned their music off at a reasonable hour, woke up early the next morning, went to their front lawn, cleaned up the empty beer cans and pizza boxes.

Sojourner opened a document on her computer, pulled out her notepad, cracked her fingers, started copying notes.

Then she stopped.

She popped into Matteo's office, tapped her head against the metal doorframe, waited for him to look up from a paper stack covered in red scribbles. She knocked her head again, coughed, tapped her chest.

"A second," Matteo said without looking up.

"I need some air," Sojourner said.

"Air is everywhere," Matteo said.

"I'm serious," Sojourner said.

"What am I?" Matteo asked.

"I'm going for a walk," Sojourner said.

"It's your day off," Matteo said.

Here, Matteo looked up.

When he'd first interviewed Sojourner for the job, a few years ago, he knew she would leave at a bad time, abrupt, in a hurry. He didn't think she would come in on a day off, carrying a suitcase, looking adrift, beer still on her breath. He thought this day would come in a dramatic and loud whirl. He had imagined Sojourner upturning her cubicle, sending papers fluttering, stomping on these stupid and pointless stories. Matteo understood how the small-town grind ate at a person. Once, decades ago, Matteo had interned for the *Wall Street Journal*. He talked fast, had thought his future contained corruption scandals and white-collar conspiracies. Somewhere in his twenties, he'd fallen in love, had children, moved to a small town, took the first job he could find. He'd learned to appreciate his rural and mundane cycle. He was happy. Matteo, however, wasn't Sojourner. Sojourner needed to get the hell out of here, start over, she said. She needed a break to figure out what starting over looked like. Maybe she'd move to New York, hustle a job at a bigger publication. Maybe she'd join a nonprofit focused on clean water. She could get a doctorate in city planning. She needed time to think.

Matteo couldn't look away. Sojourner looked back. Her lips trembled.

"Call when you land," Matteo said.

Sojourner wanted to thank Matteo. At that moment, she didn't know why. She couldn't describe the urge toward gratitude. Years later, she would understand. It would come to her during quiet reflection. She wanted to thank Matteo for giving her permission, for looking at her and understating what Sojourner couldn't, at the time, explain.

Matteo dropped his eyes again, waved for Sojourner to leave. He didn't look up when she turned around, walked back to her desk, picked up her suitcase, her bag, left her notes, didn't turn off her computer, headed for the front door. He didn't look up when the door slammed.

She was leaving, yes. That was decided. Still, where?

She had friends; not many, not enough, no real good ones, a few minor enemies—nothing serious. She could make some calls. That could wait. She decided to walk.

She took her bags, headed downtown.

At an intersection, four blocks away from the office, Sojourner noticed soaring birds in loud groups overhead, coming home

from Florida or Europe—maybe Africa, Argentina, India, or the
Azores. Sojourner didn't know this type of thing, didn't bother
asking anybody. She waited for the light to change, the birds to
pass. She waited for the world to show her a sign. She thought
the deer from this morning, maybe, had been a sign. No, she
thought, that was meditation. That was different. That was a
door opening, the universe telling her to set out, move on. Now,
she was out. Now what? She waited for the light to change. More
birds passed, stragglers fought against the unseen currents. A
semitruck made a wide right, huffed, splashed her feet with curb
water, moved slow down a narrow avenue.

Not a sign.

Sojourner did not acknowledge her wet feet. She squished
across the intersection.

Over there, a park. She could sit under a chair and sleep,
wait for a sign, go from there.

Rascal pushed into her mind. Fuck him, she thought.

"I'm sorry," Sojourner said out loud.

No, she thought, fuck him.

Sojourner found a water fountain between two benches,
took a metallic chug, pushed Rascal out, smiled, a little, not
enough to draw attention.

She drank the clean water. Bullshit, Sojourner thought.

Injustice made Sojourner sweat. Once, another therapist, a
Black man with thin glasses and a wide tie, warned Sojourner
against projecting her unhappiness onto the world. Sojourner
told the therapist about child slaves. Here. In America. Child
slaves. What place is this? All this opportunity. All these jobs.

Money. Obscene money. Jay Leno with his garage filled with hundreds of cars. Jay Leno. Jay Fucking Leno. Child slaves. Not in Africa. Not in Asia. Not in a developing country still reeling from colonization's strangling grasp. Not a dictatorship. America. Can you believe it? The therapist asked Sojourner to stop yelling, please sit down.

Sojourner drank more clean water, thought about child slaves. She sat on a bench. She looked out on the street.

She wondered how park benches felt in Marseille. How did morning traffic sound in Rome? Were there birds like this in London? Sparrows, maybe. Sojourner wasn't sure. Sparrows were birds she knew. Sparrows hopped near the water fountain, chatted, argued, laughed. Sojourner thought about Esther, her impenetrable insights. She wanted to call Esther. Inappropriate. She had to call someone. At some point, she had to get up and get going.

Rascal pushed his way into her ear, got stuck there. She heard him back home, curled up in bed, talking to his mother, crying to his mother, yelling into his pillow. She closed her eyes. She saw him in the meadow. She saw rain clouds coming over the tree line, fat with dramatic rain.

She opened her eyes, smiled her smile.

She thought about utopia.

A place with safe drinking water, safe children, sane neighbors letting young people party. A place where people worked together for a common good, with purpose, with intention, where every day felt meaningful.

She didn't need much. She didn't need London, Rome, Marseille, Bangkok. She didn't need butlers and chauffeurs.

She needed beautiful simplicity.

She thought about standing up, walking.

She needed a place to go. She pulled her phone from her jeans, scrolled through her contacts, waited for inspiration, tried to remember favors she was promised from girlfriends once in a similar situation.

Anna.

August.

That time Brando slept on Sojourner's couch for three weeks, ate every apple in the fridge, didn't wash dishes.

Cleo.

Dianna.

She didn't need Rascal. She didn't need her own home, her own bed. Sure, someday, she'd get those things, someday soon, once she got back on her feet. She continued to sit, started calling.

Brando answered after three rings.

"He called," Brando said first.

"Who?" Sojourner asked.

"Are you serious?" Brando said.

"Oh," Sojourner said.

"He's crying," Brando said. "He says you're crazy."

"Can I come over?" Sojourner said.

"He's worried about your mind," Brando said.

"I'll see you in fifteen," Sojourner said.

"In the backyard," Brando said. "Door's open."

Sojourner took her bags, sipped clean water, slapped her cheeks, headed out.

The New Naturals

THOSE NASCENT DAYS contained gorgeous and wild confu-
sion, glowing uncertainty. They planted in the growing room
without consideration of season. Potatoes and kale, carrots
and apple trees. They unpacked boxes of donated books and
filled the bookshelves. They had decided on two libraries: one
academic, the other for fiction, poetry, drama, and children's
books. Kierkegaard, Frantz Fanon, Toni Morrison, Zora Neale
Hurston, Spinoza, Ibsen, C. L. R. James, Simone De Beauvoir,
Gogol.

Whole families had moved in, mostly from cities where
the cost of living had squeezed them out: New York, Boston,

San Francisco. There was even a young couple, expecting, from Vancouver. People wanted to try this new society. They wanted to feel like their work had purpose. They were software engineers, ex-convicts, doctors, retired lawyers, and elementary school teachers. Above ground, they were underpaid, overworked, overpaid, disillusioned, drained, depleted. All of them were lost and confused in unique ways. They were dissatisfied with how their tax money was being spent without their control. They were tired of being exploited. They came from a wider spectrum of need and anger than Rio and Gibraltar could have imagined.

Down here, in the Mountain, they could spend the afternoon painting seascapes in the art room. Or, they could run on the treadmill and listen to live jazz. The filtered air was crisp. The filtered water tasted straight from a spring. Deliveries of fresh beef and chicken arrived twice a week. The chefs were misfits, veterans of the best restaurants. They didn't have to scrounge for purpose. Purpose was everywhere.

Saturday nights, after dinner, they would gather in the theater for a salon. They voted on a governmental structure with commanders and advisors. They would drink homemade wine and moonshine. They would discuss growth, change, what they wanted from the future: more music lessons; a basketball court; better wine. Rio and Gibraltar would sit, listen, take their requests to the board, constantly work on improving.

What else could they want?

Elting

- -

ELTING USED TO interpret clouds, years earlier, when he had
found himself outside on his back. In his old backyard, for
example, he would take a six-pack to the dead crabapple tree.
He would look through the thin bare branches. He'd count and
drink until he stumbled. He'd start over, get another six-pack,
sit out there until the sun went down, until the clouds blended
into the sky and counting was impossible. He'd stare into the
dark until bed. He'd feel his way through his dark house, up
his dark stairs, into his dark king-sized bed, under his purple
bedsheets. He'd hope for sleep. Sometimes it would come. That
was before Edith. There were a few sober months right when
he met Edith, where they would go to the park, listen to free

symphonies, hold each other, clearheaded, overcome with new romance and the accompanying fear that it could all come crumbling down, that this wonderful feeling couldn't possibly last. And it didn't last. Soon, drink came back.

He would drink in the basement. She would drink in the kitchen. They wouldn't talk, except to say I love you, or I hate you. He'd fall asleep on his basement couch. She'd crawl upstairs, fall asleep on the bed. Somewhere, somehow, children showed up crying in his arms. First, a boy. Then, a girl. Then, a premature and withered husk, blue, breathless, buried; a girl named Justine. Then, a boy. Then, a promotion to team director, analysts working underneath him, a bigger house near better schools. At dinner tables, parties, parent-teacher meetings, jazz recitals, Elting wandered between conversations about finance, law, politics, suburban decline, and urban revival. He nodded, wished a fresh drink would appear in his empty glass. Soon, Edith stopped saying I love you. Soon, his children learned to avoid his liquored breath and slurred hugs. One Christmas, Elting brought home three kittens from a rescue shelter. He forgot about allergies. He forgot where the EpiPens were kept. Edith yelled as their children swelled up, broke out in hives. He held the kittens. Edith held the children. The ambulances came in time. Edith went with the children. Elting drove himself and the kittens to a 24-7 convenience store. In the parking lot, he sipped a bottle; the kittens licked and nibbled at canned tuna. In the backseat: small litter boxes and one big litter bag. He read, somewhere, cats needed separate boxes for doing their business. He sang and scratched their tiny ears on the drive back home. In his basement, he sang to his kittens. He didn't know the songs. He hadn't listened to music in years. Only jazz recitals. That wasn't music, not the way his children played. Bass and anger came from his basement radio. New rap music, he figured. High-stepping and arm-pumping to his own rhythm, he recalled hip-hop's nascent years, how it coincided with his own youth. He recalled his Adidas tracksuit. He recalled the white Kangol. He recalled his first beer. He recalled his mother yelling for quiet, shut the fuck up, turn the fuck down, get the fuck up. He recalled hearing *Illmatic* in college. He recalled hearing about Tupac's death in business school. He recalled Biggie's, a year later. He recalled making his first million. The numbness. He emptied his bottle, felt that numb mist disrupt his rhythm. He wandered to his safe, fumbled with the combination. He took out his gun and ammo.

He caught his reflection in the big-screen television. He looked like himself, a little distorted, a little phantomlike. The steel against his hard palate jolted him awake, a little sober. A song he didn't know mentioned friends and family and forever love. At his feet, the kittens clawed at his shoelaces. He cocked.

The kittens. Who would feed the kittens?

He uncocked. He put the gun and ammo back in the safe.

He fell back on the couch. The kittens joined him. He pulled a blanket over their tired bodies. He apologized for everything. Behind his closed eyelids, he counted swirling lines. He petted the kittens, found sleep. That was his favorite Christmas.

In the morning, Edith came back with the kids, yelled until he woke up head-ached and dry-mouthed.

Edith packed suitcases; Elting didn't leave the basement.

The children didn't miss their father; months passed and everyone accepted their incomplete and complicated lives— still, better than the alternative.

Elting crawled from the basement, cradled and spoiled his kittens, drank at a slow and powerful pace, didn't answer the phones when they rang, didn't open up for the mailman. That was how Elting disappeared. Soon, his beard and hair overgrew and knotted. Soon after, he sold the house, the chairs, the rugs, beds, desks, bureaus, stuffed animals, clothes, shoes, smart fridge, smart microwave, smart garbage, expensive lamps from museum gift shops, expensive paintings from middling artists. He didn't sell the car, not right away.

The kittens, now small cats: he took them in velvet carrying cases to find new owners, families. One went to a family: a brother and sister, a mom and dad, nice people in a small happy house. Two went to a young man who lived downtown, in a two-floor condo in a tall building—a finance guy making his first million. Elting freed the cats from their carrier into a large white living room. Before he left, Elting told the young man to find time for worthless endeavors. The young man agreed. Elting wrangled the cats one last time, kissed their foreheads, accepted their healing purrs, kissed them again for goodbye. The young man asked if Elting wanted something to drink, as a thank you. Elting declined. He took a long elevator ride back down to his car. In his driveway, he wrote a note explaining the perils of capitalism, as he saw them. He made up quotes from historic figures, which emphasized his stance. He slid the note underneath his front door. That was that; that was Elting.

Sojourner

BRANDO HAD A new man. Her old man had left her for a new woman. Brando had bad luck and a wide-open heart. People took advantage. This new man—based on what Sojourner could tell from the sidewalk—was doing well. Brando's old man had done well also, had one house near campus, had a bigger one in the Berkshires. The new man had a bigger house, the biggest house Sojourner had seen around town, three stories and painted lemon-white and new large windows on the façade. Like all the big houses in town, it was a colonial, a proud old American house, hints of Queen Anne. Damn, Sojourner thought. Lucky, Sojourner thought.

Sojourner opened the heavy, unlocked front door, moved sideways through it with her bags, stood in an oval foyer before a wide wooden staircase with its handrails painted white. On both sides, tall entryways led to big rooms with large couches and custom-looking wooden chairs. These are called sitting rooms, Sojourner thought.

Sojourner imagined this foyer and these sitting rooms crammed with people in suits and dresses gesticulating and spilling red wine and vodka tonics on these elaborate carpets. Months ago, Brando had invited Sojourner and Rascal to a party here, but Sojourner wasn't feeling well and they'd stayed home. Now she stood in the foyer, dropped her bags, remembered spending Easter alone with Rascal, eating precooked rotisserie chicken, trying not to burn candied yams. They'd poured apple cider into a pot, added bourbon, orange slices, sugar, let it blend on the stove. Sojourner remembered that intoxication, that subtle and slow-moving drunk. Rascal swayed her across the kitchen. They sang different love songs to each other, slurred. They ended up on the couch, let the candied yams burn in the oven.

Now, bags at her feet, Sojourner found herself standing before another woman. The woman was white, muttering in a hard Midwestern voice. She wore a maid's outfit.

"Huh?" Sojourner asked, snapped back.

"She's back," the woman said. "In the back."

"I'm sorry," Sojourner said.

"Huh?" the woman said.

"I'm Sojourner," Sojourner said, extended a hand.

The woman held small folded towels in either fist. She shrugged at Sojourner's gesture.

"Come on," the woman said.

Sojourner followed the woman into one sitting room, the one on Sojourner's left. The woman walked fast. She maneuvered the chairs, couches, ottomans, and glass tables from memory. Sojourner swung her bags at each turn, knocked into each object she passed. She got close to knocking over a vase filled with fire-red blossoms. Of course, there was a fireplace, large, framed with carved marble. Above the fireplace was a large portrait of a dog; maybe a Great Dane; something inbred, from the Old World, short-lived. Sojourner didn't have time to slow down and look. The painting, without a doubt, was oil and expensive.

The woman led Sojourner from the sitting room into a dining room. The circular table was set and table-clothed. Vases were filled with orange blossoms, some yellow popping out, brown twigs added for rustic accents. Sojourner wasn't sure if this dining room was the only dining room. She wondered if the entire house was replicated within itself. A multimillion dollar and pointless Russian Doll came to mind. She wondered if Brando would let her crash in a replica master bedroom with a Jacuzzi.

The woman turned right, led Sojourner from the dining room into a kitchen with multiple islands, stainless steel and tropical aromas. Sojourner eyed apples pyramided atop a glass tray. She wanted a beer. She needed breakfast. If I stop, Sojourner thought, she'll leave me, and I'll die in this kitchen.

The woman turned left. The woman stopped. Sojourner bumped into her, knocked the small folded towels onto the tiled floor. They were in a sunroom, surrounded by floor plants with obnoxious petals. Some plants had vines running up the walls. Sojourner helped the woman pick up her small towels.

"Fine," the woman said. "Fine. Fine. It's fine."

"Sorry," Sojourner said. "Sorry. Sorry. Sorry."

"She's outside," the woman said. "It's fine. Outside."

Sojourner smelled lemon and bleach on the woman's skin. Her breath was a coffee, mint mouthwash, cigarette, and orange mixture. Up close, face-to-face, she was younger than Sojourner first thought.

"What's your name?" Sojourner asked.

"Huh?" The woman said. "She's outside."

Sojourner stood up, helped the woman, apologized again, almost knocked over a palm, picked up her bags, walked past the woman, opened the back door.

Of course, there was a pool. Of course, Brando was next to the pool in a lounge chair, sunning herself, holding a sweating drink. Sojourner considered Brando's bikini, wondered how much it cost, wondered if you were allowed to wear it and swim. From Sojourner's perspective, Brando looked like a dame in a hard-boiled detective mystery. She looked for show.

Brando tilted her sunglasses onto her forehead, squinted at Sojourner.

"Are those bags?" Brando yelled.

Sojourner shrugged her bags.

"Like I said," Sojourner said, "on the phone."

"Mary-Anne!" Brando yelled. "Bags!"

Mary-Anne appeared at Sojourner's side.

"Bags," Mary-Anne said to Sojourner.

Sojourner shrugged again.

"It's fine," Sojourner said.

"Ridiculous," Brando said to blue skies beyond her sunglasses.

"Please," Mary-Anne said. "Bags. Please."

Sojourner looked down on Mary-Anne, who was bent over at the waist, hands hovering above Sojourner's hands, primed to take the bags and run. Sojourner tightened her grip.

"Come." Brando beckoned Sojourner with a delicate wave.

With ease, Mary-Anne wrestled the bags from Sojourner.

"Room?" Mary-Anne asked Brando.

"Third floor," Brando said. "The big one. The yellow one."

Mary-Anne nodded at Brando, nodded at Sojourner, nodded at the pool, disappeared into the green room. Sojourner watched her duck under wide leaves, scoot past stout plants with thorns and sharp petals.

When Sojourner first met Brando, they were both drunk off well tequila, eating fried pigskin, greased and sad. It was an English department party at a Guatemalan hole-in-the-wall. The English department liked partying at diverse eateries to prove how diverse their intentions were, if, still, their students and colleagues were from places like Connecticut, Plymouth, Catskill, Vermont, and Keene, New Hampshire.

Brando, like Sojourner, was a tagalong, an arm piece. Brando's old man was a tenured professor in Polynesian

Literature, Ivy League, an obscure genius. Sojourner's old man was Rascal—a nobody. Brando was from Toledo.

Now, Brando asked if Sojourner needed a bathing suit.

"It's a little cold," Sojourner said.

"It's heated," Brando said. "The perfect temperature."

Brando laughed; Sojourner cried. Brando sat up in her chair, moved her legs, made a space for Sojourner to sit. There were open chairs everywhere. Sojourner sat on Brando's, put her hands on Brando's knees.

"Thank you," Sojourner said.

"Drink," Brando said.

Brando reached under her chair, retrieved one of those too-sweet margaritas in a tall can with a little beer mixed in. Brando opened the can, shoved it into Sojourner's gut. Sojourner wiped her eyes, gulped half the can, burped.

"Tell me," Brando said. "What the fuck happened?"

"Can we not," Sojourner said. "Later. Not right now. Can we, please?"

"Communication," Brando said. "I knew it."

"I started meditating," Sojourner said.

Brando choked, spittled down her chin.

"I do yoga," Brando said. "You don't see me in crisis."

"I'm not in crisis," Sojourner said.

"You're here with bags," Brando said. "On the phone, crying."

"I wasn't crying," Sojourner said.

"I know crying," Brando said.

Something in the tall hedges around Brando's pool sent small birds flying, crazed, yelling. They gathered in a frantic cluster above the pool chairs. Sojourner covered her head with a beer-less hand; Brando stared straight up, hands at her side, knees still up, bored. The birds dive-bombed another hedge, settled down, chirped at a moderate level.

"Sparrows," Brando said. "I think."

"I think I'm hallucinating," Sojourner said.

"Me too," Brando said.

"What?" Sojourner asked.

"Drugs," Brando said. "You know?"

"I'm talking about sober," Sojourner said. "Like real life isn't acting right."

Sojourner tipped her can straight up, finished, burped. Brando handed her another, turned her sunglasses and eyes back toward the sky. Sojourner cracked the can, put her chin on Brando's kneecap.

"It wasn't working," Sojourner said.

"These things are difficult," Brando said.

"It never worked," Sojourner said. "We never cared at the same time. We were never in sync."

"Tough times," Brando said.

"What things?" Sojourner asked. "What times?"

Brando pushed her sunglasses onto her forehead. She rested her beer between her legs. She would've sat up if Sojourner wasn't leaning on her, chin on kneecap, arms, now, around legs. Sojourner stared at Brando, and Brando smiled like she did when people stared, a polite reflex. People often stared at Brando, looked her up and down, whistled low, followed her around, brought her things. She was Persian and Ethiopian;

she was a competent architect with Prairie influences and two degrees from MIT. Lying next to the pool, Brando made Sojourner think of luxurious cars and champagne. Sojourner stared at her moving mouth, couldn't hear a thing.

"And," Brando said. "You're not even listening."

"I am," Sojourner said. "I am."

"What did I say?" Brando said.

"I'm not," Sojourner said. "I wasn't."

"Have you talked to him?" Brando asked.

"It wasn't that long ago," Sojourner said.

"What does that mean?" Brando asked.

"Hours," Sojourner said. "Too soon."

"At some point," Brando said. "You have to start making sense."

"It's a lot," Sojourner said.

"It's too much," Brando said.

Sojourner tilted her can back again, burped. She twisted her head, let Brando's knee impale her cheek.

"I'm not crazy," Sojourner said.

"Of course you are," Brando said.

Brando slid her sunglasses down her forehead, back onto her button nose. She leaned her head against her chair, focused her eyes on the infinite space above Sojourner's head. She put a hand on Sojourner's hair.

"It all came at once," Sojourner said. "My soul should be right here."

Sojourner poked below her own chest, between gut and ribs.

"There's nothing here," Sojourner said. "Empty. It drained away. I used to care about work. Life. The world. I used to like working hard. I used to care about other people. Now, there's nothing. Nothing here."

Sojourner kept poking her chest.

"Do I look crazy?" Sojourner asked, turned her face back toward her friend.

Brando put down her drink. She grabbed Sojourner's face with both hands.

"What do you think?" Brando said.

"Why should I stay with him?" Sojourner said. "Why should I stay here, if I'm unhappy, if I'm empty, if each day feels pointless, if staying with him makes me feel alone, if I'm alone when I'm with him. Why should I stay?"

"Did you tell him?" Brando asked.

"He knows," Sojourner said.

"Knows what?" Brando asked.

"I'm not coming back," Sojourner said.

"Not what I mean," Brando said.

"Knows what?" Sojourner asked.

"How you feel?" Brando asked.

One of the birds came back, louder. Sojourner and Brando looked up at the chirping blob. It circled, swooped, dived, scattered, disappeared again, into a hedge further away, almost in the neighbor's yard.

"Did you see that?" Sojourner asked.

"Don't change the subject?" Brando asked.

"Am I crazy?" Sojourner asked. "You know me."

"I know you," Brando said. "Everyone's crazy."

"For doing this," Sojourner said. "Am I crazy for leaving like this? Am I crazy for imagining there is something better?"

"A little," Brando said. "Doesn't matter."

"We're not married," Sojourner said. "We don't have kids. We don't have bank accounts and shared debts."

In praise, Brando raised her palms skyward. She lowered her chin against her chest, shook her head.

"Come on," Brando said.

In the sunroom, Brando ran her hands through the plants, stuck her face into a few blossoms. Sojourner stepped on her heels.

In the kitchen, Mary-Anne was looking into the wide sink with a blank expression. Her hands were intertwined above her aproned stomach. Sojourner peeked over Brando's shoulder, looked at Mary-Anne and the sink; the space between Mary-Anne and the sink. Brando fake coughed. Mary-Anne, startled, turned around.

"Excuse me," Brando said.

"Bless you," Mary-Anne said.

"The sitting room," Brando said. "Drinks, please."

"It's before noon," Mary-Anne said.

"Something with juice," Brando said. "Orange juice, or something."

Mary-Anne nodded, relaxed her fingers. Sojourner followed Brando into the sitting room, which was different from a living room in ways Sojourner didn't understand. She didn't bother asking. Brando told Sojourner to sit on a blue couch. Sojourner sat on a purple couch.

"Is she alright?" Sojourner asked Brando.

"I talk to her," Brando said. "Like talking to a squirrel."

"Hey," Sojourner said.

"Huh?" Brando asked.

"Not nice," Sojourner said. "She's a person."

"I know that," Brando said. "Of course."

"Can I stay here tonight?" Sojourner asked.

"Then what?" Brando asked.

"Maybe tomorrow?" Sojourner asked.

"You should talk to him," Brando said.

Sojourner adjusted her hair, felt haywire strands.

"I did," Sojourner said. "I tried."

"I know these things," Brando said.

"What things?" Sojourner said.

"Running out," Brando said. "Packing bags. Coming back. Running back."

"Look at you now," Sojourner said.

Brando pulled her sunglasses up. She looked around the room. She started with a smile, which faded as she scanned the portraits and furniture and intricate fireplace molding and large curtains pulled over the large windows.

"Sure," Brando said, pushed her sunglasses back down.

"He's an economist?" Sojourner asked.

"The best," Brando said. "Countries ask him for advice."

Brando yawned. Now, she looked bored, an unassuming femme fatale.

"How does it work?" Sojourner asked.

"They call him," Brando said. "He picks up. He talks."

"Not what I mean," Sojourner said.

"Tell me," Brando asked.

"You," Sojourner asked. "How do *you* work?"

Mary-Anne knocked into a coffee table, almost dropped her tray, swore twice, offered them swamp-green drinks with a bow.

"Hell is this?" Brando asked, lifted her sunglasses, held the glass beneath her crow's feet.

"Good for you," Mary-Anne said.

"Thank you," Sojourner said.

"Is there vodka in here?" Brando asked. "Gin? Tequila? Rum? Anything?"

"Yes," Mary-Anne said.

"Thank you," Sojourner said again.

Mary-Anne bowed again, tucked the now empty tray under her arm, whispered something harsh in the entryway, her back toward them.

"I heard that," Brando said.

Mary-Anne turned around, bowed at them again, exited.

"I didn't hear anything," Sojourner said.

"She hates me," Brando said, forced her drink down.

Sojourner finished half the glass with a full gulp. Exhaustion settling in, she slumped into her couch, extended her legs, dropped one hand onto the carpet, which was harder than she expected, made with fibers that scratched. She pushed an index finger into the material.

"You're mean to her," Sojourner said. "You're unpleasant."

"She's racist," Brando said.

"She's your employee," Sojourner said.

"She's in love with Brian," Brando said.

"You're insecure," Sojourner said.

"Look at me," Brando said. "I'm Cleopatra."

Brando sat up, put her elbows on her knees, put her fists under her chin. For a moment, she forced a smile. Then, her mouth tightened and she started crying. Sojourner wasn't surprised. Sojourner wanted to roll off the couch, across the carpet, hold her friend. She wanted Brando to look up, look around, get a hobby, take stock, appreciate doing nothing except drinking maybe too much. What a problem to have: maybe drinking too much during the day, not hurting anyone, getting plenty of rest, going to bed early, drinking plenty of water, rarely waking up with a hangover, rarely having to work. Brando could design a million-dollar private residence, or she could sit around and read *Ulysses* and the accompanying literary theory. Or, she could fly to Amsterdam and live under an alias for seventy-two hours, tell Brian she was on a work trip. If there was an emptiness inside her, if she was struggling to find purpose, she had plenty of time and freedom and resources to figure it out. She didn't need Sojourner's help. And Sojourner wasn't in the helping mood. Instead, Sojourner finished her drink with a gulp and watched her friend sob, then go quiet, then shake. She saw Mary-Anne pop her head around a corner. What was Mary-Anne's expression? Was she smiling?

"You okay?" Sojourner asked.

"What if we leave together?" Brando asked.

"You don't want that," Sojourner said.

"Thelma and Louise," Brando said. "We can drive off a cliff."

"Haven't seen it," Sojourner said.

"You should," Brando said. "That's us."

"You can't leave this," Sojourner said. She punched the carpet twice, thrice, until she felt something.

"Think about it," Brando said. "A rented Thunderbird suspended in midair."

"What's wrong with you?" Sojourner asked.

"What's wrong with us?" Brando asked.

"I think I'm crazy," Sojourner said.

"I believe that," Brando said.

"What about you?" Sojourner asked.

"I think I'm too restless," Brando said. "I guess I'm too complacent."

"Nope," Sojourner said. "Doesn't make sense."

"Listen," Brando said. "Look. Look at this shit. This isn't me."

Brando, who had first tried to ignore her swamp-green drink, was now chugging it down. With her free hand, she was waving at the room.

"Look," Brando said. "Listen. This fucking couch cost—guess how much this couch cost."

Brando slapped her couch, groped the armrest.

"I don't care," Sojourner said.

"You don't want to know," Brando said.

Once, months ago, Brando and Sojourner had split a whiskey bottle and broke into a library. They wanted to see if the

Mystery section was bigger than the Cooking section. They wanted to resolve a bet made earlier in the night, when the whiskey bottle was full. Together, they were reckless drunks; apart, they were normal sad drunks, mumbling, sleeping deep in dark rooms. Brando could remain idle forever. Her sadness wasn't crippling. She could remain supine on a fluffy rug for days without moving. Sojourner needed movement. She needed something better.

Once, Brando and Sojourner climbed a tall tree with a six-pack and two rum pints. They made up songs about lovesick birds. They rolled empties down the trunk. Sojourner got a rash from the bark. Rascal thought Brando was a bad influence.

"Am I going to miss him?" Sojourner asked Brando, now, drunk and tired on a purple couch.

"Of course," Brando said.

"Another drink," Brando said.

"Please," Sojourner said.

Brando yelled for Mary-Anne; Mary-Anne trudged in. Brando held up her empty glass, pointed at Sojourner, held up two fingers, snapped.

"It's ten thirty," Mary-Anne said.

Brando snapped again, held up two fingers. Sojourner experienced a sinking feeling, like she was trapped in a repeating cycle, stuck on a malfunctioning tilting and whirling machine.

"One day," Sojourner said. "She's going to poison you."

"Understandable," Brando said.

Sojourner had to regain her balance. She closed her eyes,

tucked her head into her clavicle, covered her closed eyes with her fingers. The blender shredded in the kitchen.

Her calves cramped. Her guts twisted and tightened.

"My head," Sojourner said.

"Bathroom?" Brando asked.

"It's too bright," Sojourner said.

Two hands grabbed Sojourner's shoulders. She kept her eyes shut tight, covered with her fingers. The hands turned Sojourner upright.

"Didn't you eat anything?" Brando asked.

"It's still morning," Sojourner said.

"That doesn't mean anything," Brando said.

The blender kept shredding. A knife went to work on a cutting board. It was all claps and whirs inside Sojourner.

The hands on Sojourner's shoulders went under her armpits and lifted. Sojourner got to her feet. She felt sideways, ready to slip and disappear. Now: her back—the entire thing rippled. Sojourner covered her mouth.

She realized she was walking. She tripped and felt Brando's body keep pushing her forward. They made two turns, went down a few stairs, turned left, then right. Then a door closed behind Sojourner.

"Don't leave," Sojourner said before opening her eyes. She didn't look for a light. She got on her knees and groped for a toilet seat. Above her head, Mary-Anne yelled something. She couldn't hear. Through the door, Brando yelled for Mary-Anne to calm down, wait a moment, give us a second, leave it on the table.

Sojourner noticed lavender in her nostrils. She found the toilet lid. Some vomit splashed back into her face. She kept heaving.

"No," Brando said. "No, no, baby."

Sojourner felt better, drained. She needed the tiled floor to turn into a bed. She needed blankets stacked on her fetal position. She went back into the bowl. She finished, flushed, slapped her cheeks, felt better. For the moment, she felt better. Sojourner opened the door, and Brando fell into Sojourner, held her. Sojourner, eyes opened, saw her friend crying.

"I'm okay," Sojourner said. "I feel better."

"Look at you," Brando said. "You got puke running down your nose."

"I need to go home," Sojourner said. "I need to tell Rascal. Talk to him."

"Mary-Anne!" Brando said through the ceiling. "Towels!"

Brando and Mary-Anne had Sojourner on her back, on a different couch, in a different sitting room, under a different chandelier. Brando held Sojourner's sweating hands. Mary-Anne rubbed warm washcloths over Sojourner's chest and face. Sojourner kept her eyes open, stared into her helpers' eyes.

"I need to go home," Sojourner said again.

"Water," Mary-Anne said. "You need water."

"Don't disturb her," Brando said to Mary-Anne.

"A couple of drunks," Mary-Anne said to the room.

Sojourner tried to sit up. Brando held her legs down. Mary-Anne pushed a fist, wrapped around a towel, into Sojourner's empty chest. Brando kept her hands around Sojourner's ankles.

"Just a minute," Mary-Anne said.

"Why did I leave?" Sojourner asked.

"*Him*?" Brando asked.

"*Her*?" Mary-Anne said. "*She* left someone?"

"She has good days," Brando said to Mary-Anne.

Mary-Anne nodded, wiping Sojourner's face, skeptical.

"Almost done," Mary-Anne said.

"My bags," Sojourner said. "A car."

Again, Sojourner's insides turned sideways, jerked right side up, settled into a gurgling lump. She shut her eyes, covered them with both hands. She wasn't going to throw up. She was going to feel better. She was going home. She drifted off the couch. Mary-Anne and Brando bickered far away, moved further away still. Sojourner was underwater, riding a transglobal current. The infinite space around her was emerald green and sliced with sunrays. She heard whales calling to other whales. She heard their love songs, their pleading ballads. Sojourner wondered what she'd sing to Rascal when she walked in the door. She thought about the flowers she'd pick on the way back. She recalled the new blossoms in their driveway. She'd go home; she'd meditate each morning. Yes. Meditating worked. See, look at her now: floating with singing whales. She'd learn to love Rascal. She'd find happiness through routine, repetition. There was Rascal above her head, floating on his back, that thin pale surface patched with thin hair. She wanted Rascal to know what she had learned. She wanted to give Rascal another chance to make her happy. She tried to scream. Her mouth filled with water.

Again, she convulsed.

She opened her eyes. Through her fingers, she saw Mary-Anne shaking her. Brando stood behind Mary-Anne, gaping.

Mary-Anne dropped Sojourner.

"She's alive," Mary-Anne said.

Brando relaxed into a crouch, hands on knees, pumping air.

"Bags," Sojourner said. "Car."

Outside, on the front steps, anxious, Sojourner tapped her bags with her fingers, her foot. Brando sat at her side, green drink in hand.

"You need to eat more," Brando said.

"I know," Sojourner said.

"Need food," Brando said, sipping her drink.

"I know," Sojourner said.

Cars passed. Birds stopped, hopped atop fallen leaves. Brando offered Sojourner some drink; Sojourner declined. They were waiting for a red minivan driven by a blonde woman. They had forgotten her name.

"You need help," Brando said.

"I know," Sojourner said. "I know, I know. I know."

"You're not crazy," Brando said.

"I know," Sojourner said.

"The world's on your shoulders," Brando said.

"I know," Sojourner said.

"For no reason," Brando said. "For no one."

"I see all these tunnels," Sojourner said. "I'm in one tunnel. And, I've reached a fork, all these tributaries spreading directions. All of these options. All of them are dark. I can't see the end. I just see *how* it ends. You know? There are echoes."

"You need a professional," Brando said.

"I know," Sojourner said.

"I have numbers," Brando said. "These people come to my parties."

"I will," Sojourner said.

"Today," Brando said. "When you get home."

"I need to sleep," Sojourner said.

"After sleep," Brando said. "Sleep, then this."

"I know," Sojourner said.

Brando started to say another thing. She stopped herself. She wanted to tell Sojourner that everything will sort itself out for the better. You go through stagnations; you want to leave; you don't; you come out the other side, learn, want to leave again, go through another stagnation, want to leave, don't; hopefully, discover an epiphany when you're not expecting an epiphany. In the past months, Brando had felt time picking underneath her fingernails. Doctors had found benign lumps near her right hip. They took them out; they sighed with relief. In the examination room, waiting for results, Brando was alone with her mother's ghost. She had loved her mother. She had pages in old diaries devoted to loving her mother and missing her mother and wishing her mother would scream at her again and wishing her mother would apologize again and give her a kiss. In the examination room, waiting for results, Brando told her mother's ghost about this void in Brando's stomach and soul. Brando's ghost mother made a joke about ghosts not having organs, teeth, hair, or body odor. Brando laughed with her ghost mother. The doctor walked in. Everyone sighed with relief. There: a ghost, an epiphany.

Sitting next to Sojourner, on the steps, Brando wanted to talk about her ghost. Brando didn't know how to put it. So, she said nothing.

Sojourner listened to her own uneven breaths. She listened to the birds. She hoped the birds she heard were real. She jumped up when a car passed, sat back down when the car wasn't a minivan. Until the car *was* a minivan. She hugged Brando. Neither said anything. From the curb, while loading her bags, Sojourner saw Mary-Anne peeking through a curtain. She waved.

Mary-Anne went away.

Brando went away.

Sojourner thanked her driver—Artemis—and stared out her window, at the blurred houses. The world beyond the window felt destroyed by wide brushstrokes. Too vague. Herself, impossible to understand. What was wrong? What should she do? She closed her eyes and tried to go somewhere else. A beach at low tide; all that sand between her and water. Everything blurred. Still: everything blurred. What was that deer doing on the horizon, on a small boat, waving its arms and antlers?

She opened her eyes at a red light. Two young men looked at their phones and spoke with each other, laughed. They exchanged phones and laughed some more. One stepped into oncoming traffic. The other saved him from a bus. They hugged and laughed some more. Behind them, an annoyed older man sipped from a steaming mug. The light turned green; Sojourner went away.

Now, she was in a vague pasture with rolling hills and windmills. Gray mist spilled into her valley. Riding the mist: that deer, or a different deer, on a large boat with many sails. Sojourner made a mental note to study deer, species and types.

She opened her eyes on the highway.

She closed them near a farm.

She was standing in her old living room, her own living room, before Rascal. She saw this clearly. Plates with crumbs and dried-out sauces stacked on the coffee table. Mugs with molded coffee on shelves, on the ground. Books and dirty laundry on the couch. Where did she sit?

A knock at the door. Another knock. Knocks. Two knocks at once. A forehead. A light tap. An old boyfriend. The boyfriend before Rascal. The Desperate Boyfriend. Sojourner didn't answer. The Desperate Boyfriend just wanted to know if she was okay, still alive, eating well, willing to talk. One day, fed up, empty, feeling trapped, Sojourner had left the Desperate Boyfriend at dinner, with the bill, without a follow-up phone call. The knocking went on for a couple days, stopped without drama. Sojourner still didn't leave the apartment, wouldn't leave for days. One day, she felt better. She showered, called Matteo, went to work, sat in a city council meeting, interviewed a senile assemblyman, went back home, cleaned her dishes, laundry, books, mugs.

A week later, she met Rascal in a beer garden.

Months later, knocking at her door after she'd left him the first time. Rascal didn't want to reconcile; he understood Sojourner had her reasons for leaving. He wasn't perfect, he knew that. He was doing personal work. He was trying to understand himself better, how he came off to other people. He didn't want to see her; he wanted to hear her voice. He wanted to know if she was alive, eating, going to work, talking to her family, reading. Sojourner listened to him for thirty minutes. She stood on her unvacuumed carpet, naked, looked at the door.

Months later, Sojourner and Rascal sat on her clean couch, in her clean apartment. They toasted cheap champagne in clean glasses. They wished each other Happy New Year's. They kissed. They were too tired for sex. They talked about darkness in bed. Sojourner turned on the bedside lamp. Rascal covered his eyes. Sojourner apologized for that urge to crawl into a hole. Rascal hid his eyes in her ribs, accepted her apology. He grabbed her thigh. Sojourner thanked him for loving her and all her horrible qualities. Rascal said her qualities weren't horrible—they were beautiful. Soon, they were talking about nothing, romantic platitudes, and shallow reassurances. Why had she gone back again? It was all empty. She didn't feel anything. Sojourner had thought about leaving him then, waiting for him to snore, packing a suitcase, hitting the road.

From the front seat, Artemis called Sojourner's name.

Sojourner didn't answer.

Artemis called again.

Sojourner opened her eyes.

"Here," Artemis said.

"Home," Sojourner said aloud by accident.

"Nice home," Artemis said.

Sojourner thanked Artemis.

On the highway, Artemis hoped she wouldn't grow into a woman like that: day drunk, luggage, sick and sad, unable to stay awake. Artemis hoped to leave this place. Maybe a beach. Maybe a meadow. Maybe a different college town, out west, settled down with a professor. Artemis forgot Sojourner's name. Still, she would remember Sojourner's face, that doomed look when her eyes opened and her house came into view.

Sojourner took five deep breaths at the doorway. Unlocked. She dropped her bags just inside. She didn't want to call Rascal's name. She wanted to find him in bed. She wanted to climb in and not say a word. She wanted to sleep next to him and wake up as new people, different people, better people. She walked past the fridge, didn't want a beer. She took a glass from the cabinet, filled it with tap water, sipped, emptied the water down the drain. She gripped the sink, took in the silence. Not total, not complete: birds in the bushes, in the field, on the roof. She licked her teeth. She wanted to brush her teeth. She wanted to kiss Rascal's neck with fresh breath.

She went into the bedroom. No Rascal. Bed a mess.

Sojourner paused to make the bed. She pulled and tucked the sheet stained with juice and wine. She pulled and tucked the blanket, torn in a strange place. She arranged their three pillows—two for Rascal, one for Sojourner. She pulled the comforter above the pillows, folded it down. She patted her job, smiled. She thought about love's small rituals. She went into the bathroom.

She found the note in the sink, dry.

Sojourner took it to bed, laid atop pulled, tucked, folded layers. She read on her stomach.

There was a moment when Sojourner stopped crying. Hours, minutes, days later—Sojourner wasn't sure. She held Rascal's note again. She was on the porch with an empty water glass. She counted leaves as they fluttered onto unkempt piles. She read the note again and again. He wasn't mad at her. He was mad at himself. He was disgusted with himself. All his short-comings and failures stacked on wild sentences and misplaced commas. He described the cave inside his gut. He rambled through poetic self-analysis. Typical indulgent Rascal. He was an asshole. He understood that now. A self-obsessed asshole. He said goodbye.

He was driving to Ohio, to stay with family, to get his head straight, to forget about her, get better, regain himself.

Sojourner said goodbye to the note. Then, she stopped crying, for a moment. She heard his voice in a leaf, turned and looked for his hair. She was alone. She knew that. He wasn't coming back. Still, she heard his voice. She turned and looked for his hair. She called Brando and cried again. Ghosts, Sojourner said. One ghost, Brando said. Ghosts, Sojourner repeated. She had to leave.

"Get out," Brando said.

She hadn't unpacked her luggage.

Okay. Leave.

She rented a car and drove further east, into the mountains and hills, up, then down—away.

Elting and Buchanan

MOST MORNINGS, SOMEONE yelled at the expressway. When it rained, more people than usual crammed under the underpass. It had rained last night, hard, with thunder and tree-splitting lightning. Elting had seen it: a tree exploded. Buchanan would've seen it, too, if he wasn't looking at the ground, looking for dropped silver coins and such. This morning was like most mornings—someone yelled. The person was new.

"The government!" the person started.

Elting hated when people yelled about the government. Everyone knew about the government. Tell us something we don't know.

The person wore a rug like a dress, a small cardboard box like a hat, socks like gloves. The person yelled about tiny computers in our plastic water bottles. He yelled about planes with high-powered microphones that recorded your thoughts and e-mailed them to the president of Turkey.

Elting had heard enough. He punched Buchanan in the ribs. They needed new blankets, bigger blankets, warm with enough room.

"Fifteen more minutes," Buchanan said without looking up.

Elting punched him in the pelvis, kicked his feet. "Rain stopped," he said. "Breakfast."

Days were getting longer; sun came up earlier.

"My dream was about you," Buchanan said.

"Tell me as we walk," Elting said.

Buchanan folded the blankets into their garbage bag. Elting tucked his plastic water bottles into his coat. Their leaving interrupted the yelling person. Elting waved to his friends and the unacquainted.

On Armitage, Buchanan told Elting about his dream. There was a fire and a boat and waves of fire and an impossible path between start and finish. Like all his recent dreams, Elting was at his side, telling him everything would work out, even when it didn't.

"What does it mean?" Buchanan asked.

"Like it always means," Elting said.

"What's that?" Buchanan said.

"We'll die together," Elting said.

"Not so bad," Buchanan said.

"Not so bad," Elting repeated.

They reached the alley and a door; they knocked a secret knock, twice, pause, twice, pause, thrice, once. Romeo opened, handed them fresh cinnamon-raisin bagels.

Back on Armitage, Buchanan told Elting about his fears.

"A meteor," Buchanan said.

"What's that about?" Elting asked.

"All that fire," Buchanan said. "In the water."

"What water?" Elting asked.

"The dream," Buchanan said. "The *dreams.*"

"Dreams," Elting said. "Dreams. Dreams. Always dreams."

"I know," Buchanan said. "I try to stop."

Shamed, Buchanan ducked his head, took small bites from his bagel. Elting softened at a stoplight. Morning rush hour pulsed and honked, swore from rolled-down windows. Elting knew Buchanan was sensitive.

"Tell me," Elting said. "I want to hear."

Sometimes, Buchanan's dreams came true in abstract ways. There was one about a desert mountain. The mountain imploded, covered Elting and Buchanan in sand and brimstone. That dream came true. Elting and Buchanan saw a burning car from the highway. That was last winter, during a snow storm, sleet coming into their faces at a severe angle. Buchanan remarked how the sleet felt like sand, how Chicago was a desert waiting to explode. Elting didn't know what to say, where to start, how to handle this. Elting decided Buchanan was right.

Buchanan found a tree in the park, leaned against it, slid down. Elting sprawled out on the beaten-down grass.

Buchanan put the bagel in his pocket; Elting put his nose through the bagel's hole, rested the bagel on his face, then pocketed his bagel, too, turned his head to Buchanan's feet.

"Want to see the water?" Elting asked.

"Why?" Buchanan asked.

"To see if it's water," Elting said. "Still, water. No fire."

Buchanan agreed. They stood, brushed themselves off, headed east.

Sometimes Buchanan saw his dreams in reality, happening right there, right in the street, on the sidewalk. Like, now, walking with Elting down Armitage, for instance, that skeleton riding a city bus, surfing, something unnatural. Buchanan slept in intense bursts, never more than a few hours a night. Years ago, a doctor told him the hallucinations were connected to insomnia.

Elting pulled coins from his pockets, counted them with a single finger, pushed the nickel and copper around his palm, did quick math in his head. Satisfied, Elting walked into Lucky Liquors. Buchanan waited against a lamppost.

Elting emerged with a wine box and two plastic cups.

Buchanan remembered cooking his wife small breakfasts and calling for her when the bacon was crisped. Buchanan remembered his daughter, remembered his son, remembered his dog and cat cuddling each other on the living room couch. Buchanan smiled at his memories.

Elting smiled at Buchanan; Buchanan smiled at Elting.

Together, they smiled and kept strolling.

Walking from the underpass to the water took hours. Buchanan and Elting played games to distract their sore feet.

They needed better shoes. They played guessing games: Where is that truck headed? Which child disappoints which parent? Which sports car would hit a guardrail going eighty miles per hour? Why did that couple fight this morning?

There, across the street: two children—boy and girl—in backpacks, scowling; two adults—man and woman—in matching sweaters, scowling and sipping coffee from matching mugs.

"Dad," Buchanan said. "This morning."

"What happened at breakfast?" Elting asked.

"Not this morning," Buchanan said. "Last night."

"What happened at dinner?" Elting asked.

"Not last night," Buchanan said.

"Make up your mind," Elting said.

"Ten years ago," Buchanan said. "Fifteen years ago. Dad was in a bar. With coworkers. Banks. They all worked for banks. They were drinking scotch and yelling at each other about the government and banks. Dad was leaned against the bar, ordering another scotch, going on about the government and banks."

"Typical," Elting said, shook his head.

"Yelling," Buchanan continues. "All this yelling, hoping someone hears him and gives him more money."

"Can you believe it?" Elting said, walked into the intersection, heading straight to the family.

"Then," Buchanan said. "The yelling stops. Dad stops yelling. He doesn't want scotch anymore."

"Why?" Elting asked. "Tell me. Tell me. Why?"

"You won't believe it," Buchanan said.

"I believe anything," Elting said.

Once across the street, Elting and Buchanan turned around and stared at the family's backs. They saw the father pat his wife's back, rub, kiss her cheek, stroke her brown hair.

"Dad," Buchanan continued. "He needed an excuse to change. He wanted an excuse. He was tired of yelling at bartenders. All those years and hours spent yelling and bossing around."

"And," Elting said. "This woman walks into the bar."

"Now," Buchanan said. "You're getting it."

"And," Elting said. "This woman takes the empty space at the bar."

"Mom," Buchanan said. "That woman was Mom."

"And," Elting said, "Mom orders a sweet white wine splashed with sparkling water."

"Now," Buchanan said, "you're focused on insignificant details."

"Insignificant?" Elting said. "How? A drink order describes a person."

Elting lifted the wine box above his head, slapped one side. They headed east, let the family walk west, disappear.

"Not this woman," Buchanan said. "Not Mom."

"Then," Elting said, "describe her."

"Dad felt this presence," Buchanan said. "This life-changing aura at his side."

"Too spiritual," Elting said.

"Today," Buchanan said. "Dad thanked God for giving him Mom."

"Then what?" Elting said. "What's the point?"

"What's your point?" Buchanan said.

"Look at them," Elting said, turned around, tried to find the family again, saw a passing bus with an advertisement for groceries on the side.

"I did look at them," Buchanan said.

"Why were they so unhappy?" Elting asked.

"Dad's an asshole," Buchanan said. "Dad sucks life from people."

"Why didn't he change?" Elting said. "He could change."

"When it's too late," Buchanan said. "He will."

They hit another stoplight. They watched other families walking. They saw single people looking at their phones, staring into space. They saw a friend from the underpass. They waved. Elting asked Buchanan to carry the wine. They watched people watch them. Green light. They walked.

Here, they passed slim new homes with modern facades, million-dollar edifices built up three, four, five stories. These homes hadn't been here last year. Every day, when they passed these homes, Buchanan and Elting would look for street-facing windows with the curtains pulled back. They wanted to look into these living rooms, see how deep these buildings went, see where they ended, see how people made life work. Today, the curtains were closed; the houses still dark. Instead, they wondered what this block looked like twenty years ago. They stopped at a driveway, allowed a large Porsche to back into the street and speed off.

"It was all Europeans," Elting said.

"Eastern Europeans," Buchanan said.

"No," Elting said. "No, no, no."

"Ukraine is in Eastern Europe," Buchanan said. "Poland is in Eastern Europe."

"No, twenty years ago," Elting said. "This was punk rock."

Elting took his free hands and tried to play an invisible guitar. He used a foot to tap an auto-tune pedal, distort his voice. He did a strange Peter Frampton impression. Buchanan kept walking. Elting opened his eyes, ran after him.

"I can see the future," Buchanan said, unprompted, halfway through an intersection.

"I know," Elting said. "I know."

"The future looks bad," Buchanan said. "I think."

"I'm saying," Elting said. "The present doesn't look good either."

"Not like this," Buchanan said. "Not like what's coming."

"That's true," Elting said. "That's always true."

"Always true?" Buchanan said. "It's not always true."

"When Napoleon arrived in Egypt," Elting said, "do you think the Egyptians thought the future looked better, or worse, than the present, or the past?"

"Unrelatable," Buchanan said.

"You're here," Elting said. "I'm here. Someday a bomb will kill us both."

"Another subject," Buchanan said. "Can we talk about something else?"

"No," Elting said.

He grabbed Buchanan's shoulder, twisted him so they faced each other, took up the sidewalk, made pedestrians squeeze between them, squeeze around them.

"Yes," Buchanan said.

"Here's how it goes," Elting said. "All people, throughout human history, look in the future and see lakes of fire. They see the world changing and see change as a destruction. Change is a vision of water turning to fire."

"So?" Buchanan said. He shook from foot to chin.

"So?" Elting said. "Every person thinks they have seen burning water in the future."

"How do you know that?" Buchanan said.

"I've seen studies," Elting said.

"So?" Buchanan said.

"So?" Elting said, grabbed Buchanan. "It hasn't happened. We're walking to water right now, at this moment. Once we get there, we won't see fire. We'll see dead fish, used condoms, beer cans, and extra-large chip bags, empty. We won't see fire. Unless we find some cigarettes. Unless we find some matches. We will make our own fire, if we must."

"You're wrong," Buchanan said.

"I'm right," Elting said.

"I know what I see," Buchanan said.

Buchanan broke free from Elting, kept heading east. Elting stood, waited for the moment to pass, ran, caught up at the intersection.

Elting put an arm around Buchanan's waist, pulled him close.

"See," Elting said, pointed over the cars, to Lake Michigan. "No fire."

"Not yet," Buchanan said.

"Not yet," Elting repeated.

Now, they walked south, turned into the underground passageway.

Again, the city had painted over the graffiti—gang tags, homages to dead friends, declarations of romantic love, platonic love, impossible-to-categorize love, love too big. The concrete tube was painted a hard, untouched white.

"Hey," Buchanan said. "Stop."

"Can't you smell the sand?" Elting asked.

"Should we open this?" Buchanan asked. He outstretched his arm, showed the wine box.

"Not yet," Elting said.

"Not yet," Buchanan agreed.

They unfolded their sleeping blankets on the sand. They took their coats and shirts off. They revealed old torsos and scars, drooping skin, strange fat rolls in odd places. Elting opened the wine tap, poured their glasses full. They toasted the absence of fire. They toasted another trip completed. They thanked the skies for clearing up. They thanked the sun and the shine from the lake. They cheered the state of Michigan, all the way over there, that distant place they'd never seen. They sipped. They cheered the man jogging along the sand. They cheered the dog jogging with him. When the man and dog passed, Elting and Buchanan cheered the relative peace and quiet; the humming traffic behind them; the water lapping before them, feet away.

They finished their glasses, poured another, finished that, poured another, dug shallow holes in the sand for cup holders.

"Can you believe it?" Elting asked, after some silence.

"Not at all," Buchanan said.

Elting lay on his back. Lake breeze flowed through his nostrils into his brain, out of his ears. A tapping on his chest.

"Look," Buchanan said.

"I'm sleeping," Elting said. "I'm dreaming."

"Look," Buchanan said. "Look. Look. Hey. Look."

Elting looked. He saw blue sky and Rorschach clouds. He saw Buchanan's finger pointing north. Elting turned his head sideways, put his ear on the blanket.

Elting saw two sideways figures walking toward them, fast.

"Friends?" Elting asked Buchanan.

"Cops," Buchanan said.

"Cops?" Elting asked. "How can you tell?"

"I saw this," Buchanan said. "I know how it ends."

"I want my own dreams," Elting said.

He looked back at the sky, closed his eyes.

Seconds or minutes passed before Elting heard feet shuffling on sand. He felt more tapping on his chest. This time: rapid, hard.

"Look," Buchanan said.

Elting opened his eyes. He stared into a cop's face. He saw pimples, red and white-tipped, on the cop's cheeks and forehead, one between his thin eyebrows.

"Good morning," Elting said to the cop.

The cop turned to his partner, who was standing over Buchanan with hand on gun. Elting's cop was Black; Buchanan's was Black too, lighter-skinned, mocha, with jade eyes and pock-marks running up his neck.

"You can't do this," Black cop said.

"You know you can't do this," mocha cop said.

"Sirs," Elting said, sat up. "Please beg our pardon."

"We'll leave," Buchanan said, stood up, frantic.

Elting grabbed Buchanan's ankle, tried to steady Buchanan's shaking legs.

"Please stand up," Black cop said to Elting.

"I was dreaming," Elting said.

"He was dreaming," mocha cop said to Black cop.

"We'll leave," Buchanan said to everyone.

"Sit down," Elting said to Buchanan.

Buchanan, nervous frown pulled tight, looked down at Elting.

"No," Buchanan said to Elting. "We'll go."

"Kids come here," mocha cop said to Elting.

"Kids shouldn't see you," Black cop said to Elting.

Buchanan noticed a familiar expression slide from Elting's eyes down to his lips. Buchanan had seen it before, in similar situations, when Elting needed to chill and wouldn't chill, couldn't chill, refused to chill. Buchanan braced himself.

Elting reached for the wine box. Black cop kicked the wine box over.

Buchanan held his breath, swallowed. Mocha cop kept his eyes on Buchanan, kept hand on gun.

"Stand up," mocha cop said to Elting.

"Sirs," Elting said. "You have interrupted our picnic."

"Please," Buchanan said to Elting. "We'll leave. We'll go home. We'll sleep at home."

"Out here," Elting said to Buchanan. "We have peace and water."

"You don't have peace," Black cop said.

"We don't have peace," Buchanan said.

"Listen to your friend," mocha cop said. "This is a family beach."

"We are family," Elting said to Buchanan.

"One last time," Black cop said. "Stand up."

"You spilled my wine," Elting said.

Buchanan couldn't believe the speed. First, Black cop kicked Elting in the stomach. Elting knew something hard was coming—he curled into a ball and covered his head, like he always did when a severe beating was imminent. Mocha cop grabbed Buchanan's right arm, pulled it hard behind Buchanan's back. Buchanan did not see it coming. Something popped in his shoulder twice. He yelped and gasped. Mocha cop kicked Buchanan in the knee, sent Buchanan's face into sand. Elting took his repeated blows in silence, in the stomach and ribs. They heard radio chatter, cops talking in numbers. They heard backup called, locations given, descriptions of Buchanan and Elting—middle-aged Black males, drunk and disordered, aggressive. Buchanan couldn't see Elting through the sand. Mocha cop planted a knee into Buchanan's back.

"Keep your spirit!" Elting yelled to Buchanan.

Buchanan closed his eyes and saw fire, felt steel handcuffs pinch his wrists.

They heard radio chatter, static voices confirmed reinforcements.

In his ear, Buchanan heard mocha cop's voice soften.

"Didn't you see this coming?" mocha cop said. "Don't you know?"

Buchanan heard the blows against Elting stop. He heard handcuffs click and pinch.

Soon, they were in a small plastic back seat, moving slow toward the police station, hands behind backs, without wine, blankets, water, clouds, peace.

Buchanan looked over Elting's face. No bruises; no cuts; no blood; some sand in his wrinkles.

Soon, mocha cop and Black cop led them through a fluorescent lobby, steel doors painted blue, dirt-stained linoleum hallways, steel doors painted green. Elting and Buchanan kept quiet, listened to the howls coming from interrogation rooms, the laughing detectives slapping each other's backs. Elting and Buchanan were dumped in a cell with one other person.

"Wait here," mocha cop said. "Keep quiet."

The other person was young, in a thick black fur coat. He was extended on the metal bench, asleep, mouth open, twitching through his dreams, unfazed by metal bars creaking open and slamming shut.

Elting and Buchanan knew this process. Wait, relax; wait for them to see you're not a threat, let you go.

Buchanan waited for mocha cop and Black cop to leave. Then, Buchanan punched Elting in the chest. Elting banged his head against the bars. The young man on the metal bench stayed in his dreams.

"I know," Elting said.

"Our whole day," Buchanan said. "Ruined."

"I know," Elting said.

"Our nice day," Buchanan said. "Relaxation. Gone."

"I saw my kittens," Elting said.

"Oh," Buchanan said.

Buchanan moved across the cell, leaned against the wall, left Elting leaned against the metal bars.

Buchanan slid to the concrete floor, next to the steel toilet.

"They didn't have to kick me," Elting said.

"They can kick you," Buchanan said. "They can kill you."

"Didn't you see this coming?" Elting asked, slid down against the bars.

"Not this," Buchanan said.

Elting asked more questions about the fire. Buchanan didn't listen. He was focused on a rusted drain in the middle of the cell, between him and Elting. He watched a bug with many legs crawl down there. He wasn't sure if his hallucinations were coming back. Most times, he'd hallucinate bugs like that one, squirming into the earth, crawling up his forearm, along his thighs. Sometimes, the bugs were real. He kept staring at the drain. This drain looked like all old drains. It looked like the drain in Buchanan's old basement, back in South Shore. It wasn't Buchanan's basement. It was the house he shared with his brother, Filmore. The house Filmore bought and allowed Buchanan to sleep in. When Filmore went to work,

Buchanan had to stay in the basement, on his twin bed, stare at the drain, look at bugs with many legs come for his skin. He read long books about centuries-old military invasions. He took his pills and swallowed them with tap water. Sometimes, he turned the lights off, let darkness calm his mind, all that electric energy rattling his skull. He told himself, curled up at night, that Filmore's basement was better than that hospital up north, near the lake, where the guards took your food if you screamed too loud at night. Buchanan's mind had been getting better. Buchanan had been sure of it. There were tranquil days, full weekends spent driving around with Filmore, revisiting their childhoods, eating hot dogs near the expressway, watching fireworks and White Sox home runs. Through all the noise, Buchanan had kept his head. He laughed at nothing; he hugged his brother; he thanked his brother's love; he'd felt better. He did. True. His brother was proud of him.

Then, one day, Filmore didn't come home. Buchanan waited at the basement stairs, waited for the basement door to unlock. He listened for footsteps above his head. He listened for an opening refrigerator, a bottle cap's pop and drop. He stared at the drain. He waited for the many-legged bugs to invade his fragile peace. He paced. He practiced breathing slow. He sat on his bed and rocked. He tapped his head against the concrete walls. Hours or days passed. Police broke down the front door. Buchanan heard that. Buchanan heard several feet rushing over his head. Voices yelling Buchanan's name; loud voices; voices reaching frantic harmony, sharp. Police broke the basement door down. They found him curled under his bed, holding his knees to his chin, eyes shut tight, teeth clenched, muscles taut and strained. They dragged him out, carried him, balled-up, to a waiting ambulance. They told him about the car accident. Before Filmore slipped into a coma, he told them about Buchanan, his sweet brother. They took Buchanan to the hospital up north. They force-fed him pills and flavorless food. They sent mental professionals into his room. Everyone he met had a concerned expression, spoke about trauma, misfiring neurons, permanent breakdowns.

One night, in a blizzard, Buchanan heard a gentle voice calling him. He snuck past sleeping guards. In his hospital gown and thin slippers, he followed the voice through snow. He felt his lips go numb. His chattering teeth behind his blue lips. The voice led him to an overpass, the expressway, cautious cars slipping through sleet and wind. The people under the overpass offered him blankets and booze. The voice faded. That was Buchanan.

Here, Buchanan, now, stared down a rusted jail cell drain, braced for insects, ignored Elting's questions. Elting, annoyed, stood up, walked over to Buchanan, punched his shoulder.

"We're not going to make it," Buchanan said.

Elting threw his hands up, grabbed his head, twirled in a circle.

"More of this," Elting said. "All this negative thinking is bad for my liver."

"He's right," a voice said.

Buchanan jumped at the voice, closed his eyes, covered his ears. Elting looked around. They had forgotten about the young man sleeping on the metal bench, who was now sitting up, leaned back, eyes closed.

"We're not going to make it," the young man said.

Buchanan opened his eyes, relaxed his arms.

"You don't know us," Elting said. "You don't know our journey."

Buchanan stared at the young man's calm face. He traced the young man's smile from his dimples to a wide scar on his lip, right under his nose.

"During times like these," the young man said, "haven't you thought about leaving?"

"I do," Buchanan said. "I think about taking a hot-air balloon across Lake Michigan."

"You don't," Elting said.

"I do," Buchanan said. "I think about starting a blueberry farm."

"You didn't tell me," Elting said.

"I did," Buchanan said. "I tell you and you don't listen."

"Blueberries?" Elting asked. "Balloons?"

The young man stood up, walked over to Elting and Buchanan, leaned down, whispered.

"I know a place," the young man said.

Elting gave a low moan, turned away.

"What place?" Buchanan whispered back.

"Far from here," the young man said. "In the hills."

Elting turned back around.

"What hills?" Elting asked.

"Let him tell us," Buchanan said to Elting.

"Tell us what?" Elting asked.

"Massachusetts," the young man said.

"Don't listen to this," Elting said.

"Let him tell us," Buchanan said to Elting, pleaded, embarrassed.

Elting walked over to the bench, lay down, closed his eyes, listened to the young man whisper about Massachusetts.

He spoke, whimsical, quiet. He explained. He told them about Rio and Gibraltar, Baby Drop, underground—a new world, hidden, cloaked in promise. They were growing. They were making their own food. They were making their own art, writing books, sculpture. Soon, they would build a lab. When our society above collapses, their society below will keep on, remain fresh. There was no inequality down in the Mountain. Racial. Economic. Sexual. Nothing. No exploitation. Everyone had exactly what they needed. They will keep growing. They will keep building. Keep going deeper. Now is the time to go there.

Once the young man stopped, Elting and Buchanan had questions they didn't ask. They pondered in silence, exchanged looks. Why a mountain? Why run away from the world? Why not use that money, those brains, on making our society better? What do they know that we don't? Are we so far gone? Is there no turning back? They sat huddled in their corner.

Moments passed again in silence. It grew dark outside. There were small windows in their cell, close to the ceiling. They could see lights from apartment buildings and office buildings and mixed-use tall buildings with offices and apartments and retail spaces for expensive clothes and expensive salons for expensive hair. They saw Chicago's peaks from their low vantage point. Buchanan and the young man sat next to each other, backs against the wall. Elting sat up on his bench. Somewhere down the hallway, in another cell, a person screamed out for his mother. The voice apologized for stealing, lying, cheating on his wife, doing drugs, not paying attention in Calculus. The voice stopped midsentence. Soon, crying followed, soft and choked-up, muffled. Then, the crying stopped. Each man recalled times they had cried and screamed.

Moments passed, again, in silence.

"How long's the bus ride?" Elting asked, didn't look at Buchanan or the young man.

"About eighteen hours," the young man said. "If nothing happens."

"Is there stuff to look at?" Buchanan asked. "Like, outside the windows?"

"You get some mountains," the young man said. "Out in New York, Massachusetts."

"We find the man?" Elting asked. "And he gives us tickets?"

"In the morning," the young man said. "First thing."

The three men settled into uncomfortable positions for the night. They used coats as pillows. They ignored the cops leading nonviolent criminals down the hallway, pushing too hard, saying rude things, laughing in an abusive manner. They ignored the yelling, the cold floor; the introduction, in their cell, of other vagrants, tired drunks with coats they'd also use as pillows. One new cellmate blamed Ronald Reagan for his problems, father and son Bush, the Clintons, too, Obama, those Trumps—all of them no good. Someone responded that the oil companies burned holes in our air. Them too. What about the European Union, with their Byzantine bureaucratic processes, controlling too much, dictating too much, just a front for the Germans, a cover for the Fourth Reich? Them too. What about the tech companies looking at us in the bathroom? They're the worst evil. Them too.

Somewhere in the chatter, Elting and Buchanan and the young man fell asleep, dreamed, awoke to a cop opening their cell and freeing their drifting lot into the world.

"I have a cousin in Massachusetts," Buchanan said.

"You don't," Elting said. "Stop making things up."

"I do," Buchanan said. "He's a professor."

"You don't," Elting said.

"I do," Buchanan said. "I know all my kin."

Elting knew when to stop pushing Buchanan for the truth. With friends, let them lie, when the lie doesn't matter and you'll go with them anyway.

PART THREE

Bounce

THERE, OUTSIDE HIS window, Bounce saw two birds dive-
bomb a bread loaf, over and over, lift dust-sized crumbs to a
hidden nest. Bounce wished he knew the species. He wanted
to understand their ritual. Bounce wished he was outside,
strolling, headed to work, confident and focused. Downstairs:
a kettle whistled, a stove clicked. Soon, his sister would shout
his name, tell him to get his ass up and moving. Soon after
that, his sister would move closer to the stairs and yell louder,
sending her voice echoing around the narrow corridor, tossing
her command between old family portraits and new family
portraits. Snow, his beautiful sister, would then walk up the

stairs and pound on his door—Bounce was not allowed to be alone in the house, not when everyone was at work or school or out in the world, doing something, anything.

Now, Snow was at the door, attempting to twist the locked doorknob.

"I'm up," Bounce said. "I'm up. I'm up."

"Then," Snow said, soft, through the door, "get your ass up."

Bounce got his ass up, stood next to the bed until Snow's footsteps thudded back downstairs.

Bounce got his ass into the bathroom, which he shared, for the past few weeks, with his twelve-year-old niece, Aviary.

Aviary was experiencing a profound phase, one centered around macabre interpretations of the world and life and society and youth. Her bathroom mirror was framed by printed-out pictures of roadkill, staged portraits of weary-eyed starlets with nooses around their necks.

Bounce studied his face, pulled at his thin cheeks and forehead. He fiddled his neck tattoo: a closed zipper keeping his head attached. He rubbed at his cheek tattoo: two floating fingers, symbolizing peace. Across his chest, shown backward in the smudged mirror, written in sharp letters, big and thick: I AM WIDE AWAKE. With a canvas like Bounce's torso, he could paint a horrific portrait of impressive scale. When Bounce was his niece's age, he'd wanted an expert to carve the devil on his back. He, too, had experienced a dark and annoying phase. He, too, had seen sadness and anger in everything. Once, in college, when Bounce was on a date with a Tri-Delt, he looked over his date's shoulder at a typical sunset and said, without prompting, that sunsets reminded him of death and hell. The date pulled away from him, didn't call back, told other Tri-Delts not to date that Black soccer player with tattoos.

Nowadays, Bounce kept those thoughts to himself; he muttered them in his niece's shower.

Snow kicked the bathroom door.

"I'm moving," Bounce said. "I'm drying off."

Bounce dried off, brushed his teeth, sprayed his armpits with some prepubescent perfume, gave his cheeks several firm slaps.

"Wake up," Bounce told the mist. "Wake up. Wake up. Come on."

He snatched sweatpants and a hoodie from his duffel bag, sniffed areas prone to stink, grimaced, put the sweatpants and hoodie on his crumpled clothes pile. He pulled another pair of sweatpants and a hoodie from his duffel bag, sniffed, approved, got dressed. He didn't smell his socks or underwear—he knew what to expect.

Bounce checked the window before heading downstairs: the birds and bread loaf were gone. Not even a crumb remained. Maybe, Bounce thought, my mind is broken beyond repair. The other day, Bounce thought he saw a dog riding a horse down by the lake. And that was just one example. He shook his head at the window and went downstairs.

"When is Uncle Bounce leaving?" Aviary asked over her pancakes.

"Avi!" Snow snapped over her tablet.

"What?" Aviary asked. "I don't want him to leave. You do."

"Avi!" Snow snapped again.

Bounce kept spooning his fruit and yogurt, winked at his niece.

"When's dad coming home?" Aviary asked.

At that, Snow stood up, wiped her eyes, exited the kitchen, cried in the living room.

"Take it easy," Bounce said to Aviary.

"Why don't they get divorced already?" Aviary asked.

"That's not how it works," Bounce said. "You know that."

Aviary understood love in a distant and fogged-up way. Once, looking out her window, when a thunderstorm raged, she saw two fire-haired women kissing hard against a parked car. This was during a spring afternoon, during a sickness Aviary embellished and milked for a three-day vacation from school. She watched their hands make soft movements in the lifeless street. She watched them switch positions, twirl, gyrate, mouth loving words Aviary couldn't hear. One red-haired woman had green eyes; the other, dead black. One moment, Aviary looked into green eyes. Then, after some gyration and twirling, Aviary looked into infinite blackness. Aviary couldn't square it: the contrast, those eyes. Then the rain stopped; the sky opened up bright and blue. The two people pulled their mouths apart, embraced, searched the sky for more rain, embraced tighter. The two fire-haired people caught Aviary in her perch, waved. Aviary barrel-rolled to the floor, out of view, felt rude, stuck a hand above the window, waved back until her arm hurt.

That was love, Aviary thought, somehow. All of it was love.

"I don't know how it works," Aviary said to Bounce after a moment.

"Neither do I," Bounce said, finished with his yogurt.

"I know it's hard," Aviary said. "It looks hard."

"Most of it's hard," Bounce said.

"What?" Aviary asked. "Most of what?"

"All of it," Bounce said. "You know? Most of it."

"I'm a child," Aviary said. "You have to explain things to me."

"I'm trying," Bounce said.

"So I can understand," Aviary said.

"I forgot what we were talking about," Bounce said.

"We weren't talking about anything," Aviary said.

"Right," Bounce said. "Right. Love."

"Once," Aviary said, sensing an opening, "I saw two women kissing in a thunderstorm."

"Okay," Bounce said.

"They had fire hair," Aviary said.

"Okay," Bounce said.

"They saw me," Aviary said.

"Okay," Bounce said.

"That's something," Aviary said.

Most conversations between uncle and niece went like this: each left wishing they had said more.

Somehow, Snow ended up outside the kitchen window, jingling her car keys.

"Late!" Snow yelled at Aviary.

"Out!" Snow yelled at Bounce.

Bounce took Aviary's plate to the trash, dumped out cold pancakes, took Aviary's plate to the sink, left it there, went back to the table, picked up his bowl, saw Rorschach yogurt streaks at the bottom, took his plate to the sink, left it there.

Later, Snow would yell at him in front of Aviary to wash the dishes, put them away, behave like a civilized human, show some compassion, show some appreciation, don't act like an animal, don't act like him.

Now, Snow yelled for brother and daughter to move their asses.

Brother and daughter moved their asses.

Daughter climbed into Snow's backseat.

Brother went on his way, eyed beautiful trees for crazed birds.

When a stranger first ogled him on the street, years ago, Bounce, violent with Long Island Iced Tea, chased the stranger for three blocks before vomiting with laughter, giving up. Now, Bounce was used to the stares. He could shower more, take care of his appearance, cut his hair, shave his beard, use a laser to remove prominent and meaningless tattoos. He could sleep more, drink more water. He had perpetual maroon rings around his eyes. He could fix how he looked if he had the interest or energy. As a teenager, he'd been diagnosed with clinical depression. He was drained by apathy. No matter how hard he tried, Bounce couldn't make himself presentable. He couldn't find the strength.

When a young father pulled his young daughter close to his side as Bounce ambled past—What could Bounce do besides smile, salute, put his head down, and keep on moving? When a jogger, a block away, sped up, crossed the street, sped up, and sped up—Was it Bounce, or these menacing birds? Sparrows, Bounce thought, sparrows are a bird I know.

Snow had gotten Bounce some interviews when he first washed back into her life. One, at Snow's small liberal arts college, had been a special trauma. These men in suits and women in dresses sat around a table, asked Bounce why his soccer career didn't work out, why didn't college work out, what are you doing now, how is your life, how is your soul— Bounce, why should we hire you?

The soccer team needed an assistant coach; the soccer team was underperforming and undertalented. The other applicant was middle-aged and loved baseball. Bounce saw him in the waiting room, balding, round, smiling, confident.

Bounce couldn't stop sweating. An interviewer in a beautiful floral dress asked if he needed a tissue, if he was crying and needed a moment to gather himself.

"It's not going that bad," she said, with a genuine smile.

Bounce declined the tissue, excused himself, shook the baseball man's calloused hand, wished him luck, ran home, waited on the porch for Snow to appear.

Snow told Aviary to run inside, get washed up before dinner—Mom has to speak with Uncle Bounce.

Snow sat with her brother, rubbed his cheeks, patted his head, hugged him into her breast, told him not to worry.

Bounce didn't hear her over his sobbing, the electric storm raging throughout his brain; Bounce only heard noise.

Snow kissed her brother's thick skull. She kissed him again. Then, she went inside to deal with her own shambolic life, cook dinner, check Aviary's fingernails for dirt, imagine a peaceful world.

Bounce remained on the porch until rain pushed him upstairs without dinner.

Now, Bounce needed a place to go—he couldn't walk forever.

A coffee shop up the street had crumbling scones and fluffed croissants; the movie theater was cheap and empty because it was falling apart and covered in thick grime.

If Bounce drank, there was a bar that opened around ten and played daytime talk shows until sports started. If Bounce still drank, he could drink himself to death. So, Bounce didn't drink. Instead, when his thoughts grew too intense to ignore, he hung around the park with some burnouts and paid five dollars for low-grade weed. The burnouts didn't ogle Bounce; they taught Bounce how to throw a Frisbee, how to make it glide along wind currents.

His last option was the public library. But today was not a reading day. Bounce needed five dollars for a coffee and donut. He patted his thighs, ass, chest, and waist, hoping a bill stack would somehow materialize on his person. He didn't need much—five dollars. He just needed one bill. He patted again, with more force. He just needed five bills, at most. A minivan slammed on its brakes centimeters away from Bounce's knees.

How did he end up in the intersection, rubbing his thighs, staring through the ground, dazed?

How did he end up so far from home?

Bounce felt his big toe slide off the curb. That falling sensation, a tiny jolt, lung tossed up against his heart, all his insides lifted and dropped.

He understood how a person could want to feel their body panic. All that adrenaline ripping against your skin, shocking your hairs. Bounce could understand how a person needed that every now and then; craved it, when life turned dull. Wasn't Bounce dull, right now, toe dangling into traffic? And that jolt, that small shock, jump-started his wires.

Bounced looked at his big toe, looked through his big toe, saw hair, skin, bone, callus, asphalt, dirt, sewers, lazy water carrying filth, earth layered and ancient, shifting plates, ever-present tension, rumbling molten oceans, an expiring core, ticking, ticking. Bounce looked into his own eyes at the center of life. And there was that jolt again. There was everything. There were tears, now, falling on his shoes.

Bounce looked into time. He saw all of it. Before, after, alongside, now, right now. He saw all of it. He felt it. All of it wrapped around his body, shocking him—jolts, those jolts, millions of them, billions, trillions; his entire body lit up.

He cried at the beauty. He cried at the shame. He didn't deserve this. He didn't deserve the beauty wrapped around him, didn't deserve the air, the trees, the bed, the family, the love and care, the dangling big toe, the jolts, the tears.

Unable to look into the world anymore, he closed his eyes.

He was back in the womb. He was back in the water, a speck. He was back in the park, outside his elementary school, running up the metal stairs, running down the slide, falling, getting back up. Back in his mother's classroom, watching her grade papers, watching pictures of himself and Snow on her desk, trying to make them move with his mind. Back in his father's apartment after the divorce, listening to love explained, sitting on the couch, receiving a kiss, a hug, a promise to never leave. Back in the hospital when his mother shut down. Back in the hospital when his father shut down. Back as a child, just a child.

And he stepped back into time.

Bounce woke in a hospital bed, Snow and Aviary flanking him in low-seated chairs. Their heads hovered around his waist. He jumped, tried to run away. Snow stood, held his large body down with her small hands. Bounce felt an aching weight all over his body.

"I fell into the earth," Bounce said.

"They said this would happen," Aviary said to Snow.

"Avi," Snow said.

"They said he wouldn't make sense," Avi said.

"Avi," Snow said.

"Because of the drugs," Aviary said, pointed at an IV bag dangling from a plastic tower.

Bounce followed her finger with his eyes, saw the bag, saw the monitors and their squiggling lines, saw the white walls, saw the room grow large as his eyes adjusted, saw it shrink back down, saw their faces worry at him.

"Do you remember what happened?" Snow asked.

"We know what happened," Aviary said.

"Avi," Snow said.

Aviary huffed, pushed her feet into the tiles, slid back, hung her head.

"I was walking," Bounce said. "I was on the curb."

"Okay," Snow said.

"It was all over me," Bounce said.

"What was?" Snow asked.

Bounce passed out.

Bounce rolled onto his stomach, put his face into a weak pillow. The hospital gown was untied in the back. He felt the air, cold, on his exposed ass. He made a series of indecipherable pleas.

"Bounce?" Snow asked. Her hands pressed into his bare back. She had forgotten about this tattoo: large flames and screaming winged angels flowing between his shoulders, running from neck to lower back. This tattoo, Snow remembered, gave her nightmares.

Snow put her mouth against Bounce's ear, grabbed his head, kept a firm grip, tried to keep his brain still.

"Please," Snow asked. "Come back. Come on. Please. Come back."

"Sorry," Bounce said into the pillow. "Sorry, sorry. I'm trying."

"I know," Snow said. "We know."

"You got hit by a car," Aviary said.

"Avi," Snow said. "Please."

"There's a video of it," Aviary said. "It's everywhere. My friends keep sending it to me."

"Avi," Snow said.

"You're flying in the air," Aviary said, shaking, crying. "You look like a superhero. It doesn't make sense. You're alive. And the car is all messed up."

"Avi!" Snow was an inch from her daughter's face. Their tears almost touched.

"I'm sorry," Bounce said, showed them his face, proved it.

"We know," Snow said, turned back around. "I know."

"I was on the curb," Bounce said.

"Then what?" Snow asked.

"These jolts," Bounce said.

"Jolts," Snow said, looked at her daughter, worry again, all tears and worry.

There was a miracle. The driver saw Bounce standing at the curb. The driver, a man late to work, when interviewed by police, described a strange feeling while heading to the intersection, seeing, in his periphery, this man teetering on the edge. The driver didn't slow down. Why would he slow down? Why would Bounce walk into the street? In the moment the driver collided with Bounce's body, the driver saw Bounce's face calm and serene and accepting. The driver closed his eyes, jerked forward, violent, the airbag smashed his face, broke his nose. He couldn't believe it, the wreckage, his car, a solid car, dented, mangled. Like he hit a tree. Like he hit a moose. What was he going to do about his car?

The driver, when interviewed by police, got this miles-away stare, had to get shook back to reality. The driver had a sister, back in his hometown—Erie, Pennsylvania—who had claimed to see the future and feel the universe change against her skin like the weather, like atmospheric pressure. She was sent into the woods, to a hospital for people with jumbled internal wiring. She lived a long and confined life. She never stopped complaining about her mind and nerves. The brother got that mile-away stare again, had to get shook back to reality again. "I guess," he said to the police, standing in the park, watching Bounce get loaded into the ambulance, "I guess we're all connected with invisible currents." The police took their notes, went back to the station, went back to their homes, sat with their dinners, sat on their couches, laid in their beds, looked at their ceilings, couldn't sleep, wouldn't sleep for days after, would study flowers in the wind and try to decipher their flow. It was one of those cases that glues onto your heart. It was one they would tell grandchildren, when they were old enough to contemplate such things. It was one they would understand in hospice, when a bright light came raining down.

The Indestructible Man.

There was convalescence. There was a broken leg, a few splintered ribs, a split in his forehead, bruises polka-dotted around his limbs.

There were days and nights in the hospital bed. There was Bounce in a tube, getting scanned. There was still a miracle.

Dumb luck. A bus. What if a bus was coming? What if it was garbage day? A truck carrying too much weight to slow down. What would it take to kill Bounce?

And Aviary, those days and nights in the hospital refusing to leave. And Snow, telling her daughter it was okay to go to school and come back. Snow crusted to her chair, started to smell, watched her brother sleep, noticing unnoticed aspects of his face. Like that mole above his left nostril. Like that faded scar poking from his left eyebrow. That small cut in his right ear, just about where the earlobe starts to round. What about the phone call with Dustin in the hallway, in the elevator, outside smoking a cigarette, walking and talking, knocking into corners and garbage cans? Giving the details, wondering how it would affect their daughter, years later, when she felt like walking into traffic. Wondering, without saying, how it affected them, if this was the event that would reconnect them, bring the house together again, brush small differences under the carpet, reignite. Knowing, without saying, nothing had changed between them. Understanding, without saying, that this had nothing to do with them. That this was about Bounce. This was about getting Bounce right. What about the fear? What if this was Bounce forever? What if the doctor had a point? What if Bounce couldn't go home? What if Bounce needed that hospital across the valley with constant surveillance and medication and walks along those trails and game night? What if Snow shouldn't have told the doctor to fuck off? There was an "I love you," another "I love you" through the phone, hang up, back upstairs.

There was Bounce, asleep.

There was Aviary, standing at the window, looking miles away.

Those first few days, Bounce caught some of it. He heard the voices, some words and feeling clear and weighted. The worried doctor. The worried sister and niece. The calming nurse saying it was normal, sleeping like this, the spasms. His body was a healing bruise; he needed time.

Most often, there were dreams. He was back in high school, late for class, running through the halls, trying to find the right room, trying to find his pants, feet in quicksand, taking wrong turns, missing a test, expelled. He was flying to Tokyo in first class, an earthquake out his window, the ocean waving up and down, touching his window. He was a child at the grocery store, holding his mother's hand, feeling it strong, feeling it weaken, feeling her presence soften, looking up and seeing her face round, bronze, full, and smiling, seeing her face thin, sharp-boned, dull; seeing her veins and feeling her veins, feeling her blood slow.

He shot awake in a dark room.

The calming nurse had put a cot in the corner. There was Aviary sprawled with limbs dangling off all sides. There was Snow in the bedside chair, sprawled too, head back and snoring. There were tubes and wires tying him down.

Now, a burden. That was Bounce. How could he repay them?

He saw his mother in her hospital bed, in her gown, apologizing for the hassle, the fuss. He had stood against the furthest wall, a scared and silent teenager. Snow had leaned over mother's bed, given her water, wiped her chin. Bounce had stood in the hallway, on the phone, whispering to his father, telling him to come. Not much time. The exchange of fear between father and son, pulsing in electronic waves.

When his father's time came—he sipping water, poked with tubes and wires—Bounce leaned over his bed. Snow, in the hall, peeking in, silent, moving between the hallway and the lobby, still estranged. His father expressed regret. Like a movie, those apologies splashing at Bounce. All these wishes. Bounce had wanted him to stop. His father said it was a hard thing forgetting about a person you love, an impossible thing, a horrible thing to ask. Of course he hadn't forgotten his wife. Twenty years, two kids, five kids if you count the miscarriages, which his father did, often. He once drove to the hospital, parked in the garage, sat there crying, punching the airbag, losing it. Don't you think I wanted to come in? Didn't you think I wanted to hold her? You don't just forget about a person. You fall in love with a person. You live a life. You walk around the house screaming, stomping, begging for it to get better. When it doesn't get better, you don't forget about a person. When it gets worse, you don't forget about a person. Didn't Bounce know that? You don't forget about your children. You don't forget about your parents. You don't forget about your childhood dog, breaking free from the leash, running into the road, getting crushed. You don't forget about your honeymoon in Mexico City, the altitude pressing against your heart, changing your love, making each word more precious than it had ever felt before. You don't forget the children that made it. You don't remember their first steps, their first words, their first ice cream, banana, mango, avocado. Still, you don't forget. Those emotions are always there, tiny pulses in your memory. You don't wake up one morning clear minded, wiped clean, a new person, a new day, weightless. You don't die weightless. Don't you know that?

Now, in his turn in the hospital, Bounce, a burden, knew that.

In the darkness, he knew. Of course he knew.

A dream about flight one night. Bounce, knapsack over one shoulder, worked through a dense forest. Somehow, he understood the need for silence, creeping. Shush, shush, a voice would say when he cracked a twig. He knew to pause when he heard nearby scurrying. He knew to hold his breath. He couldn't pause for too long. He was alone out there, wherever he was. If he stopped moving, they would catch him. So, he started breathing again, kept working, pushed away branches, hugged trees when he fell. He knew the voice shushing him. The voice saying his name. *Bounce. Bounce. Bounce. Bounce. Bounce, bounce, bounce, bounce.* A creek drizzled down the hill. He stepped on a glowing mushroom and heard it scream. *Shush, shush.* He took the creek in three steps, in the low valley, across the other side, up the hill. The voice told him freedom was yards away, feet now, pause. Bounce paused. *Breathe. Push through.* Bounce pushed through leafed limbs.

And there Bounce saw the golden field and sun and wild grass up to his ankles, tickling.

Somehow, Bounce knew what to do next.

He put down his body. He put down his knapsack. He pulled out a baguette, still warm. He pulled out salami, a peppered tube. He pulled out spring water, clear, cold, in a big bottle. He pulled out a blanket, unrolled it, wrapped it around his shoulders. He pulled out a pillow. He pulled out a spinning record player, running arias he didn't understand beyond their beauty. And then the voice was gone. And the sun was rising. And there wasn't a shadow around.

Bounce was gone.

Bounce was full and alone.

Bounce was discharged. Snow hugged the doctor. Aviary hugged her uncle, gentle. The doctor left. The family cried, thanked each other, thanked the universe, and performed inaudible prayers for life. After they wiped their eyes, cleared their throats, patted their backs, patted their heads, sniffled, and wiped their noses—anger and disbelief came upon them with tonnage and precision, right into their ribcages, up into their guts.

Bounce lifted his head, bumped Snow. Their bloodshot eyes met.

"It's okay," Snow said. "Fuck, man. It's okay."

"I'm trying," Bounce said.

"I know," Snow said. "It's okay. I know."

Near the doorway, Aviary stood. She figured, yes, this was love, writhing love. And, now, love terrified her.

Somewhere in his sedated mind, Bounce was gliding across an iced-over river, arms outstretched, sucking in wind and delicious clouds.

Bounce awoke, for a moment, in a spasm, at a red light. My head, Bounce thought, my head is detached from my neck.

"My head," Bounce said.

"Bounce," Snow said from the driver's seat.

Bounce couldn't look at his sister; his head wouldn't turn.

"My head," Bounce said. "It's stuck."

"We're going home," Aviary said from the back seat, not knowing what else to say.

Bounce couldn't wipe drool from his cheeks. Again, stuck.

"My arms," Bounce said.

Red light turned into green light; cars honked; Snow drove.

"You're hurt," Snow said, looking at the road, moving slow. Cars passed, rubbernecked.

Bounce tried to wiggle his toes, roll his ankles. Stuck. Like his feet were encased in bricks.

"My body," Bounce said. "My body."

Atop his head, Bounce felt something stroke and crawl across his hair.

"You're okay," Aviary said.

"Avi," Snow said. "Pills in my purse. Put one in his mouth."

"My body," Bounce said, couldn't stop saying in a mumbled loop.

Aviary found the pills, popped the cap, put two in her palm, leaned between the adults' seats, turned toward her uncle.

Snow fumbled around her feet for something unseen, swerved a little, kept her eyes above the steering wheel, just.

She returned upright with a mangled water bottle, a few sips left; she passed it to her daughter.

"I'm good," Aviary said.

"Not you," Snow said. "Him."

"Oh," Aviary said. "Oh, oh, oh."

Bounce, again, looked asleep. Aviary tried not to stare at her uncle; she couldn't help it. His firm neck brace; slings wrapped around his upper body, encasing bruised arms; plastic and thin casts Velcroed on both his legs, running from knee to toe.

"His damage is more mental," the doctor said. "His body is among the strongest in the world. His mind . . ." the doctor trailed off and left the room, paged to a better disaster.

Aviary held palm and pills before Bounce's lips.

Bounce mumbled something, as he hadn't stopped doing.

"Shove them in," Snow said, sensed her daughter's unsureness.

Aviary listened to her mother, shoved the pills between her uncle's lips.

"Remember?" Snow asked.

"Right," Aviary said. "Water. Right: water."

Niece brought the distressed water bottle to her uncle's lips, tilted it up, poured it all down. Uncle received the pills and water.

Deep in there, down in Bounce's spine, pain subsided and was replaced with that floating and skating feeling. Again, he drifted, couldn't tell if the car was drifting, too, if his loved ones were stuck on the horrible ground. He wanted them to come with him. If only his eyes would open.

At the house, Snow and Aviary contemplated the passenger door, mimicked each other: rested their chins on closed fists, sighed, looked at the sky, at the ground, at the mailwoman, at the packages the mailwoman carried, at the mailwoman's awkward gait, her stiff right leg, a soft and wobbling left leg.

Snow snapped her fingers, told Aviary to get in the driver's seat.

"Push," Snow said.

Aviary put her weight into her uncle's side, felt bone through his thickness. Were his eyes open?

"More!" Snow yelled.

"I'm having a heart attack!" Aviary yelled back.

"You're not!" Snow yelled back.

"I am!" Aviary yelled. "I can't breathe!"

The mailwoman, back in her truck, watched this scene and wondered if the police should get involved.

She moved on to the next house.

Somehow, they pushed, twisted, grunted, and slipped Bounce into the too-small foldout wheelchair. Somehow, they had to get this wheelchair up the front stairs.

"I can walk," Bounce muttered, drugged.

They didn't hear.

"Not gonna happen," Snow said, heaving at their front stairs.

"We could sit in the backyard," Aviary offered.

Snow nodded.

"It's a beautiful day," Aviary said. "Do I have to go back to school?"

Snow was around the house, up the driveway, rolling his Bounce toward the backyard.

"Come on," Snow said, backward, without looking.

Bounce's eyes, now open, were glassy and wide, looking straight through his niece. He was on his back; the wheelchair, discarded, in the roses.

Snow fell from her knees, onto her stomach.

"Now what?" Snow asked the grass.

Aviary waved her hands inches away from Bounce's face. Nothing.

"Does he need more?" Aviary asked.

"Why not?" Snow said.

Aviary rummaged through the purse, removed the bottle, tipped two pills into her palm, careful.

She slipped one pill into her pocket; she pushed the other pill between her uncle's lips.

"Water," Snow said. "Remember?"

"Right," Aviary said.

Inside, Aviary inspected the white pill between her index finger and thumb. She held it up to the light, at the window over the sink. The turned-on faucet overflowed a tall glass in the sink's cluttered basin. Dishes from breakfast were stuck together with syrup. This is drugs, Aviary thought. She had smelled burnt weed on her uncle's clothes. She recognized it from the cool girls that skipped gym and wore ripped T-shirts with famous and handsome faces printed on the front and back. She wasn't a baby; she had seen all types of drugs on TV; she knew not to touch needles in the park; she knew some people acted strange because drugs turned their vulnerable minds into amusement parks. She wasn't a baby. Still, this was different. This was drugs. She popped the pill, drank the over-flowing glass, refilled the glass, headed back outside.

Meanwhile, Snow chewed two pills, sitting on her ass, touching her brother's encased feet.

"Damn," Snow said. "What did they do to you?"

"Water!" Aviary announced from the porch.

Snow looked up at her daughter, admired their resemblance as Aviary jumped down the steps. She needed to admire her more often. She's tough, Snow thought, tougher than all 'em.

Those birds again, Bounce thought, stared in the only direction he could: ahead, straight. This time, the birds weren't there. Somewhere, yes, there were birds, flying, dive-bombing, hopping, whistling, and shitting. Here, however, no birds, big or small or medium. Bounce's mind still wasn't right. He was, however, coming back at a slow pace. First, he realized heat—coming down, boiling up. He tried to wipe at his brow and cheeks. He realized the slings, trapping his body against itself. He tried to stand and run. Why did he have to stand? Why was he sitting? Why was he rolling? What grass was this?

In a moment, hands were on him, pushing calm into muscle.

"Chill," Snow said.

"More pills?" Aviary asked.

"No," Bounce said. "I'm here. Where am I?"

Snow unwrapped his arms, Aviary released his Velcro, and they massaged Bounce's limbs. They giggled through big dumb grins. Snow rubbed Bounce's head, ran her finger along his overgrown hairline. Aviary fell backward in the grass, extending her arms and legs like an angel, out of place, fallen. Bounce absorbed their love, until their love was too much.

"Thank you," Bounce said. "What's going on?"

"Nothing." Snow blushed. She took a spot next to her daughter, took her hand.

"Everything," Aviary said, continued to move her limbs in bizarre ways.

Bounce looked down on his family, twisted at his hips, rolled his neck, touched his toes, raised his knees to his stomach—cracked his busted body. He squeezed between his niece and sister. Niece and sister squeezed into uncle and brother.

"Can we just lay here?" Bounce asked.

"Anything you want," Snow said.

"What a day," Aviary said.

"I felt like I was flying," Bounce said.

"Me too," Snow said.

"Yup," Aviary said.

"What?" Snow asked Aviary.

"Flying," Aviary said. "Nothing."

"Did I fuck your lives up?" Bounce asked. "I'm sorry if I did."

"Shush," Snow said, put finger on his lips.

Bounce shushed.

Like that, a little fucked up and confused, the family listened to a spinning globe. There, over the fence, in a horrible neighbor's yard, dogs attacked something that squeaked, growled at each other, misunderstood fun's definition. There, behind the garage and another fence, a lawn mower sliced at the earth, sent a wonderful smell into the currents. There, there, there, and there: life going on.

Here, Bounce held his sister and niece close. When was the last time he'd offered this much love? When was it reciprocated like this? He considered a woman in Cleveland. No, he remembered, in the morning she stole five dollars from my pants.

There had been a man somewhere in Michigan, when Bounce was drifting and wandering around the Ohio border. This man saw Bounce prone on a park bench, feet dangling off. This man offered Bounce a chili dog and a tiny cigar. This man, that man, Bounce thought, was how people should act. Still, that was months ago.

Snow moaned a sweet sound into Bounce's ribs. Aviary twitched in her sleep, swung her leg over Bounce's thigh.

A bee woke Bounce up. Snow and Aviary were gone, human-sized imprints left in the grass. He swatted the bee, remembered he was somewhat allergic, got up and tried to run inside. His battered legs made him jog, and then stroll up the steps.

Aviary and Snow were on the living room couch, sipping from steaming cups, eyes half closed, watching Bounce on the local news. "Man Walks Into Traffic." They didn't hear Bounce come in. Bounce leaned against an opened door.

Snow, jolting, turned around in her seat, saw Bounce standing, rubbing his arms.

He wasn't sure how his face looked. Whatever expression he wore was enough to terrify Snow. Jolting, again, she jumped to her feet.

"You're up," Snow said, tilting some coffee on the couch.

Aviary turned around also. She smiled at her uncle, in a way only nieces can. Bounce deflated.

"We got up quiet," Aviary said. "So you could rest."

A knock at the door.

"Upstairs," Snow said to Bounce and Aviary.

Somewhere beyond his door, below his feet, a lone sad voice greeted his sister.

This was Dustin.

And, now, Dustin was sorry. He felt sorry for Bounce. His old family. He had to pop over and see for himself.

Dustin had gone to Cornell. Somewhere between eighteen and nineteen, Dustin decided to marry Snow, that beautiful woman in his physics class. Somewhere between twenty and thirty-one, Dustin decided to explore the world and leave his wife and daughter behind.

Aviary had called him, told him she was scared. A rare impulse, calling him, usually getting the answering machine or hearing the new children, the happier children, in the background, asking their daddy to put the phone down and come play, put the phone down and tell us a joke, put the phone down and fly us around the backyard.

"I'm sorry," Dustin said. "Avi called me."

"Fine," Snow said.

THE NEW NATURALS 165

"Where is he?" Dustin asked. "Where is she?"

"Oh," Snow said. "Now you care?"

Bounce heard their voices move past the bathroom door, from hallway to kitchen, toward a place to sit. Bounce heard chairs move. Bounce thought about covering his ears and trying to sleep.

"My hero," Snow said. "Superman."

"How is she?" Dustin asked.

"She needs new shoes," Snow said. "For soccer."

"Did you get my check?" Dustin asked.

"Yes," Snow said.

Somewhere, water boiled, whistled, poured.

"This is nice," Dustin said.

This is worse than prison, Bounce thought.

"This isn't nice," Snow said.

"You should go," Snow said.

"Please leave," Snow said.

Somewhere, a glass shattered on a hard surface.

Medium-sized footsteps scurried, picked up speed, ran down the front stairs.

"Dad!" Aviary yelled.

"Avi!" Snow yelled. "Upstairs!"

"Oh," Dustin said. "Please."

"Everybody!" Snow yelled. "Listen!"

Bounce, legs tucked, had his ear against the wood. The drama came to him in vibrations. He considered joining his family, changing the subject, providing a distraction and relief; he decided his place was here: tucked and listening.

"Snow," Dustin said. "I was worried. I'm just checking."

"Now fuck off," Snow said.

"Things never change," Dustin said.

Another glass broke.

"Mr. Superman," Snow said. "My fucking hero."

"Please stop swearing," Dustin said.

"Shut the fuck up," Snow said.

"Not in front of our daughter," Dustin said.

"Where are you?" Snow asked. "What planet are you on?"

"Baby," Dustin said.

"You are a living mound of poison," Snow said.

"Mom," Aviary said. "He's just trying to help."

"Right," Dustin said.

Another glass broke, a bigger glass. Maybe, a small plate.

"Right?" Snow asked.

"Right?" Snow asked again.

"Right?" Snow asked once more.

"Right," Dustin said. "I'm just trying to help."

"He's worried about Bounce," Aviary said.

"Right," Dustin said. "Bounce."

"Right?" Snow asked. "The same Bounce you called a 'threat to society'?"

"Now," Dustin said. "That's not fair. That's out of context."

"Right?" Snow asked. "The same Bounce you called a 'bad influence'?"

"Please," Dustin said. "This is hurtful."

"Bounce," Snow said. "My brother. The person you don't want around my daughter."

"Our daughter," Dustin said.

This time: a series of plates went crashing.

"Mom!" Aviary yelled.

Bounce stood.

"Please!" Dustin yelled. "Control yourself."

Bounce was down the stairs in a moment.

Dustin and Aviary cowered in a corner, hugging. Behind them: a cabinet filled with expensive glassware, the stuff for parties and celebrations, anniversaries, funerals, birthdays. Dustin had Aviary's head clutched in one hand. With his other, he protected his own head. Snow, it seemed, hadn't thrown anything at anyone. The floor took the beating.

Bounce walked over to Snow, stood between her and the frightened others, kept his hands up, nonthreatening, kept his back to Aviary and Dustin.

"Yo," Bounce said to his blazing sister.

Snow collapsed into her brother, wrapped her arms around his waist, dug nails into his spine, pushed her forehead into his stomach. Bounce rubbed her back, absorbed her heaving breaths.

"Why won't he leave?" Snow asked Bounce's body.

"Hey," Dustin said. "Hey. Bounce."

"He just wanted to check," Aviary said. "He just wanted to make sure you're okay."

"I saw the video," Dustin said. "It's everywhere."

"He cares," Aviary said.

"My coworkers," Dustin said. "Played the video."

"Leave," Bounce said. "Please."

"Oh," Dustin said. "Come on."

"Leave," Snow said.

"Why won't he leave?" Snow asked.

"Leave," Bounce said again.

"Now," Dustin said. "Now. Hold on. One second. This is my family."

Bounce let go of his sister, turned around. Dustin was standing with his thin chest puffed up. Aviary ran around Bounce, ran into her mother's arms. Bounce stepped toward Dustin.

"Now," Dustin continued. "This is my house. I paid for this house. This is my family."

Bounce took another step.

"Leave," Bounce said.

"This is what I get?" Dustin asked. "This is what I get for caring? Fine. Fine. This is what I get."

Bounce looked down on Dustin, could smell product in his hair, cologne on his collar. When Bounce first met him, Dustin was a computer programmer with glasses and bad skin. Now, after selling some companies to bigger companies, Dustin was monied and repulsive. Bounce thought he'd always been repulsive, arrogant and insecure, fortunate to have beautiful Snow.

"Are you sure?" Bounce had asked Snow, drunk, minutes before the wedding.

"Bounce," Snow had said. "Please don't embarrass me."

Bounce gave a slurred speech during the reception, danced with an adventurous bridesmaid, lifted her in the air, twirled her around.

THE NEW NATURALS   169

Now, his whole body was a single throbbing bruise, he was all over the internet. He was Crazy Man, captured on video, stepping into traffic, getting tossed in the air. And he survived. He was invincible. People couldn't believe it. Over a million views already.

I'm just broken, Bounce thought. Sometimes, I just break. I don't hurt anybody. I won't hurt anybody. Sometimes, I just need to break.

There, behind him, his sister and niece held each other and cried. He was sick of seeing them cry.

Dustin saw emotions run wild on Bounce's face; Dustin knew that wasn't good.

"Okay," Dustin said. "I'll go. Fine. Glad you're okay. I'll go. Fine. Okay."

Aviary stayed at her mother's side, waved as her father slithered out the door.

"Wow," Aviary said. "I'm going to bed."

Snow nodded, stepped over ceramic rubble, brushed past Bounce, climbed up the stairs. Above Bounce's head, doors closed and locked.

Bounce looked in closets and cabinets for a broom and dustpan, ignored the pain, awkward in his casts.

In the coat closet, near the front door, he pushed aside fat and stale coats, kicked boots out of the way, shifted hats and scarfs and earmuffs. He waddled down the basement stairs, lowered his head, felt along the spider-webbed walls, light switch, light switch, here. Or, there? He tripped over an old rowing machine, broke it, he thought. Here: light switch.

With the light, boxes of stuffed animals, stacked against an old bookcase, tipped over and spilled. A purple bear holding fake hearts; small and smiling dogs, tails trapped in perpetual wags; a yellow bear holding bows and arrows; winding snakes with ancient patterns; a black bear with a white snout sucking on a honey-soaked paw; a teal orca, curved and majestic, smiling, covered in dust, hosting unhatched egg sacks of varying size. Bounce handled the stuffed animals, thought they revealed his niece's mental state during phases he'd missed. The snake phase, he remembered. During phone calls, she would give him honest and pleading instructions. No green snakes, she would say. Those are cliché, she would say. She used to learn words from Dustin. This is a catastrophe, she would say. This is an abomination, she said when Bounce forgot about the green snake rule and brought her a stuffed emerald python with long, exposed fangs. Between ages three and four, Dustin and Snow had imagined their daughter growing into a cancer-curing genius. A beautiful genius like her mother, Dustin would say and kiss Snow on her forehead. Bounce would breeze through for holidays, bloated and red-eyed. Their happiness made his chest hurt.

Bounce would look at his sister and Dustin and his niece and understand life's greater purposes. After seeing them for holidays—those were times when Bounce would change.

One Easter, Bounce came with two gin flasks tucked into his socks. But running around the backyard with Aviary, looking for eggs while Dustin and Snow cheered from the porch—that made Bounce stop drinking for six months. All that happiness, pure, not filtered through inebriation, loud. Bounce went back to his girlfriend, poured all the liquor down their green-molded bathtub while she clasped her hands and praised her lord. She was a low-grade Satanist; she praised downward. Love, Bounce had said, that's a real high. They exchanged cocaine bumps from an old packet and had sex in the living room.

Six months later, costumed for Halloween, Bounce found her overdosed in that same bathtub, needle poking from arm, spit running down cheek. She was dressed as a dinosaur. Bounce was a pirate, with a stuffed parrot falling off his shoulder.

Bounce drank at her hospital bedside.

She was better now. In Asheville, North Carolina, last time Bounce heard, which was years ago. Her new life involved an insurance salesman, a house, dogs, children, mountains, mild winters, and Hindu deities.

Bounce jumped at footsteps down the stairs.

"I needed water," Snow said.

"I was looking for a broom," Bounce said. "And a dustpan."

On purpose, Snow knocked over the stuffed animal tower.

"All this shit," Snow said to the floor. "Why does one child need all this shit?"

"She deserves it," Bounce said.

Snow nodded; Snow crouched, rubbed the fake animals, weighed them, inspected their bald patches.

Bounce turned away, continued looking for a broom and dustpan, pretended to look, shuffled his feet, slow, without purpose.

Snow righted herself, followed Bounce. She saw Bounce's back tremble, put both hands under his armpits.

"Let's go upstairs," Snow said. "We shouldn't breathe this air."

Snow held Bounce's hand up the stairs. From a slim cabinet, across from the trash, Snow pulled a short broom and slender dustpan.

"Oh," Bounce said.

"Go get sleep," Snow said. "I have a feeling today isn't getting better."

"I'm fine now," Bounce said.

"Are you?" Snow asked. "How is that possible? Are you?"

How could brother tell sister about death? How it used to keep him up at night? How he grew to accept it? Some people aren't meant to live long. Sometimes, death is inescapable. Bounce felt it; Bounce knew this world wasn't for him. Death, Bounce thought, sounded like release. What did his life matter? What did he provide? A burden, Bounce thought, I'm a burden other people don't need. He knew the world was better off without his body.

"I'm fine," Bounce said.

"Shit," Snow said. "You need medicine."

"I'm fine," Bounce said.

"Take a pill," Snow said. "Take a nap."

Bounce felt level for the first time that day, weighted. He felt surrounded with care. He couldn't keep up with his emotional pulls. He needed a nap.

"Where are they?" Bounce asked.

"My purse," Snow said. "My room. Go."

A song played in Bounce's head as he walked up the stairs, three by three. It was part of a song, a replaying snippet he couldn't place. Of course, the song was about love and trying and giving up and trying again and dying alone and trying again in some afterlife. It was a long song he couldn't remember in full. The song was too long, full of dull parts. Still, Bounce rode that melody two by two, three by three when he got going.

> There's a dog outside
> says it's hot outside
> looks just like you

It wasn't the type of song Bounce recalled in tight spots. He sang it into his sister's room. Purse, Bounce thought. What the fuck, Bounce thought. Snow didn't like him in her room. Even late at night, when she sat up scrolling through her phone in bed, she didn't want Bounce's head poking in. She'd yell good-night, I love you, sleep tight, see you in the morning, move your ass.

Now, Bounce stood on her carpet, right in the middle, some large child breaking a well-known rule. Now, Bounce stood at her nightstand, handled picture frames. Most contained Aviary, in adorable positions, at various ages. Some contained Snow and Aviary, forcing smiles, looking tough. A few, hidden in the back row, contained Dustin, Aviary, and Snow on vacation; on a green mountain; on a boat in the ocean; on a mountain covered in snow; playing in a creek, red and yellow foliage in the running water. One—just one—frame contained Snow alone, years younger. She held a diploma in one hand, a gown billowed over her shoulders. Her cap was tilted. Her lips puckered, chin tilted up; her freehand fingers twisted into a W. This was the late nineties. Snow couldn't believe they'd killed Tupac. In homage, she'd tattooed the Death Row Records emblem on her left butt cheek. That was the first tattoo Bounce saw and wanted. There weren't any pictures of Bounce. No pictures of mom and dad. Not even faded pictures from long ago, when they were all too young to hate each other, too fresh in their familial bliss, too happy to have a crew. No, not even those pictures. Bounce understood. He put Young Snow down, picked up Snow's purse, found his pills, took three, climbed another set of stairs, moved to a melody he didn't remember or understand.

Shards scraping against tile, dumping into plastic bags, over and over—Bounce heard that as he tried to sleep.

Bounce woke in darkness, in his bed, with a smaller body curled into him, arm against his chest.

"I might run away," Aviary said.

Sure, Aviary had poked around her uncle's room when he wasn't there. She wanted to find something dangerous and gross, something to show off at lunch. Maybe a gun, or something half-alive in a test tube. Maybe she just wanted to learn more about her quiet uncle, see for herself what all the fuss was about.

"What did you say?" Bounce asked.

"Oh," Aviary said. "I'm not serious."

"I get it," Bounce said. "Don't do it."

"I know," Aviary said.

"It gets better," Bounce said without conviction.

"It's not that bad," Aviary said.

"It never is," Bounce said. "Worse is always possible."

"What is wrong with our family?" Aviary asked. "What is wrong with people?"

How was Bounce supposed to answer his niece, with her closed eyes and nervous body, swaying like that next to his own body, also nervous, also swaying? Bounce knew what the problem was; Bounce was the problem. How do you tell a niece the world is better without her uncle? If he did tell her, she wouldn't understand. She wouldn't have the proper context. She wasn't there, didn't see, couldn't hear that faraway noise, those long-ago disasters. Bounce had seen Aviary's mind grow into a miracle; Bounce was there when Baby Aviary had petted a cat for the first time; Bounce had seen Baby Aviary at the zoo, pointing and oohing at the caged animals. At the aquarium, Bounce kept Aviary on his lap while an albino dolphin back-flipped through a hoop. Bounce had cheered with Baby Aviary, clapped through splashing water. Aviary didn't remember those moments when Bounce offered to remember with her. Aviary didn't remember when Bounce, a little stoned, left Baby Aviary in a shopping cart, long enough to start the car, glance into the back seat—no baby. Aviary didn't remember. Bounce remembered. Snow remembered and didn't forgive him after he told her, didn't forgive him still.

"Who knows?" Bounce said.

Aviary grabbed onto Bounce's bicep.

Soon, footsteps up one flight, a second flight, up the hall-way, at the door—stopped.

"Aviary?" Snow asked in a mothering voice. "Are you in there?"

Aviary looked up at her uncle. Bounce looked down on his niece. Bounce nodded. Aviary shook her head, no, no, I'm not here. Yes, Bounce nodded, we're here, we're fine, we're here. Red and blue siren lights played up from the street, up around their heads.

"Hello?" Snow asked in her annoyed mother voice. "Hello? Anybody there?"

Like her daughter, of course Snow had snooped around her brother's room. She had suspicions to clear, premonitions. Heroin, that was one. Bounce had sworn he would never touch hard drugs. You have coke in your nose, Snow said. That was years back, when Bounce was late for brunch. That was in the parking lot, after Snow excused herself and Bounce from the mimosas and exotic eggs. Coke is coke, Bounce had said. Just a little, Bounce had said. Clean it up, Snow had said. Get it together, Snow had said and cried a little.

When Dustin had left, Bounce needed a place to stay; Snow needed another body in the house, for balance. Over lunch, a colleague at the university told Snow about male role models and studies reiterating the importance of nuclear families. The colleague offered to get them for Snow, these journals contain-ing studies and charts. They're at my apartment, the colleague

had said. It's just up the road, the colleague said. I'm fine, Snow
had said. I have a great wine collection, the colleague said.
Snow picked up her microwaved lasagna and left without a
word. The next day, Bounce texted, asked for a place to crash.
Of course, Snow snuck into her brother's room as often as
possible. So far, she hadn't found anything evil or dangerous.
Depression dripped from the ceiling. Snow couldn't stay in
that room for long.

"Come in!" Bounce yelled.

"Oh," Snow said and kicked a sock.

"I'm sorry," Bounce said.

"That's it," Snow said. "'Sorry' is a banned word. No more
'sorry.'"

Snow had banned an eclectic mix of words, books, websites, and phone applications. Bounce had tried to show Aviary
a viral video, a compilation of Brazilian drive-by shootings.
Bounce had tried to teach Aviary basic Vietnamese swear
words. Bounce had said sorry then, when Aviary unleashed
a sequence of unknown hard-sounding gibberish over roast
chicken dinner. And Bounce had meant it, that sorry, and all
the other sorrys.

Snow climbed in bed.

They held each other.

Bounce started to drift. Bounce's wandering mind caught
a picture on the mantelpiece, a large one in a blotched copper
frame. There, faded, Bounce and Snow sat on their parents' laps;
Snow on Dad's, Bounce on Mom's. A wide river ran behind
them, along tree-lined shores. Wisconsin, Bounce thought. He

couldn't place their ages. He couldn't remember Wisconsin, just Wisconsin stories. He remembered Dad liked to tell stories about Wisconsin no one remembered except him. Time sat on Bounce's chest. He would turn twenty-six next month. A coach, back in high school, had called Bounce "spectacular." Bounce thought about confidence, how it goes, where it went. Snow would look him over during an honest morning and ask, Where did my rock star go? Where's my superhero?

A local newspaper called Bounce "one genius in a generation of soccer idiots," which was strange and hard to prove. Still, that was Bounce, then. This was Bounce, now.

Fat and lazy and depressed and busted during senior year after a series of hamstring sprains and twisted ankles kept him sidelined, Bounce let his friend Cruise tattoo him, whatever he wanted, wherever he wanted. At a party, sitting on an antique coffee table, Bounce let Cruise tattoo a zipper around his neck.

At a pool party, sitting on a short roof, he let Cruise tattoo PEACE on Bounce's cheek. After his breakup, at a toga party, laying on a concrete basement floor, Bounce let Cruise tattoo his chest.

A local news station, back in high school, before his body got busted, had aired a five-minute segment on Bounce's speed and grace, his unique, God-given abilities.

After three days in bed, Bounce awoke alone. He removed his neck brace. Looked around the room. Ignored the pain.

He lumbered to his feet, walked over to the closet, pulled out his duffel bag. He studied the clothes piles.

"Okay," Bounce said.

Diligent, he went through the clothes piles, lifted smelly sweatshirts and sweatpants, pulled at their seams, tested their strength. The duffel bag filled, one unwashed item at time. He tried to zip the duffel, couldn't, took out some items, threw them on the floor, tried to zip the duffel again. With each unwashed sweatshirt and unwashed sweatpants, Bounce tried to calculate the sentimental value. There was a gold one from a college rec league with CHAMPIONS on the front; a red one, a gift, from a tourist trap in California with FELON printed in black on the back; blue ones from a gas station, from when Bounce bought all his clothes at gas stations; a green and black one with Nelson Mandela's face ironed on and peeling off. He left them on the floor.

"Okay," Bounce said.

"Okay," Bounce said again.

He scanned the room, double-checked, triple-checked, quadruple.

For a moment, tears welled his eyelids, made his nose run.

"That's it?" Bounce asked.

"That's all?" Bounce asked.

Yes, Bounce knew: That's all.

In the hallway, outside the bathroom he had shared with his niece, he thought about grabbing his toothbrush and toothpaste. He thought about his niece, sleeping nearby, or awake, moving about in the darkness. I'll see her soon, he thought. I'll see her again, he thought, unsure what was true, what was fantasy.

Downstairs, outside Snow's room, he touched the door with his palm, stood for a dramatic minute. He wasn't good at leaving, even with all his practice.

In the kitchen, Bounce put oranges in his pockets, filled his mouth with sink water.

He stood before the mantel, looked over the pictures and almost memories, bare recollections. He picked up a small frame, with Aviary and Snow smiling on a riverbank, fishing poles at their feet, arms around each other. Bounce put it in his duffel, wrapped it in an unsentimental sweatshirt. Okay, Bounce thought.

"Okay," Bounce said.

Bounce slid out the front door, into a full dawn, into a bird swarm.

Bounce slid down the street.

Bounce drifted.

Bounce slid.

That was Bounce.

"Okay," Bounce said.

Okay.

Gibraltar

THROUGH A BUSH, Gibraltar saw headlights rock and throw light all over trees and nesting birds, asleep. He waved; the headlights stopped. He shuffled from the bush, hopped in, nodded good morning, checked his chamber—loaded. This was a normal run: rice, beans, kale, and frozen chicken. On normal runs, he could relax and think about steadier days. He didn't talk on normal runs. He also didn't talk on extreme runs, recon runs, fun runs, or runs with unclear objectives: He hopped in, checked his chamber, went quiet, stayed quiet unless prodded, unless a deer ran across a dirt road, a hawk shot from a low-lying branch. Hey. Yo. Look out—see that?

He left the gun on his lap. He pressed cold hands against weak air ventilators, also cold, a little warm.

Part of the bargain, these adventures. The Benefactor wanted them to hone their survival skills. They had to prepare for a future without technology, or, rather, a future where technology was too powerful, where artificially intelligent monsters patrolled aboveground. Next to the cafeteria, the growing stations for crops were nearly complete. They were adding an obstacle course, which would double as a playroom for the children. Gibraltar wanted chemists to figure out how to make paper last forever underground. The moisture was a problem. He didn't want to be holding a gun.

He wondered where fall had gone. Just yesterday, he thought, I jumped into a pile of leaves. Just yesterday, he thought, I was back in Little Rock. Just yesterday, he thought, I was sixteen. Now, in this front seat, rocking along Massachusetts backways, he was past thirty.

At sixteen, he'd taken his license and driven to Memphis. He drove up to St. Louis, Chicago, Milwaukee, took a long way home, stopped in Kansas City. He'd visited an older cousin in Champaign-Urbana. She gave him tequila and took him to a party, introduced him to the basketball team, a football player, some swimmers, a golfer. Back then, he was an unskilled athlete, fit and uncoordinated, not dedicated. Now, in this front seat, awake and dreaming out a frosted window, his soft stomach touched his loaded gun.

Back then, he drank too much and threw up on his cousin's walls. That same cousin, who years later, would jump off a bridge and leave letters for each family member she loved, hand-written, in envelopes arranged on her bed. Her letter to him was all questions asking if she was a good cousin. It was one of those things you couldn't figure out. How can you get in someone else's head?

At sixteen, that same year, he drove south to Clarksdale, Mississippi, to see his saxophonist aunt. She took him to a bar with peeling murals around pool tables with peeling felt. She played Coltrane and sang Aretha. She gave him a beer, told him to never smoke. A guitarist had offered him cigarettes without filters. In the morning, with a headache, he rode with his aunt to Money, Mississippi. She sipped a beer tucked between her legs. She took him to the Tallahatchie River, pointed at the muddied waters, told him about Emmett Till, and warned him against white folks. Then, back in the car, with a fresh beer, driving up to Oxford, she softened. She guessed white folks weren't all that bad, as a whole, in small quantities. She took him to Faulkner's house, took a picture of him leaned against a big old tree. At night, she took him to another bar. In the morning, she kissed him goodbye and called him every New Year's Day until she moved to Mexico and stopped calling anybody.

Now, in this front seat, almost there, he checked his gun again. Those mysteries he found in other people—his aunt, his cousin—were now mysteries he tried to unearth within himself. Look at me, he said to his sixteen-year-old self, look at all these questions I still have.

How did he do it? How did he end up here? How was it going to end?

Elting and Buchanan

THEY WERE HEADED east, along the Great Lakes and across wheat fields, grass fields. Before Monday, they would hit rest stops in Indiana, Ohio, Pennsylvania, and New York. They would arrive in Massachusetts in time for morning rush hour. From behind the tinted bus windows, from underneath their bundles, they contemplated with awe mountains and hills older than recorded time. They climbed off the bus in a college town. They contemplated with lesser awe the old stone buildings and new glass buildings. Of course, they second-guessed their decision. They were reluctant and unsure people—second-guessing was their natural state. Wouldn't

you overthink all your decisions if all your previous decisions led to uncontrollable disasters and criminal impulses?
Wouldn't you shrink at the sight of a mountain if all you knew
before setting your eyes on said mountain was skyscrapers and
potholed pavement? Wouldn't you miss home if you stretched
your legs hundreds of miles away and felt the weight of distant loved ones pressing on your knees, making them quiver
and creak? Wouldn't you prefer familiar ghosts to unforeseen, yet certain, conflict? Yes, their knees would creak in
Massachusetts.

In a bathroom stall, in a rest stop west of Cleveland, Buchanan
looked past a yellowed toilet seat, into a pool of bright blue
water. He was afraid everyone would hear him. They all looked
when he ran in—the dads and sons and truck drivers and tourists and wanderers, twisting their heads away from urinals and
stalls and hand dryers. Something knotted Buchanan's bowels
around the Indiana–Ohio border. He spent an hour sweating
and holding his lips shut. Then, on the bus, Elting kept a hand
on Buchanan's back, moved it in small circles, paused and patted when the moment seemed right.

Then the bus stopped.

Near the rest stop entrance, Buchanan, in his hurry, tripped
over a man with a cane. Elting, out of breath, stopped, helped
the man off the asphalt, let Buchanan go.

Buchanan, alone in the stall, fought an internal explosion.
His mouth filled and leaked, until, unable to withstand the
pressure, it burst.

He flushed, wiped his mouth with toilet paper, flushed, sat on the yellowed seat. He imagined a crowd outside his stall, huddled, hushed, waiting for him to emerge. They would laugh. Buchanan, in his head, could hear their cackles. He covered his ears and swayed back and forth. They would call him dirty. Buchanan put his head between his knees. Sometimes looking at his feet helped. Now, it didn't. Not at all. Not with gum, toilet paper scraps, dried piss, dirt, and crumbs around his shoes. He tried the graffiti around him, maybe that could fill his head with gentler thoughts.

CALL ME FOR SUITS AND FUCK

JESUS LOVES CRACK

I WAS RAISED IN A SMALL TOWN, I WILL DIE IN GLORY

HELL IS YOU PEOPLE

SORRY MOTHER FATHER SISTER BROTHER MICHAEL JACKSON

PERVERTS DIRTY PERVERTS

CALL JESUS FOR FUCK

Buchanan stood back up, exploded again.

Elting waited at the bathroom's entrance, next to a claw machine filled with frayed stuffed animals. People were starting to stare, hurry past him, look back over their shoulders. The bus was supposed to leave soon. The driver wasn't going to wait again. Not after Indianapolis, when Buchanan hid under a table at Subway and refused to leave until Elting confirmed the Hungarian tourists at Dunkin Donuts weren't speaking an ancient language designed for mind control. They were thirty minutes behind schedule then.

The world outside Chicago didn't make sense to Buchanan. Elting was his guide.

As an effective guide should, Elting walked in the bathroom and screamed: "Buchanan! Buchanan! Buchanan! Buchanan—I'm here!"

Buchanan poked his head out from under the stall.

Tired and rushing men, in unison, paused and watched Elting move toward Buchanan. Elting crouched and moved in a crablike waddle, careful not to touch the floor. Elting impressed the crowd with his speed and awkward grace.

"Is everything okay?" a man in a Cleveland Browns jersey asked.

"Just call the cops," another man said.

The man in a Cleveland Browns jersey interrupted Elting's path; Elting stared at the man's thighs.

"Kick him over," a man brushing his teeth said.

"They're on dope," a man said after zipping up his pants.

"We're not addicts!" Buchanan yelled.

"We are pilgrims," Elting said, stuck in his crablike position.

"Enough!" The man in a Cleveland Browns jersey rested his right hand over his heart; the left, he rested on his hanging stomach.

With the room at attention, the man in a Cleveland Browns jersey questioned the room's humanity.

"Who are we," he asked, "to look down on our fellow humans?"

"Who are we," he asked, "to call the cops on friends?"

"Who here," he asked, "hasn't taken two hits of acid when the occasion, the setting, called for one?"

"Who among us," he asked, "hasn't heeded friendship's call when a companion has fallen ill?"

The gathered men grew bored and resumed their business—turning faucets, wiping hands, zipping, grunting, moaning, exhaling, releasing, flushing.

"Thank you," Elting said to the man in a Cleveland Browns jersey.

The man put his hands under Elting's armpits and hoisted. They were eye-to-eye, unsure how to conclude their interaction.

"Thank you," Elting said. "You are kind."

The man wiped a tear from his left eye, nodded, mouthed something inaudible, gripped Elting's shoulders, and mouthed something else.

"What?" Elting asked.

And the man was out the door. Behind him, lingering: a mysterious and kind aura.

"Please," Buchanan said to Elting.

Elting snapped back to his mission. He slid on a puddle, crashed into Buchanan's stall, slammed and locked the door behind him, and embraced Buchanan.

"Tell me," Elting asked. "What's wrong now?"

"My head," Buchanan said. "My stomach. The air."

"The air?" Elting asked. "This is a bathroom; the air is poison."

"Everywhere," Buchanan said. "The air everywhere makes me sick."

He emptied what was left of his empty stomach: opaque strings of inner fluids.

Elting knelt, rubbed one hand across Buchanan's back, placed the other hand on Buchanan's forehead.

"We're almost there," Elting whispered. "Stay with me."

"We're not even halfway," Buchanan said from inside the bowl.

"Soon," Elting said. "Time and distance won't matter."

"That doesn't mean anything!" Buchanan yelled and echoed.

Elting felt a crossroads approaching. At a crossroads, Buchanan was useless. Decisions rendered Buchanan useless. Elting was surprised they made it this far. If this was happening in Cleveland, what would happen in Erie, Buffalo, Albany? What would happen when they arrived?

No: he would not let Buchanan ruin this opportunity. They had a chance at rebirth, a chance they never thought was possible. If they stuck it through—they could transform into anyone, anything. Elting put both his hands on Buchanan's shoulders, massaged, soothed, pressured.

"Soon," Elting said. "Better is going to come."

"How soon?" Buchanan asked. His head was still hovering in the bowl.

"As soon as we leave here," Elting said. "Our destination will move closer."

"Can't we just go home?" Buchanan asked.

"Home?" Elting asked. "What home? Our blankets? Our concrete?"

"Chicago," Buchanan said. "The lake. That home. The bridges and expressways."

"Imagine." Elting placed his chin between Buchanan's shoulder blades. "A bed. A roof."

"A closet," Buchanan added.

"A closet." Elting nodded.

"What else?" Buchanan asked. He relaxed under Elting's body.

"Every night," Elting said. "We'll eat fruit cups without melon."

"I don't mind the melon," Buchanan said. "The texture isn't bad."

"Imagine," Elting said. "If your entire cup was filled with berries and peach slices."

Buchanan slipped out from under Elting, rested his back against the wall, rested his arm on the toilet seat, and sat in, at best, a puddle of leaked toilet water. Elting sat on the toilet seat, looked down at Buchanan, put a hand under Buchanan's chin, raised Buchanan's head toward his, connected their eyes, and wiped away newborn tears from Buchanan's unwashed cheeks.

"We will make it," Elting said.

"When we get there," Buchanan asked, "what happens if it's the same?"

"Nothing is ever the same," Elting said.

"What if," Buchanan asked. "We have to live under another expressway?"

"Where we're going," Elting said. "There aren't expressways."

"What if they don't take us?" Buchanan asked. "After all this? After all this journey? What if they take one look at us and . . . what if they don't like our style? After all this? What will we do?"

Buchanan tucked his knees into his neck. His fingernails scraped at his forehead; he left white lines, of varying length and width, in his dry skin. Elting grabbed Buchanan's wrists, kissed his fingernails.

"We're the type of person they want," Elting said. "Can you believe that? Us."

"What if they're wrong?" Buchanan asked. "What if this is another Jonestown? They make documentaries about this stuff. Utopias and false hope. What if there is nothing better out there? What if this world is all we have?"

"We'll still have each other," Elting said. "We still have our coats."

They both remembered a colder time, before they met. In silence, they both thanked mysterious higher powers for placing them in loving hands. It's enough, Buchanan thought, to have someone care for you. It's enough, Elting thought, to care for someone. They both stood, took exaggerated steps to unstick their feet.

They didn't hear a person enter the stall next to theirs. They didn't hear the person moan and grunt. They didn't hear the water splash through their thin walls. They didn't hear the person apologize for the smell. They didn't hear the person whimper. They didn't hear the person offer thanks—thank you for reminding me to love my wife. They didn't hear the person flush to muffle deep sobs.

They left the stall and the bathroom without washing their hands. They left the sound of repeated flushes and profound emotional revelations.

They reached the parking lot arm in arm.

They looked for the bus.

They didn't find it.

They looked for the bus.

They didn't find it.

They looked for the bus.

They didn't find it.

They looked for the bus.

They collapsed in a handicap spot.

"What now?" Buchanan asked. "What now? What now? What now?"

Above them, Ohio's sky appeared larger than before, endless, expanding still. Were those dark clouds, sluggish with rain, coming up the interstate? Yes, they were. Of course, yes, they were. And thunder: somewhere close and unseen. All those people walking past, staring, shaking their heads, unlocking their warm cars, starting their engines, heading home, heading someplace better, starting new lives, revisiting old ones, running away—did they even care? No, they didn't. Of course, no, they didn't. Again, Elting and Buchanan were alone, surrounded by dozens of strangers, outflanked, still without a home.

The Benefactor

CONVERSATIONS WITH HER accountant, the money people, the authorities, her contacts at the IRS, congressional puppets in her sock drawer. Four years. Where was the return on investment?

This was serious business. What are you doing? Where is this money going? Billions of dollars coming into Polonaise and going . . . where?

The Benefactor told them not to worry. These were insignificant sums. Money she didn't notice.

She formed more LLCs to spread the money around.

She was more concerned with the board. They were starting to express doubts. Fewer people were coming. People were
getting sick—strokes, heart attacks, bad falls—needing real
medical attention. Real hospitals. They had to let people leave
and come back. People were starting to complain about the
limited classes. They wanted college-level courses. They didn't
have enough faculty yet. They didn't have an expert on Irish
Modernism. And the movie selection, the wine. People were
starting to feel stir-crazy. They started to crave regular fresh
air, light, a light breeze from a window, hikes along the ocean,
salty sea air. Rio and Gibraltar, during the weekly conference
calls, had started to sound less energized, more drained.

These were the Benefactor's real concerns. Not money.

Disbelief, aghast. One accountant dropped dead, a heart
attack. Are you kidding me? Hundreds of millions. Maybe
over a billion.

How can you explain that? they asked her. Gone.
Disappeared. How can you explain that?

The Benefactor would listen to the whining, go back to her
current paradise, Buenos Aires, for example. From her balcony, she yelled for her advisor.

After ten minutes, her advisor appeared, out of breath, still
chewing her dinner, possibly the freshest, best steak on earth.

"What should I do?" the Benefactor asked.

"Someone will find out," her advisor said, gulped.

"It's money," the Benefactor said. "From my company. It's
just money."

"We're publicly traded," her advisor said, gulped again. "We're accountable."

"So we'll go private," the Benefactor said. "Who cares?"

Her advisor stumbled backward.

"Four-oh-one Ks," her advisor said. "Jobs. Retirement accounts invested in us."

"So what?" the Benefactor asked.

"News," her advisor said. "Attention. Questions."

"This is my project," the Benefactor said. "These are my people."

"If I may," her advisor said.

"You may," the Benefactor said.

"What's the point?" her advisor asked.

"I don't understand the question," the Benefactor said.

"Why not run for senate?" her advisor asked. "Governor? President? Why *this*?"

The Benefactor could've explained. Show me a society, on earth, as it is, that works, that is worth the effort to sustain. Show me an operational capital. Show me a system that can't be overrun with enough money and power and lame cunning. Show me a structure held together with more than duct tape. Show me promise in the world. Show me a reason not to run away. This was a new society, an equal society, sustainable, with her money, her resources, her diversified wealth and power. Sure. It wasn't there yet. They needed more time. More money. They needed to trust the vision. Still, this was the future. When the earth is uninhabitable, this society will live on. And they're building it right now. They're creating the future. This woman and her husband were Adam and Eve. And, yes, the Benefactor was God. She was distributing knowledge, creating a self-sustaining ecosystem. The Benefactor could've explained the roots of her distrust. She could've turned to her advisor—her loyal advisor, her trembling advisor, her unfortunate shadow—her hands on her advisor's shoulders, broad for her size, her face in her advisor's face; she could've explained her reasons, her fears, nights in North Carolina with that beautiful friend, walking the closed-down trails, smoking their cigarettes, drinking their stolen beer, imagining a bigger and better world, imagining themselves rich, imagining themselves friends until death at an old age. She could've explained how the friend, that dear old friend, didn't make it to college, explained how people are masters at hiding pain, explained the shock at that phone call. A friend found hanging on a beautiful North Carolina trail. She could've explained it all.

She could've. She didn't, however, want to talk in her current worked-up state. You can't call yourself a God and expect people to listen. Another day. She would explain another day.

"What did you have for dinner?" the Benefactor asked.

"Steak," her advisor said.

"Bored of steak," the Benefactor said. "Let's go to Patagonia."

PART FOUR

Sojourner and Bounce

A BLUE-HAIRED BARISTA with six face piercings called Sojourner's name, held out her latte, called her name again, placed her latte on the counter, sighed, turned back to the espresso machine. Sojourner liked how lattes sounded. She liked how writing in cafes and drinking lattes sounded, on the phone, when she told people how she was holding up. She never finished her lattes. She wrote short essays about utopias and Eutopias, both practical and impractical societies; thought experiments where society started over from scratch with new structures, like replacing representative government with true one-person, one-vote lawmaking where everyone voted on everything; radical changes to existing programs, like free higher education and a defunded military. She wanted to start a blog, get her essays published in online magazines. She'd heard a young person talking about a blog and personal essays one day in a sandwich shop. She thought she could start one. The barista called her name again. Somewhere behind her, a couple argued about which pastries to buy. She'd forgotten her headphones at home. As she tried to visualize her headphones, she craved a smoke. Smoking was another new thing. She liked how "cigarette and lattes" sounded when she looked in the mirror each morning and spoke to her reflection. She slid her computer back in her bag, slipped on her coat, left without her latte, without writing a word.

Next door, in the dive bar, Sojourner ordered a light beer and whiskey shot—another change, another pleasant-sounding thing in the mirror. Halfway done, calmed, Sojourner heard the door open.

Bounce stepped in with a duffel bag hanging at his side. He took an empty stool three spots away from Sojourner.

"Back again," the bartender said to Bounce.

"Back again," Bounce repeated.

"No luck," the bartender said.

"Tomorrow," Bounce said.

"Maybe this isn't the place," the bartender said.

"I got health," Bounce said.

The bartender nodded, pulled Bounce a beer from a cooler.

"Tab?" the bartender said.

Bounce nodded; the bartender nodded; Sojourner, watching the whole thing, nodded and wanted to salute health with her bottle.

"Might take some classes," Bounce said.

"Like dance?" the bartender asked. "Me too, maybe."

"Like history," Bounce said. "GED. Anything."

Bounce's phone rang, like it did a few times an hour. Snow, again. This time, he picked up, cupped his hand over his mouth.

"Yes," Bounce said. "I'm alive. No. No. Yes. Love you."

"Health," Sojourner said, lifted her beer at Bounce.

Bounce lifted his back.

Three beers in, Bounce moved next to Sojourner and asked how a person like her ended up in this bar, on this day, at this moment in a small Massachusetts hill town.

"This isn't a movie," Sojourner said. "We don't wake up next to each other."

"Just a question," Bounce said.

"What's with your face?" Sojourner said. "Your neck?"

"In my head," Bounce said, "there's a fuse turned upside down, misfiring."

"Health," Sojourner said, laughed, knocked her beer over.

Bounce joined Sojourner, laughed at the spilled beer foaming on the bar top. They laughed while the bartender attacked the spillage with small napkins. They were still laughing when the bartender took the empty bottle, replaced it with a full one.

"How's that so funny?" The bartender asked. "How does that make you piss your pants?"

Sojourner laughed at the picture in her head: two strangers pissing themselves in joy, in the late morning.

When Bounce could breathe again, he ordered another beer.

"That's a long tab," the bartender said.

"Just wait," Bounce said. "Tomorrow."

The bartender crossed his arms like a bartender in a sepia-toned Western film about bordellos and renegades, gold in streams, outgunned sheriffs, and stolen bank vaults.

"What about tomorrow?" the bartender said. "What happens then?"

"Same thing as today," Bounce said. "Except more lucrative."

"Maybe this isn't the place for you," the bartender said.

"Let me," Sojourner said. "On me. Today."

The bartender obliged, went out back to smoke a pipe and stare at the sky.

Sojourner and Bounce took their drinks and moved to a booth. Sojourner leaned against the wall and put her legs up. She looked sideways at Bounce.

"You look familiar," Sojourner said.

"I might," Bounce said.

"Where?" Sojourner said, squinted. "I know you."

"I went viral," Bounce said, shrugged, stared down his bottle.

Sojourner leaned back in her chair, almost fell over.

"The Indestructible Man," Sojourner said. "You got hit by that car. You're not so big."

"You're from around here?" Bounce said.

"I lived in Foxtonhollow for a bit," Sojourner said.

"Why are you here?" Bounce asked.

"Same as you," Sojourner said.

She started to explain, stopped, chugged her beer, wiped her mouth, burped, laughed a bit, sipped.

"I might leave," Bounce said.

"Already?" Sojourner asked.

"I'm Sojourner," Sojourner said.

They clanked beers, went out back, split an unfiltered cigarette, looked at mountains across the street, marveled at the deep-purple leaves mixed in with orange, red, yellow. They wondered where else on earth could you see colors like those mixed up in nature. They assumed autumn in Japan was also beautiful, worth a marvel.

"Where next?" Sojourner asked, stepped on the cigarette, offered Bounce another one.

"I'd say my place," Bounce said.

"Except you don't have a place," Sojourner said.

"Except I'm between places," Bounce said.

"And this isn't that thing," Sojourner said.

"What thing?" Bounce asked.

"A bar thing," Sojourner said. "A bed thing."

Bounce thought about a bed and got lost.

"I need a shower," Bounce said.

"You do," Sojourner said.

"Food too," Bounce said.

"There's food at my place," Sojourner said.

"A couch," Bounce said. "I could eat a couch alive."

They wound up a hill in Sojourner's crowded car. Boxes sat unpacked in the backseat. Before Bounce took the front seat, Sojourner had to remove a clothes pile, toss it over her shoulder onto the boxes. The car had a lived-in smell.

They approached French King Bridge, met some surprising traffic, a few cars moving slow, waiting for an oversized truck to maneuver across the bridge without tipping over. Bounce looked out his window, saw an abandoned restaurant on a hill, looking down on them, sad, barely peeking out from trees. Sojourner swore at the truck, now halfway across. Bounce couldn't look away from the restaurant. He wondered what they had cooked in there. What smells lingered? It was a place no one noticed. A place where no one would notice him.

What if they pulled over and went inside? Could he cook Sojourner dinner in the kitchen? Would she love it? Would they come back for every anniversary?

Sojourner sped up, swore at the truck, now across the bridge.

Bounce twisted his neck around, said, to himself, a sad goodbye.

They pulled off a small road into a small parking lot next to a medium-sized apartment complex with peeling white paint.

Sojourner's place looked and smelled like her car. Most

of the floor was unpacked boxes and clothes piles. Sojourner pulled a pot from somewhere, filled it at the sink, put the pot on a crusted burner, pulled dry pasta from somewhere, placed it next to the pot. She pulled two beers from the fridge, tossed one at Bounce, motioned for him to follow her down a hallway, past an opened bedroom door, past an opened bathroom, out a back screen door.

Her apartment building backed into untamed forest and another small parking lot. A Toyota Camry sat on cement blocks. Sojourner motioned at two plastic chairs.

"I'm getting into nature," Sojourner said after a moment.

"I tried it," Bounce said. "Somewhere in Ohio."

"Aren't you empty?" Sojourner asked after another moment.

"I'm something," Bounce said. "I can't place it."

"Sometimes," Sojourner said, "if I stare long enough at nothing, I see things."

"Clouds get me," Bounce said, looked up. "I'll see stuff up there."

"Things that aren't here," Sojourner said. "My mind makes stuff up."

"All the time," Bounce said.

More moments passed in near silence. Cars passed and birds moved from tree to tree, hopped along the parking lot, picked at sticks. Bounce and Sojourner both wondered what was real and what was their minds jumping around. Bounce checked to see if the Toyota Camry was still there. It was.

Sojourner felt new weight in her gut. She was heavy in her

chair. This was real. Her heaviness, the comfort, that wasn't in her head. She looked at Bounce, checked to see where he was looking. He was looking at the car with an expression Sojourner recognized. She wanted to hold him. She wanted to tell him everything could turn out alright.

"I have a question," Sojourner said.

Bounce nodded, kept his eyes on the car, the cinder blocks, a small bird hopping under the axle.

"Yes," Bounce said.

"Did you come here to die?" Sojourner asked.

Bounce felt his bottle slip a little, almost drop.

"Here?" Bounce asked. "Die here?"

"Up here," Sojourner said. "In these hills."

"I don't think so," Bounce said.

"Okay," Sojourner said.

"What about it?" Bounce asked.

"When I think about it," Sojourner said. "All the things wrong with me, I think, are related to me wanting to die."

"What does that mean?" Bounce asked.

"This emptiness," Sojourner said. "In my body. I have a hard time explaining it."

"We can talk about something else," Bounce said.

"Out of nowhere," Sojourner said. "I'll feel alone, empty, scared. And I want to die."

"I'm sorry," Bounce said.

"Don't you understand?" Sojourner asked, looked at Bounce's shoes, felt Bounce looking at her. "When I think of the world, when I think of a hundred years from now, the direction we're headed: running out of food, running out of land, the water coming up to our necks, the forests burned away, all the wealthy people living on floating societies or living in space. Lead in the water. Our lush valleys turned to deserts. Education run by robots. No more English departments, history departments, art history departments, religious studies, language studies—all of it gone. A world devoid of beauty, the appreciation of beauty. The quiet glory in reading a poem in another language, not understanding the words, and still feeling the language wrap around your heart. There will be only work. And stupid work. Despairing work. Work and sleep. Dull sleep. Lifeless sleep. I feel it now, most days, it feels like a hundred years from now is standing on my chest and we're already in the horrible, artless future. And I wonder if there was ever a worthwhile present, if the world was ever filled with beauty, the appreciation of beauty, the tearful, soul-burning embrace of beauty and joy and glory. Has any society, in human history, found the right way to live? Can you think of any society that functioned well for a sustained period of time? Peaceful societies were overrun by warmongers. The warmongers were eventually defeated. The libraries were burned. The citizens taken as slaves. Disease would come and decimate indiscriminately. And the world would keep turning. Another society would raise from the muck. And to the muck soon return.When you think about it, when you take a second to think about our capacity to change anything, to do anything meaningful with our stupid lives, to make a difference in the world, to figure out what different even looks like, when you think, really really think, about how to make the most out of life—Don't you feel hollow?"

"Right now?" Bounce asked. "Here with you?"

"Yes," Sojourner said.

"With you," Bounce said, "I don't feel like that."

"Me neither," Sojourner said.

"Want to talk about something else?" Bounce asked.

"Okay," Sojourner said.

Bounce looked for a conversation starter, a fresh beginning, tapped his bottle against his knee, hummed a song he didn't know.

"I'm looking for work at a hardware store," Bounce said.

"I'm trying to write more," Sojourner said.

"Get back in touch with my body," Bounce said.

"I want to control my mind," Sojourner said.

"Yeah," Bounce said. "That type of thing."

"A sign," Sojourner said. "If you believe in them."

"Signs?" Bounce said.

"Like you," Sojourner said. "Meeting you in a bar."

"I'm trying to drink less," Bounce said.

"There's good in you," Sojourner said. "I can feel it. I need good."

"Thank you," Bounce said.

"I'm not just saying it," Sojourner said. "To sound nice and romantic."

"Thank you," Bounce said.

"I'm not romantic," Sojourner said. "That's not my thing."

"I didn't think so," Bounce said.

"This is a good place to die," Sojourner said. "Alone, if you want."

"I'm going to take classes," Bounce said. "Learn about history."

"I'm not always like this," Sojourner said.

"Like what?" Bounce said. "How are you acting?"

"I don't sit here," Sojourner said. "Drink and look at the forest, the hills."

"We can go inside," Bounce said.

"We can go inside," Sojourner said, nodded.

"Not like that," Bounce said. "We can talk on the couch."

"Let's go inside," Sojourner said.

Soon, they were standing in the kitchen, talking about their past lives, Bounce's tattoos, Rascal, the times they fell in love, the moments they wanted to give up, the hope, fleeting, derived from great despair, the bright lights that kept them awake through darkness. They forked pasta covered in cold marinara. They stood there for hours, switched to water and tea, wondered aloud why life suddenly felt worth living, why their emptiness was gone, and, together, they felt full.

They fell asleep early. Bounce woke up before sunrise. He opened the front door and woke Sojourner. She kept her eyes closed, told him to stay, put his bag down, sleep on the couch. Bounce listened, laid on the couch, listened to birds outside. A car started out back. He was dreaming; he was sure.

The Benefactor

NOT ANOTHER PARADISE. A rented apartment in New York City. Central Park, dark now. Her advisor, asleep, in one of the six rooms; the fifth, the Benefactor thinks, the one next to the second kitchen.

This was her birthday. She should celebrate. There was a cake made of gold in a refrigerator—which refrigerator? maybe the fourth refrigerator, the one in the pool room, with the tiny bottles.

In the third sitting room, the Benefactor, if she wanted, could push a button on the end table and a well-dressed man would bring her coffee, decaffeinated tea, warm rum and cream, oils and a foot massage, or a simple and silken embrace. If she wanted, the Benefactor could call the president of the Republic of Uzbekistan. She could ask how the people were doing, his people, the people toiling his fields, welding his pipes. She could offer help, offer a discount of some kind, some broad-scale economic stimulus, just because she felt like it, like she did in Guyana, built those schools and grocery stores.

She could do anything. She should get off the couch and fly to Montreal. She should rent an apartment near the Mountain, walk to Leonard Cohen's house, pray, leave an offering, something dramatic, teenage, and silly.

She could do anything, except, according to a letter from the president of the United States, take profits from her company by the billions and funnel them into some secret project and not explain it to the Polonaise board members, shareholders, or regulators.

Anything, except make the New Naturals work. She couldn't make people come. She couldn't build a hospital fast enough. She couldn't build enough greenhouses to provide corn and wheat and soy. She couldn't build a school system, a university. Or, she couldn't do it fast enough.

The Benefactor turned off her lamp. The entire place dark now.

Here's what she wanted to do: stay on the couch until she fell asleep, wake at three in the morning, like she did in college, when she'd come back home to Durham, watching movies with her dad until he fell asleep in his favorite chair and she fell asleep on the couch, until, at three in the morning, her dad would pat her forehead, goodnight, goodnight, come to bed.

She'd let her advisor sleep in. She'd drive herself. To a quarry, a river, a trail and creek, some water and some woods. She'd park the car and walk to the water, like she did in grad school, when she needed some time alone, when she needed to think, work through the jumbled equations, that five-year plan, the ten-year, the domination blueprint bright in her mind. Those thin cigarettes.

She could do anything. It was her birthday.

Anything, except another paradise. She was tired of failed paradises, big ideas, changing the world, hurtling into advanced eras. The world didn't want to change. These global structures didn't want to change. She wanted a long drive from El Paso to New Orleans. She would go smaller. She would create a world just for her. No one else.

She wanted the couch to swallow her. She wanted the Benefactor to disappear.

She'd sell each paradise. She'd divest her portfolio. She'd buy a house in North Carolina. In the summer, she'd drive to the coast and eat crabs straight from the trap.

Enough of this. She'd make the calls tomorrow. The project was over.

It was her birthday.

It was time to sleep.

Gibraltar and Rio

HER FINGERS MOVED along the Connecticut River, swerved with bends and followed tributaries. Rio kept coughing, used her free hand to cover her mouth, kept her watering eyes open. Gibraltar patted her back, turned his head away, hid his worry.

"What does the doctor say?" Gibraltar asked once Rio stopped.

"I have a fever," Rio said.

"We can go to a hospital," Gibraltar said.

"We have a doctor here," Rio said.

"We need a real doctor," Gibraltar said.

"We have a real doctor," Rio said.

"We need machines," Gibraltar said. "A whole staff, nurses, lab work."

"We can ride our boats south," Rio said, dropping her finger at Springfield.

"Then head west," Gibraltar said, nodded.

"At night," Rio added.

"At night," Gibraltar said, nodded.

A saxophone and trumpet riffed through their office wall. A piano and drums tapped along.

"I hate jazz," Rio said.

"You always say that," Gibraltar said.

He rubbed her back, removed his hand from the map, extended it to his wife.

"I don't feel like dancing," Rio said, eyes and finger still focused on a slim tributary.

"It's good for you," Gibraltar said.

He grabbed her hand and pulled her away from the desk. Rio gave one cough and relented. Gibraltar kicked off his slippers; Rio kicked off her pair, coughed again. On the carpet, Gibraltar pulled her into his chest. They obeyed the notes and harmonies, glided toward the couch, spun near the bookcase filled with map collections, theses on social theory, biographies of revolutionaries. Gibraltar led Rio across the rug, kissed and dipped her underneath the portrait of Toussaint Louverture. The saxophone settled into a smooth solo. Gibraltar lifted Rio back up, noticed sweat on Rio's forehead. Rio buried a cough in her shoulder. He pulled her close and cupped her chin. They swayed under their light.

"When do we tell them?" Gibraltar asked.

"Tell them what?" Rio asked.

"About the money," Gibraltar said. "How she's not sending more?"

"Can we talk about this later?" Rio asked.

"We're running out of food," Gibraltar said.

"We're running out of space," Rio said and coughed into Gibraltar's armpit.

"We can take you to a hospital," Gibraltar said.

"I can't leave. This is my home," Rio said.

"I know," Gibraltar said.

"We have a doctor," Rio said. "I'm fine."

"I know," Gibraltar said. "I know. Still . . ."

"Still," Rio said. "Still nothing."

Rio pushed away from Gibraltar, made her way back to the desk while the trumpet went for a walk. She leaned close to the map.

"Someday," Gibraltar said. "You'll have to leave here."

"I know," Rio said.

"Why not tonight?" Gibraltar asked. "We can make it safe."

"Not yet," Rio said.

"What if it's never ready?" Gibraltar asked.

"If you believe that," Rio said, "why are you here?"

Gibraltar sat on the couch, put his head against the wall, turned away from his wife, who was turned away from him. A cymbal crashed. Soft applause. A break.

Gibraltar was looking at the carpet under his bare feet. He stood up, picked up his slippers, put them on while standing, almost fell.

"You know what I'm saying," Gibraltar said.

"What you're saying isn't helpful," Rio said.

"I'm going to dinner," Gibraltar said.

"I don't need anything," Rio said.

In the hallway, Gibraltar heard Rio coughing for a minute. He timed it, held himself together. Next door, the band started up again.

This hallway—the Main Hallway—held classrooms and offices. On Tuesday afternoons, Gibraltar taught basic entrepreneurship to adolescents. On weekends, Rio oversaw study halls and discussion groups. Gibraltar walked past a classroom and heard a retired professor explain the Boer Wars. Through a closed door, further down the hall, students shouted about Reagan's War on Drugs.

At night, sometimes, you could hear parents calming children. The children didn't understand why they'd left the world above for this cave with tiled floors and wood-paneled walls. Why couldn't they call their friends? Why couldn't they eat pizza and watch comedies? Why was everything fruit, beans, rice, chicken, long documentaries, and Spike Lee Joints?

Gibraltar turned away from the cafeteria and theater. He wasn't hungry after all.

In their identical rooms, advisors and commanders each had one queen-sized bed, one dresser, one closet, one reading chair, a bookshelf, and a landline phone in case of emergency. Their wood-paneled walls were painted midnight blue, to mimic a country night sky, a comforting celestial embrace.

Gibraltar threw his shirt on the reading chair. He crawled

into bed and continued to convince himself that everything was worth it.

Curled up in an empty bed with an empty stomach, he replayed pivotal life moments, like he did each afternoon. First, in high school, all that wasted potential. Gone for what? Now, lying in bed, decades later, he couldn't remember more than a few late nights spent drinking cheap beer out of cans and smoking cheap weed from resin-crusted pipes and bongs, fat-rolled blunts with some cheap coke sprinkled among the dry brown leaves. What if he had finished his Political Science homework? What if he had hit the weight room between basketball practices, worked on his jump shot, worked on his handles, watched tape? He didn't think he was NBA material. Still, he could've spent some time in Europe, or Asia. Basketball was big in Brazil. On most continents, there were teams hungry for mediocre talent. If he had finished his Political Science homework, he could've gotten into politics, run for alderman or mayor. On his back, staring at a rock ceiling, Gibraltar imagined himself as a man of the people. He saw himself leading a joyful parade. He saw himself howling on city hall's steps, part of reality, not underground building a fantasy.

He heard knocking on his door. Real knocking. Now.

He told the knocking to wait; it didn't. He slid from bed, didn't pick up his shirt.

"I'm sleeping," Gibraltar said.

"It's Amadou," a voice said.

"It's Trayvon," a voice said.

Gibraltar turned the knob and the two men entered and pushed him back, whoa, whoa whoa. Amadou had once played defensive end at Northern Iowa, for a semester. Trayvon, before moving here, had lived in Queens and worked in a Szechuan kitchen, cutting hot peppers and mixing them into thick sauces. Amadou was once called Justin; Trayvon, Anthony. They'd changed their names when they arrived here, wanting something more militant; they were in charge of security and recon. Trayvon was small compared to Amadou, who ducked and squeezed through doorways.

"Apologies," Amadou said.

"We apologize," Trayvon said.

"I just said that," Amadou said, pushed Trayvon in the chest.

"Rio sent us," Trayvon said.

"We need food," Amadou said.

"We have to wait," Gibraltar said.

"We know," Amadou said.

"Rio sent us," Trayvon said.

"You said that," Gibraltar said.

"What time are we leaving?" Amadou said.

"They're showing a movie," Trayvon said.

"*She's Gotta Have It*," Amadou said.

"We were wondering," Trayvon said, looked at his slippers.

"Can we leave after the movie?" Amadou said.

"We were going to take dates," Trayvon said, looked up, smiled at Gibraltar.

"Too much information," Amadou said, pushed Trayvon again.

"We'll leave after three," Gibraltar said.

Amadou and Trayvon saluted, turned away on their heels, shut the door, high-fived in the hallway.

Gibraltar wondered why they saluted all the time. It made Gibraltar seem important, so he didn't say anything. He stood there for minutes before his stomach churned. He either needed to eat or throw up. He stood for minutes more, trying to decide.

Dinner was the same as lunch: two thick white bread slices, an orange, vanilla ice cream, black-eyed peas with pork bits. Lunch was the same as breakfast. Gibraltar took his tray to the commanders' and advisors' table, felt eyes following him, staring at him sop up beans with the bread. This tension had persisted for days. Murmuring, sometimes shouting, averted eyes. Until last week, Gibraltar had eaten every meal with Rio, sitting hip to hip, laughing with their mouths full. Was it last week, month? When did the sickness get so bad? How did he let it get so bad?

Gibraltar dropped his orange, watched it roll across the tiles, watched it stop against a young woman's foot, watched the young woman notice something against her foot, watched the young woman kick the orange away without looking down. His eyes followed the orange between tables and feet and tiles. He felt malnourished.

"Whose orange is this!?" A young man yelled from across the room.

Gibraltar didn't raise his hand. He sunk down, wanted to sneak out.

"Who is wasting food!?" Another young man yelled from a corner.

"It's mine!" Another young man yelled.

"He's lying!" A woman yelled.

"You don't know that!" The lying man yelled.

"I'm your wife!" The woman yelled.

"Come on," the man said, hushed, leaned into his wife's ear.

"Sit down," the woman said.

The lying man sat down.

"Give the orange to a baby!" An older man said with his hands raised.

"Yes!"

"A baby!"

"Give it to a baby!"

The older man kept his arms raised, scanned the room.

"Does anyone have a baby?" The older man asked, put his arms down.

"I do!" The lying man yelled, stood, triumphant.

His wife yanked him down.

Deep in the crowd, hidden by the adult bodies, a baby started crying. The older man sat down, weighed down by epiphany: this is no place for a baby.

Gibraltar snuck out when the crowd went silent.

He found Rio in bed, coughing, sitting up, reading her Napoleonic War maps. Gibraltar handed her a water glass from the carpet.

"I'm feeling better," Rio said without looking up. Her eyes were in Upper Egypt, near the pyramids.

"There's a movie tonight," Gibraltar said.

"There's always a movie," Rio said. "I pick the movies."

"Want to go?" Gibraltar asked Rio.

"Not tonight," Rio said, looked up, softened her bloodshot eyes against Gibraltar's obvious worry.

"People are getting weird," Gibraltar said. "Something is about to crack."

"Food helps," Rio said.

"A purpose helps," Gibraltar said.

"We have a purpose," Rio said.

"A plan," Gibraltar said. "A goal."

"We have a plan," Rio said.

"A plan that works," Gibraltar said. "Money. Support."

"I have a back-up plan," Rio said. "I found a small river and a target."

"Where?" Gibraltar asked.

Rio put the maps in her lap, rubbed her eyes, coughed, ran fingers through her hair.

"The bank," Rio said. "Foxtonhollow Savings and Loan."

"A bank?" Gibraltar asked.

Rio jumped from bed, dragged Gibraltar to the bookcase, pulled a leather-bound volume from a low shelf—*Massachusetts Topography.* She opened to a dog-eared page about rivers and mountains in Western Massachusetts.

"We're thinking too small," Rio said. "We don't need a benefactor. We don't need a board. We're creating something new."

"A bank," Gibraltar said.

Rio nodded. "Perfect," she said.

"Rio," Gibraltar said, took a step away from his wife.

"We need something big," Rio said.

"That's too big," Gibraltar said.

"We need money," Rio said.

"They'll find us," Gibraltar said.

"How?" Rio said, closed the book, threw it on the reading chair.

"It's too big," Gibraltar said.

Rio grabbed her husband by the thighs, coughed into his chest, pressed her forehead into his sternum.

"We need this," Rio said. "We're not Jonestown."

"We're not thieves," Gibraltar said.

"We're something more," Rio said.

"We're a hundred people," Gibraltar said. "In a mountain. Stealing food and sleeping bags."

"They can't find us," Rio said. "That's it."

"That's not it," Gibraltar said.

"We're meeting in the morning," Rio said. "We'll figure out what happens next."

"That's it?" Gibraltar asked.

Rio climbed back into bed, picked up her maps.

"You can sleep next to me," Rio said.

"I know," Gibraltar said.

"I'm not contagious," Rio said.

"I wouldn't care," Gibraltar said.

"You can't sleep?" Rio asked, looked at Napoleon's eastern front, the Pyrenees, the stubborn Iberians. Gibraltar nodded.

"I can't sleep before raids," Gibraltar said.

"I know," Rio said.

Around half past two, after hours of watching Rio cough in her sleep, Gibraltar jumped at a knock on the door.

He pulled his raid outfit from the dresser's bottom drawer. He changed into the black sweatpants, black sweater, black socks, black gloves; he put the black ski mask on his head, rolled up like a normal hat, a nonthreatening hat, a hat for a cold walk.

In the hallway, Amadou and Trayvon were dressed the same, with big high-schooler grins and wide-open eyes. They walked in silence into Classroom Eleven—modern history. Inside the tall picture frames: autographed famous-athlete jerseys and famous-musician posters. There was Prince in Barcelona, Jay-Z in Rio de Janeiro, Miles Davis in San Antonio, and Tracy Chapman in Montreal. Donations from a board member, some record producer who was once a Black Panther.

Trayvon went to the hatch in the middle of the room, opened it, poked his head down—coast clear. Gibraltar and Amadou climbed down the ladder. Trayvon followed and shut them in darkness.

"We need lights down here," Amadou said, bumped into Gibraltar's back.

"Stop saying that," Gibraltar said.

They walked about a hundred yards, until they hit the other ladder, the big ladder. Trayvon climbed first, opened the hatch, poked his head up—coast clear. Amadou and Gibraltar followed.

They crawled out from under the empty buffet table. They looked around, scanned the booths and tables. Amadou went into the emptiness, checked for intruders, yelled when he didn't find anything. Trayvon stood in front of his favorite mural: a panda eating bamboo next to a stream, a smiling red dragon flying about the panda, sprinkling the scene with gold coins. Gibraltar, on his way to the door, stopped at a table, found a pencil.

"She needs to stop coming up here," Gibraltar said aloud without realizing.

Amadou and Gibraltar had their ears pressed against the door.

"Someone's going to see her. You have to talk to her," Amadou told Gibraltar.

"I do talk to her," Gibraltar said. "It's none of your business."

Amadou went to speak again; Trayvon grabbed his shoulder, shook his head no. Once, when Trayvon first arrived, months ago, he saw Gibraltar make someone bleed from the ears.

Amadou cracked the door, peeked his head out—coast clear.

Soon, they were down the hill, across the French King Bridge, into the woods, running low across a field, down a dirt road, hiding in a roadside bush.

"What time did you say?" Gibraltar asked Trayvon.

"Any minute," Trayvon said.

Soon: tires shifting rocks and pebbles. This time: a minivan with a medium-sized trailer attached.

Lori poked her head from the driver's side window.

"Yo," Lori said.

"Yo."

"Yo."

"Yo."

"In," Lori said.

They rocked along unpaved paths, roads, decommissioned train tracks, and hermit trailers tucked away from civilization. Lori cupped a hand over her cigarette's ember, exhaled out her nose. Trayvon, Amadou, and Gibraltar sat in the back row, knees, elbows, and shoulders touching. Daytimes, Lori worked as a substitute teacher at a boarding school two towns over. Nighttimes, she hotwired cars, then drove them into the Connecticut River when she finished her missions. In the darkness, her bald head reflected moonlight back at her passengers. Before she'd moved to Massachusetts, Lori had studied mechanical engineering in Germany. What was she doing in a van in the middle of the night?

"Where?" Gibraltar asked Lori.

"Under you," Lori said without looking back.

Under them were three compact guns with rapid triggers and long bullets, war guns acquired from an armory in New Hampshire. They checked their chambers. Loaded. They flipped their safeties. Their knees, elbows, and shoulders bounced with nervous energy.

"Why can't I calm down?" Amadou asked.

"It's your body," Lori said.

"Remember," Trayvon said. "You've done this before."

"A hundred times," Amadou said.

"Ten times," Gibraltar said.

"Hundred," Amadou repeated, added centimeters to his bounce.

"Same drill," Lori said. "He's waiting."

"Hop out," Gibraltar said.

"I watch the loading dock," Trayvon said.

"I load," Amadou said. "With him."

Harsh light appeared through the thicket. Big-Chain Stores lined up, closed for the night, wide squat buildings made with big bricks and neon façades. When they came above ground and saw things like this, they all felt nostalgic. Trayvon recalled taking his high school girlfriend to get her ears pierced in a mall. They'd eaten in the food court after and Trayvon remembered the slime-covered pasta and cardboard pizza. His girlfriend drank a two-gallon lemonade because, she said, her ear hurt too much to eat. Now, holding a weapon in a minivan, the memory made Trayvon sniffle. Gibraltar had spent his first professorship paycheck on an obnoxious television. Rio said he'd regret it and make them broke doing stupid things like that. He remembered their fight and reconciliation over a large-screen viewing of *Reservoir Dogs*. Amadou wondered if his mother still worked overnight shifts, packaging, labeling, and shipping. He pictured her getting home now, dozing off in their driveway until sunrise, then making herself bacon and toast and eating it in bed, before falling asleep again. Amadou, like most big young men at some point in their teenage years, had wanted to play for the Kansas City Chiefs and buy his mom a luxury spaceship, or whatever. He thought about his mother in orbit over Mars, watching the sun reflect rainbows off frozen oceans.

Lori pushed through the thicket, glided toward a loading dock, looked around, stabilized her shaking hands on the steering wheel.

Lori found purpose in aiding, like the man in a blue security guard outfit smoking on the loading dock. If Lori could have moved into the Mountain, she would have. She'd first heard about the Mountain, the restaurant, and the people living underneath while she sat at a bus stop, pretended to read a book about self-improvement. A disheveled man had whispered to her, asked if Earth, for her, felt like a barren maze with endless dead ends and dimwitted Minotaurs. The disheveled man told her, if she wanted change, to visit a Salvation Army near Greenfield, ask to speak to the manager, tell him she was looking for a new world underneath the old world. Lori told the man to fuck off. The disheveled man told Lori that she was a perfect candidate; he had watched her; she had impressed him; she was impressive and sad. Lori didn't say anything. She took a bus to the Salvation Army, asked for the manager, said she was looking for a new world underneath the old world. Could she leave today and never come back? the manager asked. Lori said yes. After elation coursed down her shoulder blades, Lori said no, I have a brother, a sister, a cat, bills, responsibilities. The manager said they could come, forget your bills, forget your job. Lori said no, you don't understand, my brother, my sister, they're sick, like fiends, dope sick. Oh, the manager said. Lori took a bus to work, apologized for her lateness. She didn't have a sister or brother.

Amadou, Trayvon, and Gibraltar hopped out, circled their heads in every direction, followed their eyes with their guns. They shook the security guard's hand. Amadou took a drag from his cigarette, bowed, saluted. The man and Amadou went inside. Gibraltar gave Lori a signal to back up. Trayvon walked around a corner, kept lookout. The man and Amadou made a few runs with a pallet, unloaded, smoked, laughed. Gibraltar leaned against Lori's fender, faced the forest, let his gun dangle from his hand. When Amadou gave the signal, Gibraltar would call Trayvon, Trayvon would come back, they would hop in, Lori would drive straight, take the same route back to French King, wait for another signal from the restaurant, wait for the mountain garage to open, drive into the new world underneath the old world. Then, she would drive out, dump the car in the Connecticut River, take a pill, walk home, go to work, settle until called again.

Now, sitting there drumming her hands on the steering wheel, Lori thought about her warm bath and warm high.

Then, Trayvon came running into view, waving his hands. Gibraltar jolted, pointed his gun past Trayvon, in the direction from which he'd run.

Trayvon ran to Amadou and then to the man. The man ran inside. Amadou hopped off the loading dock, ran next to Gibraltar, stood and aimed. Trayvon knocked on Lori's window. Lori rolled it down.

"If it turns bad," Trayvon said, "keep going."

Lori imagined what "turning bad" meant. In her mind, she saw army tanks and war helicopters with wide searchlights.

"Got it," Lori said.

A compact SUV with PRIVATE SECURITY stenciled on the side turned the corner, parked.

Lori saw the driver's face, saw his brains firing. First, he was tired, confused. Then, he noticed the guns, the van, the trailer, the Black men pointing the guns at him, these guns made for killing many people quick. Lori saw him fumble with his radio. Before he could speak, Lori saw Amadou put a bullet through his window. Gibraltar and Trayvon followed, kept their fingers on the trigger.

It was quieter than Lori expected, muffled. Gibraltar got in the minivan. Amadou closed the trailer, got in the minivan. Trayvon opened the security car, checked the guard's pulse, listened to the radio, didn't hear anything relevant, ran back to the others.

Back in the woods, driving down a familiar dirt road, they crept in silence. Until Gibraltar punched the seat in front of him.

The signal came from the restaurant, the mountain garage's door opened, a patch of grass on the mountain's far side, away from street view. People came out to unload. Lori left when it was finished, didn't say anything to anyone.

She dumped the car, took a pill, walked home, took another pill, ran a warm bath, took another pill, got dressed, went to work. At lunch, sitting at a bar, she saw breaking news coverage of an overnight robbery, death, bullet casings.

She didn't go back to work. She took another pill and fell asleep in the bar bathroom.

Sojourner and Bounce

SHE SMELLED BURNING before she saw thin white smoke creep under her bedroom door. Her dreams contained wide plains, grazing animals, spaceships, masked villains, and a dead president with a face she didn't recognize. Was he a president at all? Or just a senator? Maybe a corrupt mayor? His voice had a moneyed cadence. She smelled burning when she pushed the ejection button and found herself floating in space, alone and happy.

"Bounce!" Sojourner yelled from her tangled sheets. "Are we going to die!?"

"Not yet!" Bounce yelled from the kitchen.

She loved living with Bounce. She loved driving him to class. Most days, they were bettering themselves, together, growing.

She hated when he cooked.

She tried, without luck, to reenter her dream. She wanted to talk to a therapist about this pulsing emptiness coursing through her gut and into her heart. Why did she hate waking up? She reached into her book bin, pulled out her journal, found a pen underneath her pillow, added "interrupted dreams" to the list of things she hated, right under "Bounce's old socks." Overnight, it seemed, her sheets had gotten itchier. The pile of clothes on her bedroom floor wasn't a pile anymore. It had spread into a flood, covering every inch of stained carpet. The Scottie Pippen poster on her ceiling was starting to peel off. Pippen was jumping for a block. Now, in its current state, Pippen was trying to dive into Sojourner's brain.

She dragged the closest pair of sweatpants over her feet and up her legs.

Bounce froze when she entered the hallway. He was balanced on a chair in the kitchen, trying to remove the alarm batteries before the smoke hit.

"It doesn't work," Sojourner said.

Bounce eased down with an apologetic smile.

"I fucked up toast," Bounce said.

"Anything else?" Sojourner asked.

"Eggs are brownish." Bounce lifted a smoking pan to Sojourner's nose.

"Is the milk still good?" Sojourner asked.

"Tastes like it is," Bounce said. "Doesn't smell like it."

"We can get something on the way," Sojourner said. "Get your backpack."

Bounce was crashing into his next life. This one, he said to the mirror, had better work.

While in the Dunkin Donuts drive-thru, they heard a news anchor on the radio mention a shooting behind a Walmart, a security guard fallen victim to thieves. The news anchor pondered with a guest about this killing's connection with the increasing streak of robberies in the area. The robbery victims, the news anchor said, were big businesses, global chains. The news anchor wondered if last night was an escalation. They offered loving thoughts to the victim's family. The guest wanted to talk about guns in America. The news anchor had to cut to commercial.

"Who cares?" Bounce said to the radio.

"People care about stuff," Sojourner said.

"Stealing from Walmart," Bounce said. "Who cares about Walmart?"

"It's a sign," Sojourner said. "Social decay."

"It's Walmart," Bounce said. "Not society."

"Also," Sojourner said, "someone died."

"A cop," Bounce said.

"A security guard," Sojourner said. "A man driving a car around an empty parking lot."

With her dented bumper, Sojourner, unthinking, nudged the car ahead of them. The young driver got out, checked for damage, called Sojourner a bitch, noticed Bounce in the front seat, and slunk back into his front seat.

"Want me to fuck him up?" Bounce asked Sojourner while looking out his window at leaves caught in a swirling updraft.

"I want you to give me five dollars," Sojourner said.

"I'm sorry," Bounce said.

"Sorry for what?" Sojourner asked.

"Everything," Bounce said.

Sojourner could feel Bounce heading down. She put her hand on his chest and told him to breathe. It was their turn to order.

"Two large black teas," Sojourner said. "Two strawberry donuts."

"I don't know where to go," Bounce said.

"I didn't mean it," Sojourner said. She rubbed his head, patted his tattooed cheek.

"What did you mean?" Bounce, recovered, asked.

"I meant," Sojourner said after paying and counting her change, "I'm sick and stuck just like you."

"You're smart," Sojourner said. "You're capable. The world is waiting for your full potential."

They drove to Bounce's class, parked, kissed, Bounce clapped his hands, jumped out the car, sprinted into the square white building, tripped at the doorway, forgot his tea and donut, forgot to tell Sojourner how much he needed her.

Another student—a new male student, an unknown face, with a shining sweatshirt and bulky sneakers—was in his seat. Already, Bounce felt the lack of his tea and donut. He felt irritation grow from his ass, up his spine, and into his ears.

Years ago, months ago, weeks ago, days ago—Bounce would've pushed his fist down the young driver's head, down into his spine and guts. That was the Old Bounce. This New Bounce managed his emotions, didn't go around collapsing vertebrae. This New Bounce dragged his feet to the front row and plopped into a seat with rickety legs and stewed. Mr. Jason walked in, put his bag on the big metal desk, clapped his hands, wrote the day's tasks on the whiteboard with a fading green marker.

"Today," Mr. Jason said. "World War II, reading, reading, more reading, more reading—"

"Why are we reading so damn much?" the new male student asked.

Mr. Jason tried to explain his pedagogy. No one cared. They pulled out their phones and started scrolling, giggling.

Bounce sunk deeper into his chair and self. He monitored his breathing and closed his eyes. He thought about Sojourner and his donut. That tea, he wondered, was it still steaming in her cup holder?

Nothing good in Sojourner's e-mails, again. She was trying to freelance, to make some money. She had outlined an essay on the ramifications of undiagnosed mental illness in marginalized communities. She had sent it to ten places. Here was rejection ten, from a magazine specializing in women of color and their thoughts.

Sojourner's savings were running low. Bounce had asked for money from his sister, again, and she said, again, this was the last time. The combination of financial insecurity and imposter syndrome was making her limbs tingle and ears ring. What was she going to do?

Someone ordered a smoothie and her personal space was invaded by fruit, yogurt, and hemp milk, combined, shredded, violated, liquefied. Sojourner asked herself a series of questions about anger and misguided hate—why was all this bile in her throat?

"Excuse me," a man said. "Are you staying here long?"

He was standing over her, holding a croissant and laptop.

She kept her eyes on his round stomach; she didn't answer.

"Excuse me?" he asked again.

Then, minutes later, she was packed and driving down Route 2, punching the steering wheel.

She reached French King Bridge, pulled over, parked next to a minivan with fake wooden paneling across its flanks, centered her breathing like she saw in an online video about sudden anxiety. In the video, a smiling young person explained this sensation, like paralysis, that overcomes people in frantic moments. In the comments, someone had written a two-hundred-fifty-word response about modern weakness and cuckolds. In her car, now, near a bridge, dozens of feet above shallow water, Sojourner thought more about that two-hundred-fifty-word response than the video itself, more than the suggested calming techniques—close your eyes, push your belly out while inhaling, tilt your head with your breath from side to side, think about a childhood pet or imaginary friend or real friend or imaginary pet. She couldn't remember the commenter's name, their fake name, profile name; she thought it had something to do with Mission Impossible and pussies. The commenter thought anxiety was a social construct created and sold by soft-hearted liberal welfare merchants. The commenter concluded: anybody with anxiety should kill themselves and make room for competent humans.

Now, there was Sojourner, out of her car, feeling her pockets for cigarettes and a lighter, measuring, in her head, the distance from bridge to river.

Breathe.

She found a bench and didn't sit. She found her cigarettes. She walked around the green-painted bench, counted her steps, clapped her hands when she got to twenty, started over. She kept the cigarette in her mouth, allowed the ash to grow long before it crumbled into her path.

She didn't notice the man, woman, and children posing for pictures next to French King Bridge. They weren't posing anymore. They followed Sojourner as she made her laps. They forgot where they were headed. Someplace with a good burger, the dad thought. Mom and children, worried for Sojourner, wondered what type of help she needed most.

Sojourner snapped back into her surroundings, decided to sit down. The minivan was gone. Nothing took its place. She turned her head back to the bridge, except this time she looked beyond it. Above the bridge and herself, on an overlook, across the river, an old restaurant looked ready to slip into the water. It was slanted to the right, painted cream with a pointed roof. The windows were blacked out. In another century, Sojourner guessed, this had been a church. This was once a holy place, where mysteries were answered by prayer and miracles. How many times had she driven across this bridge, past that restaurant, without looking away from the road? A few times, she recalled now, something strange had caught her eye, Once, for example, a pickup truck overflowing with apples flipped on the bridge, spilled, bruised, and crushed more apples than Sojourner had ever seen in one place; a line of idling cars extended a few miles back. And then, with a coworker driving back from the shelter with the coworker's new puppy, when that old restaurant was hosting a party. They glimpsed a tree filled with red Chinese lanterns, cars in various states of decay and disrepair waiting for the valet on the steep driveway; inside, through the street-facing windows: dancing, yelling, live rock music guided by a crooner Sojourner heard from the passenger seat, a disco ball and strobe lights. Outside, on the lawn, in a cage, was a . . . bear? A big dog? Sojourner couldn't remember. She remembered asking her coworker if she wanted to stop and sneak into the party, wedding, whatever it was. The puppy had started to whine and pee and they kept driving and never spoke of it again. The coworker took a job in Dallas, took the puppy, and stopped returning Sojourner's e-mails.

Now, on her feet again, gripped, Sojourner decided to explore.

During lunch, Bounce stood in the parking lot and looked up, through the shedding trees, at a face-shaped cloud. Whose face was it? Bounce wasn't sure. Maybe a person he'd never met. Blood filled the top of his skull and his neck started to hurt; Bounce looked down.

"Anything good up there?" Mr. Jason asked.

Was he standing there long?

"Just cool shapes," Bounce said.

Mr. Jason held a peanut butter and jelly sandwich in one hand, a peeled orange in the other.

"That one looks like a face," Mr. Jason said.

"I know," Bounce said.

"Looks like Larry Bird," Mr. Jason said.

Bounce wanted some space. Mr. Jason's shoulder was almost touching Bounce's middle ribs. Bounce looked down on Mr. Jason's dandruff and gray roots, then slid a few inches to the left.

"Larry Bird had a longer face," Bounce said.

"You played ball?" Mr. Jason asked.

"A little," Bounce said.

"It's a beautiful game," Mr. Jason said. "More violent than people think."

Bounce slid a few more inches to the left.

"I don't like it anymore," Bounce said.

"Did it hurt you?" Mr. Jason asked.

"No," Bounce said.

"Oh," Mr. Jason said. "You weren't good enough."

"I guess," Bounce said.

"Well," Mr. Jason said. "You're good enough to pass the test."

"I played soccer," Bounce said.

"Well," Mr. Jason said. "I'm going to eat this orange and this sandwich and drink vodka."

Bounce watched as Mr. Jason crossed the parking lot.

Bounce turned his eyes back up, tried to find that face again.

Looking down on the river, halfway across the bridge, Sojourner watched a broken log, headed to Connecticut, bump along half-sunken stones. She spit at the broken log and missed. She slid her fingertips along the concrete ledge as she walked; she jumped over a broken sparkling water bottle, fresh, still bleeding and bubbling and spilling into the gutter.

The old restaurant clung to an unimpressive hilltop. Two paths to the top were available to Sojourner. Half a century ago, a skilled landscaper had carved a staircase into the hill with red bricks and cement. A less-skilled landscaper had paved a driveway leading from Route 2 to the front door. Both the staircase and driveway, now, from Sojourner's perspective, looked made of dust, as did the grass, trees, bushes, sky, and the single railing running up the stairs.

What if a brick in the staircase came loose and she tripped and stumbled onto Route 2 and a semi-truck carrying industrial-sized tires flattened her without stopping? No: that was not how her death looked. No: that wouldn't fly. Sojourner chose the driveway.

Above her head: a red awning with jagged holes, the sky peeking through, clouds moving too fast. Was that a face? She looked back down and searched for signs of life inside the restaurant. Empty tables, an empty front desk, an empty buffet with no one standing in line, and a chandelier hanging over it all. The only light came from underneath a faraway door. Sojourner opened the door, peeked her head in. A bell chimed; she jumped.

"Hello?" Sojourner asked no one.

"We're closed!" a voice yelled back.

"The door was open!" Sojourner yelled back, stepped further inside.

Hushed conversations crept from the kitchen.

Now, Sojourner was under the chandelier, looking up at intricate spider webs, which were also empty.

"We don't have food!" a voice yelled.

"What is this place?" Sojourner yelled back.

"A restaurant!" a voice yelled.

Now, Sojourner stood at the buffet, the dust-caked trays.

Hushed conversations continued.

"Leave!" a voice yelled. "Or we will call the police!"

"The door!" Sojourner yelled. "Was open!"

Now, she was at the kitchen door, watching shadows move against the slim light. She noticed the carpet for the first time: red, thin, and speckled with burn marks.

She swung the door open. A Black woman stood in the light, revealed, for a moment, the tiny room, empty, except for a table covered with sheets of paper.

Sojourner froze.

"Oh," the woman said. "Are you here for me?"

"Did you come to me?" the woman asked.

Sojourner tried to answer. She couldn't talk.

"Sister?" the woman asked.

"The door was open," Sojourner squeaked.

The woman looked over Sojourner, didn't know what to make of this unexpected visitor.

"Don't call the cops," Sojourner said. "The door was open."

"You're not here for me?" the woman asked.

"Why would I be?" Sojourner asked. "Who are you?"

"You're not answering the call?" the woman asked.

"What call?" Sojourner asked.

"The movement," the woman answered. "The New Naturals."

Sojourner, scared, backed up, easy, easy, easy.

The woman moved with her.

"Sister," the woman said. "I'm here for you."

Sojourner ran out the door, down the hill, into her car, without looking back.

Mr. Jason had them take turns reading, out loud, in a circle, one paragraph at a time, an article detailing Japan's attack on Pearl Harbor. Bounce read his paragraph, felt like a third grader, one about the Japanese planes moving across the Pacific before sunrise. Bounce read and drifted off. He imagined himself stuffed into a cockpit, floating, on a mission. What would it take? What would make Bounce do something like *that*? To intentionally explode his body. Would he feel relieved, no longer a weight on his sister, on Sojourner?

Once, when he was driving down Route 2, in a subdued dawn, he'd considered moving against a bend in the road, veering left, through the barrier, into buttressing woods. For a moment, he'd drifted. Alone on the road, he scraped against the barrier. He accelerated. That sound, he could still hear it now: metal rubbing against metal, sparking. He shut his eyes, clenched his jaw, heard a different sound, teeth against teeth, grinding. Sweat made the steering wheel slip. And that was it. Back home, in the driveway, he cried for a minute, wiped his eyes, walked in, faced his mother in a bathrobe, at the kitchen table, poised with cold coffee and questions about where he stayed last night, why didn't he call, who did he think he was, what did he think this was—didn't he know how much she cared? And he cried again, for a minute, wiped his face, apologized, went to his room, and disappeared. His mother woke him up minutes later. What the fuck happened? Who the fuck do you think you are? Are you okay? Are you okay? Are you okay? Are you listening?

"Bounce," Mr. Jason said, now, standing over him. "Bounce."

Bounce looked up, sweating.

"Everything alright?" Mr. Jason asked.

The class looked at him, scared, waiting for an outburst, or who knows what.

Bounce wiped his face, asked if he could use the bathroom. He walked out without waiting for an answer. He left his bag. Outside, he leaned against a tree, spitting up on a pile of dead leaves.

Sojourner lit another cigarette off the stove, kept pacing and tried to tell Bounce what she saw. Bounce sat on the counter.

"Wait," Bounce interrupted. "What was this person doing there?"

"You're missing the point," Sojourner said.

"You're right," Bounce said.

"Will you let me finish?" Sojourner asked, desperate.

"And she attacked you?"

"Not attacked. She came at me."

"How did she come at you?"

"She talked all this nonsense. She called me sister."

"Do you know her?"

"Are you serious? I don't know anyone."

"Did you call the cops?"

"You're not listening. I felt something in her?"

"In her?"

"Not in her. *Around* her. In her aura."

"Aura?"

"Before I went in there, I felt dead, dull, you know? When I left, I felt alive, fast."

"Like you're feeling now?"

"Now, yes: I'm moving, now, and I want to keep moving."

"What does that mean?"

"I mean: let's go back."

"And do what?"

"I wasn't ready before; I'm ready now."

"Ready for what?"

"She saw something in me. She recognized my fear."

"What does that mean?"

"I don't have the words yet."

"And you want to go back."

"And I want *us* to go back."

"For what? Why?"

Sojourner hopped on the counter, squeezed next to Bounce. Her feet floated next to Bounce's knees; her smoke burned his eyes, settled above their heads. Bounce leaned back; Sojourner leaned forward.

"I know you feel it too," Sojourner continued. "Whatever is happening to us right now isn't working. You know that. Don't you feel it?"

"Class is going alright," Bounce lied.

"And then what? Learn something. Then what?"

"Then I'll learn something else."

"Something like what?"

"Business. Build something. Pay you back."

"You're not a business man. You're not an electrician. You're not a lawyer."

"I don't know what I am."

"This woman may know. I don't know."

"You're not making sense."

"We have to find out. Trust me."

"How are you sure?"

"I feel it. When you meet her, you'll know too."

"You ran away. You were afraid."

"That was before; this is now; this is our future."

"Our future?"

"Us. Together. We'll find something together. Maybe."

"And, if we don't? If we don't find anything?"

"We will. Maybe."

Bounce hadn't seen Sojourner's eyes like this: wide, deep, hopeful, and electric. And her smile since she picked him up for class—that was new, too.

"Don't you trust me?"

"Yes."

"We will. We will. I promise: we will. Maybe, we will."

Sojourner punched his shoulder over and over and over and over. Her cigarette fell into her lap. She jumped up, stomped it out, pulled out her pack, went back to the stove, lit up, went back to Bounce, pounded his thighs over and over and over and over.

"Now," Sojourner said. "Let's go now. Right now. Let's go now."

Bounce grabbed his coat, followed Sojourner out, went back for her coat when she stood outside, shivering, looking for her keys.

Before speeding onto Route 2, Sojourner flattened a dead squirrel and exploded a cardinal that had swooped low, chasing something, or running away. Bounce took the cardinal as a sign, asked Sojourner to pull over or slow down. Sojourner didn't hear him over the excitement pulsing in her eardrums. Bounce kept asking, started yelling when Sojourner slammed her brakes feet away from an intersection.

"Please," Bounce said. "Chill."

"Can't you feel it?" Sojourner asked the red light. "I can. I can. I can."

Bounce could feel his heart spasm under his tight chest. He felt a tingling run from toe to shin to thigh to gut.

"I feel something," Bounce said when the light turned green and Sojourner burned onto the highway.

If you're lucky, you can glide at eighty on Route 2 for miles without seeing a cop or another car or anything except trees and hills, roadkill and soaring scavengers. Sojourner and Bounce were lucky. They were alone on the road and now, alone in the parking lot next to French King Bridge. Snow came in through Sojourner's rolled-down window.

"When did this start?" Bounce asked the flakes outside.

"At a time like this," Sojourner asked. "You're thinking about the weather."

She checked the surroundings, glanced in all directions, stepped outside.

"Don't we need a plan?" Bounce called after her.

She shut the door on his question.

Bounce joined her on the bridge, looked up at the restaurant, looked down at the Connecticut River, looked upstream, followed the river until it disappeared around a bend.

"That's it." Sojourner pointed to the restaurant.

"That's it?" Bounce asked. "I've seen it before. That's it?"

Yes, Bounce thought. This is right. This might work.

"Let's go," Sojourner said.

Bounce followed Sojourner across the bridge, up the driveway, through the snow falling harder than before, gaining speed, making them squint. He caught up to her underneath the tattered awning. He took her hand. She didn't look back at him. She kept her eyes on the door, looked for movement.

"Please," Bounce said. "This is crazy."

Snow filtered through the awning's holes. A hard wind came at their sides.

Sojourner freed herself from Bounce, pushed the door open. She looked back at him after taking a step in. He was a tragic giant covered in white specks. She felt glad; she felt like a savior.

"Come on," she beckoned.

Bounce couldn't see the car from where he stood. He couldn't see twenty feet in any direction. They were encased in a thick white gust. We're floating, Bounce thought, we're going someplace else. And Bounce caught Sojourner's smile in the dark entryway. And his heart stopped beating so hard. And the tingling slid from gut to thigh to shin to toe. And he felt alright. He joined Sojourner inside.

"See?" Sojourner asked. "Can't you feel it?"

"I don't think so," Bounce said, still looking at her smile.

"You just don't know it yet," she said.

They snaked through the empty tables, tiptoeing, holding in their breath. Underneath the chandelier, Sojourner held out her arm and stopped Bounce. She turned to him, made sure their eyes were locked. She pointed to the back door. Bounce nodded.

"Why are we sneaking?" Bounce whispered.

"Shush," Sojourner whispered.

"No one's here," Bounce whispered.

"We don't know that," Sojourner whispered.

Bounce wobbled, distracted by invisible eyes all around him. His foot ran into a chair. His hands slammed on a table. His weight brought the table down. His crash echoed.

Sojourner jumped on his body, put a hand over his mouth, dulled his moans.

Together, they braced for discovery. They listened for footsteps, didn't hear any. No suspicious yelling came from an unseen place. No doors opened. No sirens. As before: silence. Moments passed into minutes—still, nothing. Just air struggling in and out of Bounce's nose.

"Shush," Sojourner kept hissing. "Shush it. Shush."

Bounce mumbled into Sojourner's hand. Her knee stuck into his ribs. He begged her to remove it, and the hand from his mouth, and the other knee from his crotch.

Sojourner stood up, didn't help Bounce.

Instead, she paced around the room, tilted her head back and forth.

"Where is everybody?" Sojourner kept asking.

"What were you expecting?" Bounce asked, regaining his footing.

Sojourner walked over to the empty buffet, ran her fingers along the dirty aluminum. Bounce tried to balance the crushed table on broken wooden legs. He gave up and started toward the back door.

"Don't," Sojourner said. "Stop. Don't."

"There's no one here," Bounce said. "Is this the right place?"

Bounce put his ear against the door. Nothing. More quiet. Bounce placed his hand on the doorknob and started to twist. Sojourner slid next to Bounce, stopped his hand.

"This is the right place," Sojourner said. "Of course: this is the right place."

"What are we missing?" Bounce asked. "What are we looking for?"

Sojourner put her ear against the door. Nothing. Deep quiet. She let Bounce turn, enter. She peeked out from between his arm and armpit. She kept a hand on his waist. Bounce flipped the lights.

What they were expecting didn't appear. They now stood in a small illuminated room with a lone table in the center. What were they expecting? Sojourner wasn't sure. She knew this wasn't it. Bounce inspected the room.

"Where are they?" Sojourner asked.

"Are you feeling okay?" Bounce asked.

Sojourner leaned against the wall and slid down.

"Where is she?" Sojourner asked. "Where are they?"

"Are you sure we're in the right place?" Bounce asked.

"I'm not crazy," Sojourner said. "Stop looking at me like I'm crazy."

"Maybe they're in another room?" Bounce asked.

"What are we going to do?" Sojourner asked.

"Go home?" Bounce asked.

Bounce tried to sit on the table, felt the legs creak under his weight, stood, squatted in front of Sojourner.

"Home?" Sojourner asked. "That place. You call that place home?"

"Sure," Bounce said. "Why not?"

"What are we doing?" Sojourner asked.

Bounce examined the room, noticed stains patched across the carpet, walls, and ceiling. He noticed a wet smell. He noticed Sojourner's face slacken in gradual increments. He didn't know what to do with his hands. He sat in front of Sojourner and drummed against the floor.

"We're just on an adventure," Bounce said.

"Shut up," Sojourner said. "Listen."

Bounce lifted his hands off the carpet, took offense.

"What did I do?" Bounce asked.

"Not that," Sojourner said. "Stop talking; do that thing again."

"What thing?" Bounce asked.

"That beat," Sojourner said. "Shut up and drum."

Bounce drummed his right hand down on the carpet.

"Not that one," Sojourner said. "That one."

Bounce drummed his left hand.

"Hear that?" Sojourner asked.

Bounce did hear—a hollow thud against his left hand.

"Move," Sojourner said. "Move. Move. Move."

They both stood; Sojourner pushed Bounce away.

"Look," Sojourner said. "Look. Look. Look."

Sojourner pointed at a conspicuous patch of carpet, a darker shade than the rest, newer. At the edge was a small metal latch, also fresh, without dust.

"Open." Sojourner grabbed Bounce's arm.

"Open. Open. Open. Open."

Bounce bent down and opened the trap door.

Beneath the door, a big ladder descended into the earth. Cold air met their faces. Sojourner gasped at the darkness.

"Now what?" Bounce asked, stepping back, knocking into the wall.

"We go down," Sojourner said.

"What about the car?" Bounce asked. "What about our lives?"

"Down there," Sojourner said. "We'll find what we need."

"How do you know?" Bounce asked.

"Can't you feel it?" Sojourner asked.

"Stop asking that," Bounce said. "Let's think about this."

While Bounce thought, Sojourner started down the stairs.

"Hold up," Bounce said. "Hold on. Hold up. Hold on."

Sojourner disappeared into the narrow maw.

"Hurry your ass up," Sojourner echoed.

Bounce considered his options. He could follow Sojourner underground and see what destiny had in store. Or he could run out of the restaurant, down the hill, across the bridge, straight into the car. He could drive to New York, Quebec, Virginia, Florida, Phoenix, or California. He could even drive to Alaska. He could take a new identity and start over with a fresh history. He could look behind him and laugh at the person he was once. He thought of Sojourner in this new life. Where would she settle?

He went down, almost hit his head, felt cold air welcome his legs, and shut the door.

The New Naturals

THEY HAD EMERGED in the middle of a large room, up from the floor.

"What museum is this?" Bounce asked, frightened and confused, looking at the tall picture frames wrapping around the walls. Across the carpeted floor, waist-high pedestals supported small square display cases.

Inside the display cases: record players, basketballs, footballs, baseballs, soccer balls, microphones without stands, wide-brimmed hats shining with pastel colors.

There were too many objects for Bounce to digest while tiptoeing around the room, looking for an exit. Sojourner had stayed at his side, looking over her shoulder, holding tight.

Two men came rushing in with flashlights and baseball bats. Sojourner, at Bounce's side, dug her nails into his hamstrings.

One man told them to get on the ground. Sojourner planked her body next to Bounce's.

"I'm sorry," Sojourner said. "I'm sorry. Sorry. So so sorry."

She wanted Bounce to forgive this stupid journey. What had she gotten them into? What was this place? How could they get out alive? Who was that coming through the door?

"Look up," the other man said. "Get up."

Sojourner and Bounce got to their knees, witnessed a powerful figure. Gibraltar wore all white linen and slippers. Everyone, they realized, wore slippers. His forceful eyes settled on Bounce and Sojourner, but in a calming way. Sojourner felt herself relax.

"Who are you?" Sojourner asked the man.

"I am Gibraltar," Gibraltar said. "Who are you?"

"Sojourner," Sojourner said. "What is this?"

"I'm Bounce," Bounce said and no one heard.

"Where do you wish you were?" Gibraltar asked.

Sojourner didn't have an answer. Bounce didn't either.

"Is this a club?" Sojourner asked.

"More than that," Gibraltar said.

"Is this some kind of underground civilization?" Bounce asked.

"More than that," Gibraltar said.

"Is this a mutant sewer people situation?" Bounce asked. "Are you radioactive?"

"I'm like you," Gibraltar said. "Are you a mutant-radioactive sewer person?"

"I'm sorry about him," Sojourner said to Gibraltar.

"Don't apologize for me," Bounce said to Sojourner.

"Where do you think you are?" Gibraltar asked. "Where did you think you were going?"

"A woman," Sojourner said. "I saw a woman earlier today at this restaurant."

The guards and Gibraltar shifted their stances, tightened up.

"A woman?" Gibraltar asked. "Who was this woman?"

"I don't know her," Sojourner said.

"She doesn't know her," Bounce said. "We don't know anything."

"You're here," Gibraltar said. "You know something."

"Upstairs," Sojourner said. "At the restaurant."

"We're not cops," Bounce said.

The guards pulled guns from their side holsters, pointed them at Bounce's head.

"Why would you say that?" Gibraltar asked.

"Please no." Bounce buried his head into Sojourner's side, curled into a ball.

"We're just people," Sojourner said. "Who are you?"

"This woman didn't tell you?" Gibraltar asked.

"I'm just lost," Sojourner said. "We're just lost."

"I see that," Gibraltar said.

Gibraltar motioned for the guards to lower their guns.

Gibraltar knelt in front of Sojourner, put a hand on her shoulder.

"You don't know?" Gibraltar asked. "You have no idea?"

"I want to find out," Sojourner said. "We want to find out."

Bounce nodded, remained curled.

"What did this woman look like?" Gibraltar asked.

"Smallish." Sojourner finished, "Big forehead. Cheekbones. Like she doesn't eat. Powerful. I felt power come off her."

"That sounds like Rio," Amadou said.

"Rio," Sojourner repeated. "Rio."

"And you?" Gibraltar turned to Bounce again. "Did you see this woman?"

"No, sir," Bounce said.

Gibraltar stood, went back to the door, paused, turned around.

"Take them to holding," Gibraltar said.

Gibraltar gave Sojourner and Bounce one more look over. Before he left, he whispered something to Trayvon.

Amadou helped Sojourner and Bounce to their feet.

"Are you going to kill us?" Bounce asked.

"We don't like killing people," Trayvon said.

"Only when we have to," Amadou said.

"Like intruders," Trayvon said.

"Yeah," Amadou said. "Like intruders."

"Still," Trayvon said. "We don't like doing it."

Amadou and Trayvon led Sojourner and Bounce into the Main Hallway. Through a cracked classroom door, a piano practiced a lullaby, couldn't get the swell right, the dips, sweet curves.

"Are these classrooms?" Sojourner asked.

"No more talking," Trayvon said.

"Don't look either," Amadou said.

"Just walk," Trayvon said.

"Don't kill us," Bounce said. "We're nothing."

Amadou and Trayvon pushed them down a hallway, stopped responding to their questions and pleas. Along the way, a child ran past them. Then another child. Then another. Then a group of children chasing the other children. Then adults telling all the children to slow down and watch their step, warning them the movie was about to start and they better act right and sit quiet.

Amadou and Trayvon pushed Bounce and Sojourner into a dark, closet-sized room.

"Wait here," Trayvon said.

Amadou closed the door, locked it.

Bounce and Sojourner felt for a wall, found one, leaned against it, slid down, held each other.

"If we die," Sojourner said, "I'm sorry."

Bounce didn't respond. He tapped his head against the wall, held Sojourner tight, thought about all the ways death came to him in dreams. He hadn't seen this one before. He thought, curled up with Sojourner, this wasn't a bad way to go. He hoped it would happen quick. A bullet in the head. A sword in the heart. He hoped they wouldn't feed them to dogs or bears.

"If they let us," Sojourner said, "can we stay here?"

"I don't have my stuff," Bounce said.

"Stuff?" Sojourner said. "What stuff?"

"My shirts," Bounce said. "My sweatpants."

Bounce felt Sojourner's eyes roll in the darkness. He felt her sigh on his arm hair.

"I'm going to sleep," Sojourner said.

"Me too," Bounce said.

Both of them closed their eyes and thought about new lives. Both of them admitted, to themselves, that they needed each other. If they couldn't do it together, they wouldn't do it, whatever "it" was. They decided, in their own minds, that this was the best love they'd felt. Both pretended, in quiet elation, to sleep.

The advisors and commanders had convened in the theater. Gibraltar and Rio sat in tall chairs below the big screen. The others sat in the front rows: Amadou and Trayvon, Security Advisors; Sandra, Education Advisor; Ida, Music Advisor; Oscar, Community Outreach Commander; Laquan, Culinary Advisor/Medical Advisor/Crop Specialist. Not their real names, of course.

"Let's lock them up," Oscar said, hand still raised.

"I saw her," Rio said. "Earlier. Upstairs."

Sandra raised her hand; Rio called on her.

"Can you stop doing that?" Sandra asked.

"Doing what?" Rio said.

"Going upstairs," Sandra said. "It's dangerous. It's stupid."

The whole front row grunted and nodded in agreement, snapped their fingers.

"It's easier for me to think," Rio said.

Rio coughed and hacked. Gibraltar held her upright.

Laquan raised his hand; Rio pointed to him with her free hand, the hand not covering her mouth.

"You need a real doctor," Laquan said.

"You are a real doctor," Rio managed.

"I'm not a real doctor," Laquan said. "I was a medical student."

"You know enough," Rio said.

"No," Laquan said. "I don't."

"Let's circle back," Gibraltar said. "To the intruders."

"They stay," Rio said. "We don't need a vote. They stay."

The front row shifted in their seats and nodded in agreement.

"Next," Gibraltar said.

Amadou stood up, adjusted his shirt, cleared his throat, tapped his stomach.

"We're in some trouble," Amadou said.

"Damn right," Sandra said.

"You think?" Ida asked, flipped her dreads from one shoulder to the other.

"Hell were you thinking?" Oscar said, standing up. Gibraltar motioned for him to sit back down; Oscar sat back down.

"How bad is it?" Laquan asked, leaned forward, looked up at Amadou.

"We don't know," Trayvon said.

"There's no security tape," Amadou said. "That's good."

"How could you let this happen?" Sandra asked Gibraltar.

Gibraltar rubbed Rio's back as she coughed.

"How could this happen?" Ida asked.

"An innocent man," Oscar said. "With a family."

"A brother," Sandra added. "One of us. A brother."

"A family," Oscar said again.

"He saw us," Amadou said.

"He was calling for backup," Trayvon said.

"It was a new thing," Gibraltar said. "These guards are new."

"Our intelligence was bad," Trayvon said.

"We had no choice," Amadou said.

"A brother," Laquan said.

"Killing innocent people," Ida said.

"Is that us?" Oscar asked.

"We need a plan," Gibraltar said.

"We need to chill," Trayvon said. "For a time."

"Did we get enough food?" Amadou asked Laquan.

"We'll never have enough," Laquan said.

"How long?" Gibraltar asked.

"Weeks," Laquan said. "Two weeks."

"Fine," Rio managed. "We're fine."

"We can't take more people," Laquan said.

"We're fine," Rio managed again.

"What are we doing?" Oscar said, stood up again. "Is this what we are? Killing people, turning people away—is this why I signed up? Is this why I left my daughter? I quit my job. I told my boss to fuck himself. I sold my car. I sold my Social Security card. To kill people, to turn people away."

Oscar started crying, pacing up and down the front row, rubbing his eyebrow raw, looking at his feet, the carpet, the ground underneath, the earth's core.

"And me?" Sandra asked. "What about me? I wore suits to work. I had a heated swimming pool. I had a slide. I came down here for more purpose. I am not feeling any purpose."

"A slide?" Laquan said. "I had two dogs. I had a refrigerator covered in smiling pictures. All the friends I had. We would go to happy hour and take pictures. My dogs would wait up for me."

"This?" Ida said. "This is why I left my husband? Running out of food, killing people, turning people away, wearing these clothes, eating this food, watching these movies. For what? My husband was a nice stupid man. He played the stock market and sometimes won. My husband called me Potato Cake. And, I called him Blueberry Muffin. I thought I would find someone deeper here. Someone brimming with meaning and passion. I miss my husband. What was I thinking?"

"We all made sacrifices," Gibraltar said, like he always said in these meetings when everyone started crying and doubting.

"Adjourned," Rio managed.

"Amadou," Gibraltar said. "Trayvon."

"Stay back," Rio managed.

Single file, heads down, wet-cheeked, the others left them alone, slammed the door. Trayvon and Amadou stood in front of Gibraltar and Rio.

"We're not going to chill," Gibraltar said.

"We have an opportunity," Rio said. "We have a window."

"What window?" Amadou asked.

"Window for what?" Trayvon asked, shook a little more, vibrated.

"Something big," Rio said.

"What's big?" Amadou asked.

"Big what?" Trayvon asked.

Rio climbed down her chair, punched herself in the chest, cleared her throat, inhaled, forced a wet cough into the open air.

"The college," Rio started. "We're going to smash; we're going to grab. We're going to hit two targets at the same time. First, the art museum. Second, the library. We're going to get our cause out there. If we're going to survive, we need to expand. If we're going to expand, we need more money. We need to let people know we're out here, somewhere, working for them, fighting, building, sustaining."

Amadou sat back down in the front row. Trayvon bounced from foot to foot, ground his teeth.

"You hear this," Amadou said to Gibraltar.

"She's right," Gibraltar said.

"I know 'she's right,'" Rio said, collapsed up into her tall chair.

"Smash?" Trayvon said. "Grab?"

"What?" Amadou said. "Grab what?"

"They have a Jacob Lawrence," Rio said. "In the museum. A rare painting."

"The library?" Amadou asked.

"Can you believe it?" Rio said. "W. E. B. Du Bois's letters, essays, everything."

"So?" Trayvon said.

"People collect this stuff," Gibraltar said. "Black market stuff."

"What do we know about the black market?" Trayvon asked.

"Don't worry about what we know," Rio said.

"What if it doesn't work?" Amadou asked.

"It'll work," Rio said.

"Haven't you seen a movie?" Amadou asked. "Does it ever work?"

"Sometimes," Rio said.

"You," Trayvon pointed at Gibraltar, who had his chin rested in his palm. "What do you think?"

"We have people inside," Gibraltar said. "We have maps. A timeline. Backup plans."

"And if someone sees us?" Amadou asked.

"Don't let someone see you," Rio said.

Rio kissed Gibraltar on the cheek, gripped his hand momentarily, walked out, her coughing echoing down the silent hallway.

In their small room, huddled on the floor, Bounce and Sojourner tried to sleep.

"What if I didn't know you?" Bounce asked.

"You didn't know me," Sojourner said. "Your whole life, just about."

"It doesn't make sense," Bounce said. "How I feel about you. What I'd do for you."

Sojourner pushed her head into Bounce's chest, ran her fingers along his ribcage.

"Stop talking like that," Sojourner said.

THE NEW NATURALS 263

"If anything happens," Bounce said. "I want you to know."

"Know what?" Sojourner asked.

"How I feel," Bounce said. "What I'd do."

"I know," Sojourner said.

Sojourner had a speech prepared, written out in her head, primed for a moment like this, a moment when feelings needed clarifying, debts expressed, appreciated, accepted and loved. She had romantic and gross confessions for Bounce. She breathed deep from his armpit, readied herself.

A knock at the door. A turning doorknob.

Amadou and Trayvon stood over them.

"Up," Amadou said.

"Both of you," Trayvon said.

"If you're going to kill us," Sojourner said. "Do it here."

"Come on," Amadou said.

"You hungry?" Trayvon asked Sojourner, then Bounce.

"We have some dinner left over," Amadou said.

"It sucks," Trayvon said.

"You'll eat," Amadou said. "You'll live. We'll talk."

Gibraltar took his feet off the table as Sojourner and Bounce walked into the cafeteria. Gibraltar told Trayvon and Amadou to take some peach cobbler and wait outside. At Gibraltar's table, steaming dishes were in line—baked chicken with black pepper and lemon, greens, rice, cobbler. Places were set for Sojourner and Bounce.

Bounce took five pieces of chicken and Sojourner jabbed him in the leg. Sojourner poured herself some lemonade.

"What is this place?" Sojourner asked Gibraltar. "What are you?"

"Is this a cult?" Bounce asked. "Is this a group-suicide thing?"

"Where are you from?" Gibraltar asked.

"Toledo," Bounce said.

"Chicago," Sojourner said.

"Have you seen other places?" Gibraltar asked. "Do you know what the world's like?"

"I went to Cleveland a lot," Bounce said.

"What does it matter?" Sojourner asked.

"Isn't the world horrible?" Gibraltar asked.

"Not that bad," Bounce said. "Sometimes."

"Yes," Sojourner said.

"That's why we're down here," Gibraltar said.

"Can we stay?" Sojourner asked.

"You," Gibraltar said to Sojourner. "My wife wants to speak with you."

"I have to stay with her," Bounce said.

"No," Sojourner told Bounce, patted his shoulder.

"We'll talk," Gibraltar told Bounce. "Eat."

"Where is she?" Sojourner asked.

"Outside," Gibraltar said. "They'll take you there."

Bounce made Sojourner a plate with everything.

Sojourner left empty-handed, quick.

Bounce switched out his empty plate with Sojourner's.

Gibraltar put his feet back on the table.

"If anything happens," Bounce said. "If she's hurt—"

"That not what we do," Gibraltar said.

"What do you do?" Bounce said.

"You came to us," Gibraltar said. "You mean well. We'll protect you."

"Protect us from what?" Bounce asked. "We weren't in danger."

"It's all a threat," Gibraltar said. "Every second up there."

"Sometimes," Bounce said, "things work out fine."

"You're lucky," Gibraltar said. "You're alive. You're lucky."

"I have a sister," Bounce said. "A niece. I want to see them again."

"Someday," Gibraltar said. "When the time comes."

"What does that mean?" Bounce asked.

"We don't know," Gibraltar said. "We'll know when it happens."

"What would we do?" Bounce asked. "Down here. What do you do?"

"We have a mission," Gibraltar said. "I want you to help us."

Rio told Sojourner to sit on her bed, told Amadou and Trayvon to wait outside, or go for a walk. She was standing at the bookcase, figuring where to start.

Sojourner spoke first.

"I saw you," Sojourner said.

"I'm glad you came," Rio said.

"What is this place?" Sojourner asked.

"Don't you have days," Rio started, "when all you want to do is climb into a hole?"

Sojourner nodded, took deep and hurried breaths.

"Don't you wish," Rio started again, "you could move with purpose through the world, know you're working toward something meaningful, long-lasting?"

Sojourner nodded again, looked at the carpet.

"This is that place," Rio said. "The place you always wanted."

"I drift," Sojourner said. "My therapist calls it drifting."

"You wake up," Rio said. "You go to sleep. You can't recall the in between."

"Yes," Sojourner said. "Yes. Yes. It's like that. Boring fog, you know."

"This isn't that," Rio said.

"Can I stay?" Sojourner said.

Rio pulled *The Souls of Black Folk* from the shelf, weighed it in her hands, coughed, held in a cough, jerked her head back, tossed the book at Sojourner, missed.

"Read that," Rio said.

Sojourner picked up the book and turned it over.

"I have," Sojourner said. "Twice."

Rio pulled another book off—*A Sand County Almanac* by Aldo Leopold—threw it at Sojourner, hit her in the gut.

"What about that?" Rio asked.

Sojourner flipped through the book, found her favorite essay, held it up for Rio.

"It's everything," Rio said, sat in the reading chair, caught her breath.

"I want to learn more about nature," Sojourner said.

"Tell me more," Rio said. "What else?"

THE NEW NATURALS 267

"What?" Sojourner said. "What else?"

"Yourself," Rio said. "Your mind. What else do you want?
What do you do?"

"I write essays," Sojourner said. "I try to write essays and
get them published."

"What about?" Rio asked.

"Small reflections," Sojourner said. "Personal stuff about
modern society."

"Are you Black?" Rio asked.

"Yes," Sojourner said.

"No, you're not," Rio said. "I'm looking in your eyes. I'm
looking at your hair."

"My mom's Black," Sojourner said.

"Is your dad German?" Rio asked.

"He's from Indiana," Sojourner said. "We have family in
Iowa. Minnesota too, I think."

"Why did you say it?" Rio asked. "Why say you're Black?"

"I always have," Sojourner said.

"Why?" Rio asked. "Explain."

"What else?" Sojourner said. "'Biracial.' 'Biracial' sounds
stupid, scientific."

"Why not white?" Rio asked.

"I don't look white," Sojourner said.

"You don't look Black," Rio said.

"If I called myself white," Sojourner said. "People would
laugh."

Rio laughed and coughed in a confused storm. Sojourner
scanned the room, looked for something to offer, found a water

glass. She picked it up; Rio waved her over, drank, regained herself.

"Is this place only for Black people?" Sojourner asked.

"Oh, no," Rio said. "We let everyone in, if they care enough to come. Like Travis. He was the best high school quarterback in Texas. Whitest guy. He gets sunburned all the way down here."

Rio stood, reached to a high shelf, pulled down a rolled-up map.

"Here," Rio said. "Come here."

Sojourner joined her at the desk and helped her unfurl the map.

It was Western Massachusetts. Their location was marked with a red *X*. There were other *X*s, connected with swerving red lines.

"What are these?" Sojourner asked, ran her fingers along one red line, jumped to another, followed all the tributaries without purpose.

"Objectives," Rio said. "Goals."

Gibraltar watched as Bounce spooned another chunk of peach cobbler onto his plate, tore into it with a grimy fork.

"What do you think?" Gibraltar asked.

Bounce swallowed big and choked a little.

"I'm not dangerous," Bounce said. "What did you say?"

"Smash and grab," Gibraltar said.

"I don't smash and grab," Bounce said.

"You could," Gibraltar said.

"I could," Bounce said. "I won't."

"Tell me," Gibraltar said. "Do you want to leave, right now?"

"Not without her," Bounce said.

"What if she stays?" Gibraltar said.

"Then I'll stay," Bounce said.

"Don't do this for me," Gibraltar said. "Do it for her."

"I will," Bounce said. "If she asks me."

"I love my wife too," Gibraltar said, picked a cold glazed peach from the dish.

"She's not my wife," Bounce said.

"Girlfriend?" Gibraltar asked.

"I don't know," Bounce said. "We don't talk about it."

"Oh," Gibraltar said. "Long-term unrequited love. Like, platonic high school best friends."

"We met a little bit ago," Bounce said.

"What's the deal?" Gibraltar asked.

"When I needed a place," Bounce said, "she gave me a place."

"That's it?" Gibraltar said.

"That's a lot," Bounce said. "For me."

Both men sat back and considered their wandering years, adrift and alone. They remembered cold beds, hangovers, pulled shades, and borrowed cigarettes outside loud bars. They remembered cold pizza and unclean microwaves, unclean dishes stacked with funk and mold. They thought about depression and wondered why it didn't kill them. Why were they special? Why were they spared? In their own heads, they overlapped and didn't notice. They recalled these women they

both loved now, how that changed everything, meeting someone like that, a force, a guiding light. They smiled to themselves, looked across the table, wondered why the other was
smiling, looked away, and smiled at the ceiling, table, or floor.

"I know," Gibraltar said after a moment.

"When I need someone," Bounce said.

"I know," Gibraltar said.

"Nothing like it," Bounce said.

"Finding something," Gibraltar said.

"When you need it," Bounce said.

Both men smiled again, understood why the other was also
smiling, dumb and big.

"It doesn't make sense," Gibraltar said.

"Why us," Bounce said and laughed.

"What did we do?" Gibraltar said.

"To deserve this," Bounce said.

Rio placed her whole palm on the university, smothered it,
looked up at Sojourner.

"Then what?" Sojourner asked. "You steal this stuff. Then,
what?"

"People know we stole it," Rio said. "We take responsibility."

"What next?" Sojourner asked. "Won't they find us? Won't
they find here?"

"We won't bring it here," Rio said. "We'll take the stuff
someplace else."

"That was you," Sojourner said. "At the mall. That killed
that man."

THE NEW NATURALS   271

"Not me," Rio said. "Us."

"You kill people?" Sojourner asked. "For what?"

"We don't kill people," Rio said. "There were complicated circumstances, unforeseen escalations."

"You killed a person," Sojourner said. "What I'm saying is I still don't get it."

Rio slid her palm down to New York City, tapped it once and twice, looked up again.

"Get what?" Rio said.

"I'm not sure what you want," Sojourner said.

"I want what you want," Rio said.

"What do I want?" Sojourner asked.

"A better place," Rio said.

"Is this better?" Sojourner asked, moved backward toward the door.

"Of course," Rio said. "Of course, it is. It is."

"Killing people," Sojourner said. "Stealing things. Always on the run."

"We need to grow," Rio said. "And we need to hide. We must protect ourselves."

Sojourner stopped moving, found herself stuck in Rio's glare.

"I understand," Sojourner said. "I'm trying to understand."

"We need help," Rio said, soft. "We have benefactors. We need more."

"Benefactors," Sojourner repeated.

"People give us money," Rio said. "Help us build things."

"Build?" Sojourner asked, moved again. "Build what?"

"We're moving," Rio said.

Rio went to the bookcase, pulled a binder from a middle shelf with both hands, knocked some books off, coughed into the air, right at Sojourner's face. Sojourner fell back on the bed; Rio joined her, still coughing.

"Water?" Sojourner asked. "Is there a doctor here?"

"I'm fine," Rio managed. "The best doctor."

Rio leafed through the binder to a set of blueprints. Sojourner saw a stenciled mountain range with interconnecting tunnels swirled like big digging worms. Printed across the top, in bold letters: THE NEW NATURALS.

"How did you build this?" Sojourner asked. "How does anyone build this?"

"We had friends," Rio said.

Bounce picked at his teeth with a fork, burped. Gibraltar gazed above his head at some water stains spreading across the ceiling.

"Any minute," Gibraltar said, poked at an ingrown hair on his chin.

"Did you play ball?" Bounce asked.

"Some," Gibraltar said. "Bad. Some good."

"My parents wouldn't let me," Bounce said.

"Were they religious?" Gibraltar asked.

"Which religion hates ball?" Bounce said.

"I don't know," Gibraltar said. "I don't know religions."

"They didn't want me outside," Bounce said. "On the courts."

"Books then," Gibraltar said. "You read a lot."

"I played soccer," Bounce said. "They drove me to the sub-urbs to play soccer."

"Soccer isn't bad," Gibraltar said. "Lots of Black people play soccer."

"More Black people play soccer," Bounce said. "If you think about it on a global scale."

"Who cares?" Gibraltar said.

"Sometimes," Bounce said, "I look at a ball and want to shoot it."

"Me too," Gibraltar said.

"It promises so much," Bounce said. "Possibilities and opened doors."

"When it goes wrong," Gibraltar said, "it's all regret."

"I should've worked harder," Bounce said.

"I needed a better coach," Gibraltar said.

"If I went to a bigger school," Bounce said. "A Catholic school. A boarding school in New Hampshire."

"I should've stayed in," Gibraltar said. "Went to the gym on Saturday nights."

"Do you remember any Saturday night?" Bounce asked. "Do drunk teenagers do anything interesting?"

"It gets me," Gibraltar said. "Thinking about my wasted potential."

"Isn't that everybody?" Bounce said. "Replaying mistakes and former selves."

Gibraltar worked through an answer in silence, tapped a butter knife against his kneecap. His life, stacked up like that, stared down at him. He was going to agree with Bounce.

Instead, the door opened and Sojourner walked in. Gibraltar noticed how Bounce looked at her—nascent and fierce love posing as never-ending devotion.

"Yes?" Bounce asked.

"Yes," Sojourner said, walked over, put hands on Bounce's neck and shoulders.

"Alright," Gibraltar said, stood, patted his hand a few times on the table, shook Bounce's hand, shook Sojourner's hand, and walked out.

Gibraltar walked fast to his wife. She was coughing on her back in bed with her eyes closed, lights on, blanket pulled under her chin, books in his spot. He moved the books, crawled in, wrapped his body around hers, kissed her closest body parts: neck, shoulder, clavicle, armpit, bicep, chest, ear, cheek. She leaned into him, pushed her head into his head, rubbed her cheek against his cheek.

"I'm fine," Rio said, even though Gibraltar didn't ask.

"I know," Gibraltar said.

"I like her," Rio said.

"I like him," Gibraltar said.

"Tomorrow night," Rio said.

"Okay," Gibraltar said. "Okay. Okay."

"I'm okay," Rio said.

Gibraltar watched her fall asleep, felt her breath get deeper and slower, felt her heart rest against his arm, relaxed with her. With the lights on, he saw her mouth drop open. He kissed her forehead, held her tighter, dropped into warm memories, like their first Thanksgiving together, broke grad students roasting a small chicken and large potatoes in a single pan, drinking wine from the bottle. They passed it between them, opened another when the first finished, danced to their own voices, opened another bottle when Rio wanted her own. They ate with their fingers. They made a pact to do this every year until they got tired of each other. They licked their fingers clean. Gibraltar said he'd never get tired of her. Rio laughed and wished him luck. They woke up hungover, in love.

Now, Gibraltar didn't want to turn the lights off. He wanted to stay in bed and not sleep.

Amadou showed Bounce and Sojourner to an empty classroom with sleeping bags unfurled across blankets. On the walls: timelines from the twentieth and nineteenth centuries; posters of Frederick Douglass, Bayard Rustin, Phillis Wheatley, Zora Neale Hurston, Aretha Franklin, Michelle Obama, and Satchel Paige; inspirational words in fun fonts printed on banners ran near the ceiling.

"Do you like it here?" Sojourner asked Amadou.

"Sure," Amadou said. "It's better than the world. You know, shitty jobs, shitty people, shitty everything."

"Is this plan going to work?" Sojourner asked.

"I don't think so," Amadou said. "Still, it might. Maybe."

Bounce and Sojourner put their sleeping bags next to each other, spooned like two large worms, wiggled against each other throughout the night. Bounce said he loved her. She loved him too and said it. They said they were happy, down here, together. They slept and dreamt of domestic life, family breakfasts, and trips to all-inclusive resorts.

Elting and Buchanan

SO, HERE, ON Interstate 90, outside Cleveland, cars and trucks moving east and west, sun down, rain coming down, head-lights, taillights, brake lights? Where did they go, those scared and tired bodies?

First, they went inside.

"What?" Buchanan asked.

"What?" Elting asked.

"What next?" Buchanan asked.

Elting couldn't answer. He stared at Popeye's across the food court, the people waiting in line looking at their phones, sniff-ing the fried air. Buchanan asked something Elting couldn't hear. Buchanan asked again, softer. Elting saw a woman pull a drumstick from a small box, hand it to a girl, pat the girl's head, tell her something with a smile, pat the girl's head again, walk into the rain.

So, what happened?

Did they meander through the parked trucks? Did they find a bored man halfway to his destination? Did the bored man offer them a ride for nothing? Did they find their way?

Did they find a nice family eating chicken at a small table, laughing about their trip, cataloging memories from the road, marveling at the littlest one dipping fries in barbeque sauce— how can someone sleep so much? Did the nice family give them money for bus tickets, drive them to the bus stop, wave and wish them luck?

Did they find another bus, later, and sneak on when the driver was waiting for chicken? Did this new bus stop in Erie, Buffalo, Albany, Springfield? Were they effective stowaways, clandestine, incognito? Did a nice older woman offer them pieces of her cheese, picked off a wedge with her fingers?

Did the rain stop? Could they find a rainbow across the fields and highway?

Did they come far enough? Did they get away?

Now, Elting took Buchanan's hand, walked into the rain. They got wet in the parking lot, jumped at thunder.

"We could walk," Buchanan said.

"We can't," Elting said.

No, Elting thought, we stop here. We admit some journeys are doomed. We take our seats and feel time trap us. We stand in the rain and soak, wash, drip into nothing. We accept some distances as insurmountable. We accept our unspectacular cycle in this life, hope for better the next time around. We hope the universe finds balance, evens us out over centuries and galaxies. We look into defeat and see promise.

"We could," Buchanan said.

"We can't," Elting said.

We accept highways don't have sidewalks. We accept Cleveland is twenty miles that way; Erie is sixty miles that other way; New York is a wide state with mountains; Massachusetts is a dramatic promise.

"I'm cold," Buchanan said.

"We can," Elting said, listening to tires splash.

Buchanan apologized again, looked at Elting's deluged profile, wanted Elting to look at him.

Elting wanted to tell Buchanan it was fine, this was fine, they were fine—some journeys are doomed. Some people don't get where they're going. Elting smiled into the storm. In the bathroom, Elting and Buchanan dried themselves with machines and paper towels.

The New Naturals

A CHILD TAPPED Bounce on the face with a pinky, tapped him again when he didn't wake up, tapped him again when Bounce rolled over. Sojourner groaned at Bounce's too-big body taking up too much space. She opened her eyes and saw them all: small children with mouths agape, standing in a circle.

"You're not our teacher," a girl with cornrows and long arms said.

"You're right," Sojourner said.

"Who are you?" a boy with long earlobes said.

"My name's Sojourner," Sojourner said, extended to shake the boy's hand.

"Sojourner Truth!" the children cheered.

"'Ain't you a woman'!" the children yelled.

The classroom door opened and closed.

"Class!" a short man with wire glasses yelled. "What did I say about yelling?"

Bounce grunted, pulled the sleeping bag over his head; Sojourner kneed Bounce in the thigh, pulled his sleeping bag down. She stood up, kicked Bounce, told him to stand up, too. Bounce stood, imposed. Children and teacher stepped back.

"Mr. Branham!" an Afroed boy yelled. "It's Sojourner Truth!"

"What are you doing here?" Mr. Branham asked, stepped between his students and Bounce and Sojourner.

"Gibraltar," Sojourner said. "We're new here."

"I'm Bounce," Bounce said.

"Sojourner," Sojourner said.

"Sojourner Truth," Mr. Branham said, laughed.

"'Ain't she a woman'!" the children yelled again.

"Seats!" Mr. Branham said.

The children hurried to their seats.

"We'll leave," Sojourner said.

"Breakfast is in the cafeteria," Mr. Branham said.

"Sorry," Bounce said.

"If you want," Mr. Branham said, "you can stay."

"We should eat," Sojourner said.

"Thank you," Bounce said.

"We're talking about Marcus Garvey," Mr. Branham said.

"We don't want to intrude," Sojourner said.

"You two are special," Mr. Branham said.

"Why?" Sojourner asked.

"Thank you," Bounce said.

"We're not accepting new members," Mr. Branham said.

"Why?" Sojourner asked.

"She is special," Bounce said.

"We don't have room," Mr. Branham said.

"We should eat," Sojourner said.

Mr. Branham went to his desk, told the students to pull out their maps, gave them two minutes to describe Africa in ten words. Sojourner and Bounce rolled up their sleeping bags and blankets, listened to the children mutter words like "better," "togetherness," "lions," and "sunrise."

Mr. Branham waved goodbye as Sojourner and Bounce closed the door.

More children, these ones late to class, rushed in, knocked into Bounce's legs. Sojourner swerved around a boy and girl holding hands, laughing, smiling, not looking where they were going. A man with long gray dreadlocks told the stragglers to hurry hurry, watch out, hurry, mind the clock. Sojourner asked the man where they should put their sleeping bags and blankets. The man took them, smiled, pointed to the cafeteria, told them breakfast was running low, hurry hurry.

Some crisp bacon was left, a few oranges, some pancakes, cold coffee, and empty milk cartons. Amadou and Trayvon called them over. Most people were finishing up, sucking orange slices, looking at Bounce and Sojourner.

"Sleep alright?" Trayvon asked.

"Great," Bounce said.

"What happens here?" Sojourner asked.

"We eat breakfast," Amadou said.

Bounce squeezed dregs from a maple syrup bottle.

"After that," Sojourner said. "What do people do here?"

"Anything they want," Trayvon said.

"Not anything," Amadou said.

"Close to anything," Trayvon said.

"You can't leave," Amadou said.

"We can't go outside," Trayvon said.

"Anything you can do down here," Amadou said.

"Like what?" Sojourner asked.

"The kids take classes," Trayvon said.

"Some adults teach classes," Amadou said.

"In the afternoon," Trayvon said, "adults can take classes."

"Lectures," Amadou said. "Some adults give lectures."

"What do you do?" Sojourner asked.

"We run security," Trayvon said.

"We handle security problems," Amadou said.

"Operations," Trayvon said. "Stuff like that."

"What will we do?" Sojourner asked.

"Eat first," Amadou said.

Sojourner hadn't touched her food. Bounce's hand inched toward her bacon; she slapped it away.

"Rio will tell you," Trayvon said.

"You're working with us," Amadou said to Bounce.

Bounce nodded, wiped his mouth.

"What if I want to work with you?" Sojourner asked.

"Gotta ask Rio," Amadou said.

"Rio will tell you," Trayvon said.

At another table, across the cafeteria, chairs knocked over, plates broke, people yelled.

"I can't take it anymore!" a voice yelled.

"I'm losing my mind!" another voice yelled.

Trayvon and Amadou stood.

"Talk to Rio," Amadou said.

"In her room," Trayvon said.

Sojourner and Bounce watched as Amadou and Trayvon moved across the room, grabbed the screaming people, two thin men with hands on their heads. Sojourner and Bounce watched Trayvon and Amadou put hands over the screamers' mouths and drag them out of the cafeteria. Bounce and Sojourner, like the remaining others, sat in silence, ate what little food was left on their plates, exchanged concerned looks and gestures. Like the remaining others, when the silence was too much, dropped their plates in a large bin, silverware in a large bin, and trash in a larger bin.

They streamed out of the cafeteria. Sojourner and Bounce made for Rio's room.

Down a hallway, children laughed and cheered. Down another hallway an adult voice screamed.

Gibraltar opened the door when Sojourner knocked. Amadou and Trayvon knelt next to Rio, who could only whisper, who was sweating and under a blanket mound. Gibraltar leaned into Sojourner's ear.

"She's not feeling great," Gibraltar said.

Rio whispered to Amadou.

"She says," Amadou said to Gibraltar, "she can hear you."

"She says," Trayvon said, "'Shut up.'"

Gibraltar stiffened, sat in the reading chair.

Rio whispered more things to Amadou and Trayvon then waved them away. She waved Sojourner over. Rio smelled sour and Sojourner knelt too far away. Rio motioned her closer; Sojourner obliged. Bounce stood next to Gibraltar, who stared at his lap, frowned, squinted, left the room, soon followed by Bounce.

"How'd you sleep?" Rio asked Sojourner.

"Thank you," Sojourner said. "Fine."

"It's over," Rio said.

"What's over?" Sojourner asked.

"The money's gone," Rio said. "Our backers are pulling out. We tried."

"Why don't you keep trying?" Sojourner asked.

"We're up against too much," Rio said. "The world is too stuck in a death spiral to change. Our structures are too solid. Our numbers are too small. We've lost the passion."

"I don't understand," Sojourner said.

"Leave," Rio said. "You need to leave. Find another place."

"I just got here," Sojourner said. "We just got here."

"It's over," Rio said. "You came too late."

"Don't tell me that," Sojourner said.

"That's how it works for people like us," Rio said, drifting. "At the whims of others, uncertain, in danger. Leave. Please. Find happiness somewhere else."

Sojourner stood, left, turned around at the door, of course, to see Rio, weak, fading, cold.

She found Gibraltar in a chair in the hallway, while Bounce played with kids, some type of tag where Bounce was always it, the one laughing and chasing.

There was a moment between them right then, where their imaginations spiraled into a utopian future, a wedding, a fresh banquet with vegetables and meat harvested with their hands, a calmness over their lives, idyllic, a kiss goodnight, a kiss in the morning, cooperative work, a shared life, love and life and time blended into a happy ball, a stillness, a settled beauty, Bounce looking at Sojourner, Sojourner looking at Bounce, can you believe it, my love, can you believe it, we found it, can you believe it, Sojourner looking at Gibraltar, their children playing together, powerful daughters, tender boys, happy, accepted, warm, hugged, a kiss in the morning, a kiss goodnight, can you believe it, forever like this?

"She says we should leave," Sojourner said.

"Where will we go now?" Bounce asked.

"One day," Gibraltar said. "I'm rubbing my wife's back as she sleeps, listening to birds and bugs out our window . . . I'm listening to my wife sleep and rubbing her pregnant stomach . . . I'm trying to sleep and I can't sleep . . . I'm thinking about how much I love her and how much she loves me . . . I'm sitting up in bed thinking about our family . . . I'm thinking about my mother crying . . . I'm thinking about my grandmother . . . I'm thinking and crying about how much I love my wife . . . I'm standing in my tuxedo and crying at my wedding day . . . I'm at my bachelor party, drunk and crying . . . I'm driving to the hospital and the baby's coming . . . Then I'm at my baby's grave . . . I'm at my baby's grave with my wife and crying because . . . if I lose her too . . . what am I, if I lose her? I'm calling engineers . . . I'm recruiting other people . . . I'm telling other people my wife is a genius with a vision . . . I'm telling people my wife understands the world better than anyone else . . . I'm telling people to come underground with us because underground with my wife is better than aboveground without her . . . I'm driving past a high school and thinking about my daughter . . . what if my daughter was alive? What if my daughter was going to prom? What if my daughter fell in love with someone like me? What would I do to someone like me? I'm walking past a prom dress in a store window . . . What if my daughter was like her mother . . . I'm standing in my tuxedo and can't believe it. That's how. That's how I got here. Okay. Okay."

"Do you need a moment?" Sojourner asked.

"No," Gibraltar said, wiped away all the tears he didn't notice.

"Are you sure?"

"Go."

Rio

-- --

IN HER FINAL sleep, Rio saw a waterfall. She undressed and jumped in the river, swam toward it. She felt fish and snakes rub against her stomach. She heard nymphs splashing, young women with small wings fluttering from joy. She waved. They waved back. She loved how the water carried her, made her buoyant. She let the current pull her toward the falls. She loved how the river reminded her of Oklahoma and her grandmother's land, which was her family's land, which was once some else's land, which was once no one's land, just land, beautiful land.

Under the waterfall, on the other side, she found Gibraltar and Drop sitting on a rock, holding each other's knees, laughing, saying Mom, Mom, come up here, put your clothes back on. She couldn't believe it—look how big you are, Drop. Look at your father's eyes, tucked right inside your face, looking back at me. Look at your cheeks, Drop. Just like my cheeks. She loved how the water made Drop's hair flatten into one long puff. She loved how the water settled into Gibraltar's stomach rolls and face creases. She joined them on the rock. She laughed with them. She loved how the laughter sounded just like falling water splashing into a river. She told them about the cranes, the sleeping gorillas, the lion cubs rolling in the dirt—all the things she saw on her way to them. Gibraltar pulled fish from the water and steamed it with his hands. She loved how Drop ate just like her father: mouth opened, teeth all crazy, half-choking. She hoped Drop found a husband like her father.

The New Naturals

THEY RETURNED TO the world.

The board members went back to their jobs, other boards, emeritus positions, faceless, still. They put their money and time elsewhere. They took calculated risks. Provided seed money for ventures with promise, unicorn companies, arbitrage. They would, in moments when their minds wandered, in their marble showers, waiting for a golfing partner to line up a shot, in short helicopter rides across Long Island, they would think about those two academics, the husband and wife. They would struggle to remember their names. They would think of their two years spent with the New Naturals as a worthwhile experiment, an honest try. They would eat dinner at their big tables and feel good about the state of things. The world was decent. With all its troubles, the world was still decent. And they were decent people for trying to make it better, for trying something new.

The people. The ones who went underground and resurfaced. The families, the loners, the lost. They stayed in touch. They texted. They e-mailed. They planned to meet again. They had, briefly, found their people. Found promise in their desperation. The wanted to keep in touch, see each other for Thanksgiving. But life gets in the way. Bills, more kids, work, more work, bills, taxes, engine trouble, rent increases, the burdensome trauma of living. Eventually, the texts and e-mails stopped. They would remember the mountain. They would promise to return.

Years later, they would receive a whisper.

They would hear about the new attempt. A new chance to start over, begin again. This time, it wasn't a mountain. It was an island, way up north, somewhere in Michigan, the Upper Peninsula. They would hear about this new couple, acolytes, picking up where Rio and Gibraltar left off. They had a daughter. They named her Drop. The three of them living off the land, gaining support, looking for backing, looking for bodies. Trying to change the world. Trying.

They would take buses, boats, planes. They would come. They would come to the island. They would see the couple waving on the docks, welcoming them, embracing them like old friends. The man, huge, covered in tattoos, powerful, smiling, holding his daughter on his shoulder.

The woman would appear.

"Hello," she would say. "Thank you for coming home."

"I'm Sojourner," she would say. "This is Bounce. This is Drop."

PART FIVE

Elting and Buchanan

SMILING FACES CAME into the shelter on Saturdays and ladled out two different soups into their paper bowls. They had a choice: vegetable or beef. Elting had changed to vegetable two weeks ago. Buchanan wasn't moving from beef, no matter how often Elting asked him to start caring about his body and spirit. Cleveland had made both of them bigger and content.

They took their paper bowls, took their favorite spots near the television.

"Hey," Elting told Rebecca. "Turn that up."

Rebecca was the manager, a smiling face with a degree in social work from Smith College. Rebecca turned up the television.

The news was breaking, talking about a cult in Massachusetts.

"Louder," Elting told Rebecca.

"Elting," Rebecca said. "We've talked about this."

"Please," Elting said. "Louder. Sorry. Louder, please."

Rebecca turned it louder and a crowd gathered.

"Who are these people?" the anchor asked. "Wayne, tell us more."

"Well," Wayne said. "In all my years. Well, this is a strange one."

"Who are these people, Wayne? What do they want?"

"Well, Katherine. Authorities received a tip and were alerted to what seems like an underground lair, right here in this small Massachusetts town, in this hillside, underneath an abandoned Chinese restaurant."

"What do they want, Wayne? Who are they?"

Buchanan hated watching the news. He dipped his spoon in his soup, took small spoonfuls, dipped and sucked his bread. He thought about his kin. His cousin in Western Massachusetts, nieces in Nevada, an aunt in Seattle, nephews spread about the Rust Belt between Buffalo and Detroit. He wished them health and love and peace like he had found. He thought about Lake Erie. He thought about the walk Elting and he would take after breakfast. He wanted to smell the foul water. It wasn't as deep as Lake Michigan. Still, he could put his feet in and feel the same. Today, he'd dip his feet, no matter how cold. Then, he'd dry off and they'd walk past the ballpark. They'd walk past the basketball arena. They'd walk past the

Rock & Roll Hall of Fame and he'd think of a joke that would make Elting laugh. Tonight, like every night, they'd come back here and sleep under a roof. They'd stay warm and stay away from trouble. Tomorrow, if they wanted, they'd get a wine box and drink the whole thing. They'd spend the afternoon drunk on their backs, warm. Buchanan loved his mind nowadays. He loved his calm visions. It felt natural.

Acknowledgments

- -

THANK YOU, CHICAGO, Buffalo, Western Massachusetts, North Carolina. Thank you, everyone I love in those places, for helping me grow, holding me close with patience and understanding.

Thank you, Algonquin Books.

Thank you, Kathy Pories. Thank you, Alexa Stark. My champions.

Thank you, love you, Lauren and Simone.